The Pilgrims' Bounty

A Historical Mystery

ACKNOWLEDGMENTS

Garry Reading for finding mistakes even after editing and advising me of them in time for corrections. Dr Robert Milton for his candid review of the content. Clemency Hinds for a great book cover.

The Pilgrims' Bounty

A Historical Mystery

Ken Bloomfield

NEW HAVEN PUBLISHING LTD UK

The Pilgrims' Bounty

Second Edition
Published 2014
NEW HAVEN PUBLISHING LTD
newhavenpublishing@gmail.com
www.newhavenpublishingltd.com

All rights reserved
ISBN:
ISBN-978-0-9930000-1-0

DEDICATION

To my wife with grateful thanks for her patience and understanding while I was writing this book.

Content

The Pilgrims' Bounty

The Pilgrims' Bounty

1

On a Russian Battlefield: 1620s

The sabre slashed down murderously towards the tsar's exposed neck, only to be deflected at the last instant by Theo's dagger. This was followed by an upward thrust, and he plunged the blade deep into the assailant's ribcage, piercing his heart.

"One I owe you, Theo," said the tsar, already parrying blows from another of the opposing Polish army.

Theo, too, was busy making sure he survived the battle and could only nod and grunt in reply to Mikhail. The whole field was a surging mass of men engaged in killing each other. There was so much blood that Theo could feel it swirling around his feet. The noise was a roaring cacophony of clashing blades and shouts and screams that defied imagination. He had little time to absorb all this, however, because he was too busy trying to stay alive and at the same time protect his friend, Mikhail Romanov, tsar of all Russia.

At just twenty-eight years of age, Theo was in his prime and had been trained for battle since the age of nine: two thirds of his life. Born Theophilus Clinton, he succeeded to the title of Earl of Lincoln early in life but soon became bored with an England at peace. Along with the title, he inherited a small standing army of loyal followers, who had trained alongside him and were restless for action. They were given the opportunity when Theo offered his services and those of his men to aid Mikhail in his struggle against his Polish aggressors.

Poland had been attempting for some time to claim the titles and territories of Russia, but since Mikhail had become tsar, the tide had definitely turned. The Poles tried to install their own imposters on the Russian throne. They wanted control, but it was to no avail. Unfortunately for them,

Mikhail's claim was genuine and unassailable. His people recognised this and swarmed to his side.

Using all the opportunities available to him, including help from mercenaries like Theo, he was able to take on the might of the formidable foe that was Poland at that time.

This final battle brought the opposing army to its knees, and at Deulino, on 11th December 1618, the Poles signed a peace treaty that lasted fifteen years.

In Moscow, there was much celebrating and Theo was in the thick of it. More than once on the battlefield, he had prevented an entirely different ending to the conflict. Mikhail, although a strong and accomplished warrior, was more than aware of the debt he owed Theo and intended to reward him handsomely for his assistance and loyalty.

A few years older than Theo, Mikhail left behind the beautiful love of his life to go to war. At home, housed in his apartments in the Kremlin, Maria Vladmirovna Dolgorukova awaited his return. Mikhail was first introduced to Maria, who was related to an earlier royal line, as a possible political match. A union seemed prudent, but regardless of the reason behind the arrangement, it was soon evident that this had indeed become a real love match. Nevertheless, it did of course help consolidate his already strong claim to the throne.

Expedient though it may have been, politics were not the reason Mikhail wanted to make her his tsarina.

He loved her from the first moment he laid eyes on her, and after he got to know her, his love for her only deepened. He couldn't imagine life without her. The first thought he had each morning when he awoke was of her, and that thought always brought a smile of contentment to his face. Now, he was racing towards Moscow with news of the victory and a copy of the peace treaty in his hand to present to the woman he loved.

When he arrived in Moscow, crowds lined the streets to welcome him and his victorious army. Theo sat next to him in the carriage, absolutely enthralled by the adulation shown to his friend: a friend he had come to love over the last year of bloody fighting and standing shoulder to shoulder on the battlefield, a friend who was obviously much loved by his people as they cheered, 'Mikhail, Mikhail, Mikhail the tsar'.

As the carriage pulled up by the steps to the Kremlin, Mikhail leapt out before the carriage had come to a standstill. As he ran up the steps, he called out, "Come and meet Maria, Theo!" The guards sprang to attention as Mikhail sped through the giant ornate doors, closely followed by Theo. As they turned the corner into a long straight corridor, Theo saw the most beautiful woman he had ever seen running towards them. At night and in between battles, it was not Russia, his people or his duty Mikhail talked about. It was Maria, only Maria. Seeing the object of this infatuation, Theo understood the tsar's fixation. She was breathtakingly beautiful. Arms outstretched, she careered into Mikhail, laughing and giggling all at once.

"You look wonderful, Mikhail, so fit. No war wounds, thank god," she said as she held him at arm's length, looking him up and down. Hugging him once again, she began to cry.

"What's this, my darling? Tears? What's to cry about?"

"I was so frightened. I thought you might be killed or badly wounded. I'm not sad. I'm just so relieved you're home safe and sound. I think the tears are all that bottled-up fear flowing out of me." The smile re-appeared as she spoke and seemed to fill the room with happiness.

"Well, my darling," said Mikhail. "I think my friend, Theo, here, might be owed some gratitude for my safe return. He saved me on the battlefield more than once."

Maria seemed to notice Theo for the first time.

"Then I must thank you, Theo, for ensuring the safe return of my love. Come, let's start by getting you both a drink. You must be thirsty after your journey."

She led them into a drawing room, where they sat around a low table in large comfortable armchairs and quaffed large quantities of kvass while they recounted some of the highlights of their adventures to Maria.

As the afternoon turned into evening and the servants went in to light the candelabra, they were still enjoying reminiscing when the tsar made an observation.

"Why is it, Maria, that Theo and I are getting more and more intoxicated on this beer, yet you haven't touched a drop? You used to be my best drinking partner."

"I don't need beer or wine to make me happy, my darling. Just having you home takes care of that. However, I do have a surprise for you."

"A surprise?" said Mikhail. "How intriguing. Now let me see…a new white stallion?"

"You don't want me to tell you in front of Theo, do you?

"But of course. Now that you've mentioned it, he'll be as curious as I am."

"Very well, my darling, but perhaps you should have one more drink."

"Now I *am* getting worried. Out with it, woman," he said smiling. "Don't keep me in suspense."

"Well, Mikhail Fedorovich Romanov, the woman whom you say you love, but whom you have yet to marry, is carrying your child."

Mikhail dropped his drink as his mouth fell open in shock. He quickly recovered and laughed gleefully, hugging and kissing the woman he loved so very much.

"If that's the case, my darling, we'd better get married right away, don't you think?"

"I think that sounds like a very good idea. I've taken the liberty of making some arrangements in anticipation." She laughed.

"Congratulations to you both," said Theo. "I can see you'll be very happy."

"Please stay for the wedding, Theo," said Mikhail.

"Of course," said Theo. "I wouldn't want to miss it."

"That's settled then," said Maria. "All that's left is for you to fix a date."

"Let's arrange it for a week from to-day," said Mikhail. "I can't wait to make you my tsarina."

And so it came to be. A week later, in the Cathedral of the Archangel in the Kremlin, Mikhail Fedorovich Romanov, the first Romanov tsar, made Maria Vladmirovna Dolgorukova his tsarina.

From the Bell Tower of Ivan the Great, the bells pealed, and in the streets, the people cheered.

The tsarina was dressed in red and gold and looked magnificent as she was married and crowned on the same day. The tsar looked no less stunning in his uniform of white and gold. The happy couple travelled in an open carriage through the streets from the cathedral to the reception, where they entertained both members of the Russian nobility and royals from surrounding countries.

Both within the palace and in the homes of the people, the celebrations went on for three days. Theo felt proud to have been invited, and he acted as equerry to the tsar throughout.

When the celebrations eventually came to an end, Theo asked the tsar for permission to leave.

"Of course, Theo, if you feel you have to return home, but I'm organising a party that might appeal to you more than these somewhat stuffy orthodox celebrations. It's almost Maria's twenty-first birthday, and I'm going to surprise her by inviting all her young friends to a dance held in her honour. There will be no ceremony, just lots to drink, lots of fun and the most enormous cake you've ever seen."

"It sounds tempting, but my men have been away from home a long time, and I know they're eager to return to their families," said Theo.

"Then let them go, but you must stay. Did I forget to mention that an excess of beautiful women will be invited? Probably five women to each man," said the tsar, mischievously.

"You didn't mention that, but now that you do, I'm convinced." He grinned. "I'll stay."

"I'm sure you've made the right decision." The tsar laughed.

"But my men must be allowed to go home," said Theo.

"Of course. They have my permission. They can leave today if you wish, and I shall give each of them a bonus as an extra reward for their service."

"That's very kind but unnecessary. They've been well paid."

"Nevertheless, I wish to show them my personal appreciation and send them on their way with fond memories of Russia."

"As you wish, Your Majesty," said Theo, bowing.

"What's this 'Your Majesty'? I prefer Mikhail from my friends." He winked. "Now, Theo, we've got a party to organise."

"So that's why you wanted me to stay."

The two friends laughed and walked off to ensure they were out of earshot of the tsarina while they made plans for a party to remember.

The best musicians and entertainers were hired, and interior designers were commissioned to turn the ballroom into a fantasy land. The best chefs and bakers were employed to produce the most exquisite dishes and confections. No expense was spared, and all were sworn to secrecy. The tsar was adamant the party was going to be one his beloved tsarina would remember forever.

2

Scrooby, England: Early 1600s

In the village of Scrooby in Lincoln-shire, young William Brewster was discussing his religious beliefs with his brother. Their father was a dissenter or separatist. He agreed with the ninety-five points raised by Martin Luther nearly a century earlier, which condemned the running of the Catholic Church: the idolatry and the plain old-fashioned greed displayed by the clergy. A classic example was when people in mourning for their loved ones were coerced into buying indulgences purported to save them from eternity in purgatory.

The Church of England, although not Roman Catholic, was the same in all but name, with the only obvious difference being that Henry VIII had broken England's allegiance to Rome. Now, in the time of Charles I, it was not easy to worship outside the mainstream Church of England. In fact, there were laws against it. However, as always in history, whenever people of conscience developed a deep conviction, they usually followed it, regardless of the penalties. William's father was such a man, and although he exerted no undue pressure on the boy, William shared his views on the matter. James, his brother, agreed with them both but feared the consequences if caught engaging in their preferred method of worship.

"I'm worried about the chances Father takes when preaching at gatherings of our friends," said James. "It only takes one person to inform the authorities and he could be imprisoned and maybe worse."

"That's hardly likely," said William. "First, as you say, they're friends with the same convictions, and secondly, Father has the protection of the old earl. He'd never allow him to be arrested. After all, his eldest son, Theophilus, attends most of the meetings. Theo told me his father has no love for the church and is sympathetic to our cause."

"I know you're right, William, but I do worry, and I'm more than aware of the sly and conniving ways of the spies of the Church and king."

Nevertheless, William senior was never arrested, and many years later, young William decided it was no longer desirable to remain in a country that did not allow its people to worship in the manner they felt was right. The old earl passed away, and Theophilus inherited his title and became Earl of Lincoln.

3

Ekaterinburg, Russia: 1991

Ivana was fascinated by the picture of the aristocratic young lady that hung above the huge fireplace dominating the drawing room in the manor house in Ekaterinburg, owned by her father, Vladimir Dolgorukov. The subject of this painting was seated, smiling, wearing a green silk gown, positively glowing with happiness. Her hair was piled high in the fashion of the day, and she had a pretty, small, white poodle-type dog on her lap. Apart from her incredible beauty, she wore a stunning jewel-encrusted crucifix on a chain hanging from her waist. This, Ivana's father told her, was a gift from the tsar to the woman in the picture, the tsar's wife. Ivana was her direct descendant, and should the cross be found, it belonged to the Dolgorukov family.

As a nine-year-old at the time, she had many wonderful dreams about the tsar and his beautiful tsarina.

When she was older, she learned that many treasures of old Russia had disappeared after the revolution. That this or any of the missing or stolen items would ever find their way back to their owners was at best unlikely, so her father's optimism was unrealistic. He hung his hopes on the fact that the British and the Spanish had returned from revolution to constitutional monarchy. "Why not Russia?" he would often say.

The revolution had not brought the people the prosperity they envisaged. Communism had been a hard master, and with this new found democracy, things were little better for the ordinary person. Corruption throughout the corridors of government was insidious and had spread throughout many spheres of business. Since the fall of communism, the Russian Mafia had spread like a cancer over all parts of the once-proud nation. Could a reversal be achieved? Was the return of the monarchy a real possibility? The Dolgorukov family were closely allied with the Romanovs, having intermarried over the centuries, and would undoubtedly have shared in any return to power.

As she approached adulthood, Ivana realised this was one dream of her father's that was almost certainly never going to materialise. There were huge amounts of money involved in the government of Russia, and those who had access to this extreme wealth were never going to relinquish either their money or their power, not even to a constitutional monarch. Her father, though, was in ill health and getting old, so she saw no reason to interfere with or belittle his dreams. She loved him dearly and his happiness was all that mattered to her.

4

Grimsby, England: 1620s

When William came of age, he began to preach at gatherings around the county. Printed copies of the Bible were becoming increasingly available. The new printing facility recently invented in Germany made it possible to produce larger quantities, which in turn made them affordable for ordinary people for the first time. Translated into English, they helped William with his sermons. People could relate better to a book of faith in their own tongue than to one in the antiquated Latin of previous versions.

Anxious to get as many copies to his followers as possible, William narrowly missed an encounter with the law.

"Hello there," shouted William at the gangway to a Dutch ship on the Grimsby quayside. "Is the captain aboard?"

"I am he," was the gruff reply, and a tall weather-beaten man appeared.

"I'm William Brewster, and I believe you have some goods for me?"

"If you can pay the going rate, I most definitely have," said the captain. "There are two large cases for you below deck. I'll have them brought up right away. Come aboard."

On board, William and his brother, James, opened the cases eagerly. Sure enough, they were filled with beautifully presented copies of the Bible, exactly as ordered. After sharing a drink with the captain, they settled up with him and loaded the cases onto the small cart on which they had arrived

"If I were you, I'd get on my way before this weather sets in. There's a storm brewing, and those books will get spoilt if they get wet. Which road will you be taking?"

"We'll take the Gainsborough road," said William. "It'll be safer."

There was no law against having a Bible, but with so many in the cart, questions would have been asked. With no explanation to satisfy the authorities, the result could have been many months incarceration, at best.

"Why did you tell him we'd take the Gainsborough road?" said James. "I thought we were staying with Cousin Thomas in Brigg tonight?"

"And so we are," said William. "But why did he ask? I don't trust him. Don't you know there's a reward for informing?"

They were told later that a troop of the king's men, accompanied by a bishop's aide, arrived in Gainsborough that night. They called into every inn, asking if anyone had information concerning two men with a small cart. This wasn't the last time William was betrayed by a sea captain.

5

Chicksands, Bedfordshire Military Intelligence HQ: 1998

Captain Dick Brady was an officer with British Military Intelligence. He served in the Gulf War and later assisted in various conflicts on behalf of the British government. His expertise had been mainly in intelligence gathering and interrogation behind the lines, where his fluency in Arabic and many other languages proved most useful. The army, never one to look a gift horse in the mouth, was now going to make full use of this experience.

"Captain Brady, Major Davenport wants to see you in his office right away, sir," said the duty sergeant.

"Do you know what about, Sergeant?"

"Not a clue, sir. He didn't say."

Dick went to the office and knocked.

"Come in," said Davenport. "Take a seat."

"You wanted to see me, sir?"

"I did indeed, Captain. You've been selected to be an intelligence adviser to the SAS. To this end, you'll need to accompany them in combat situations. They've asked, therefore, that you report for training at their facility at Credenhill, Hertfordshire. Do you have a car?"

"I do, sir. When do I leave?"

"According to the order, immediately, so I'd get packed and on your way, Captain. Here are your papers."

Three hours later, Dick pulled up at the SAS guard house, where he was shown into the office of Lieutenant Colonel Madden.

"I understand you've done some good work in the Gulf and in Northern Ireland," said Colonel Madden. "We've got work to do in this new flare-up in Bosnia, and I need someone who can interrogate in the field. You'll need to learn the language and brush up on your combat skills. I don't want my boys putting their lives at risk by carrying someone who can't look after himself."

"What exactly will that entail?" said Dick.

"It will mean putting you through a combat training course here at Credenhill."

"When do I start?"

"No time like the present, Captain. My sergeant will show you to your quarters. Stow your gear, and be on the parade ground in fatigues in thirty minutes."

That was when Dick met Sergeant Spud Taylor and Sergeant Daniel (Danny) Jones. They put him through hell over the next six months. At times he wanted to kill one of them and at others, both of them. The training was hard but thorough. By the end of it, he could dismantle and reassemble an M16 while blindfolded, and his hand-to-hand combat skills improved vastly. He developed a bond with the two hard and rugged sergeants that would last a lifetime. He served with them in Bosnia, Kosovo, Afghanistan, Iraq and in several less-heralded skirmishes on behalf of the British government.

Eventually, they were all let go as a result of government cutbacks. The two sergeants went into the mercenary/bodyguard business. Dick, on the other hand, chose to open his own private-investigation office, based out of a small office in an arcade off Regent Street in the West End of London. Unfortunately, the recession hit, and business wasn't exactly booming.

6

Moscow: 1620s

In the Kremlin, a wonderful building with echoes of Ottoman influence, there were a number of workshops hidden away down a corridor under sweeping, richly decorated arches. They were used by many different artisans, whose patrons were the nobility of the Russian court. In one of these, Evgeny Telepnev, a master jeweller, was toiling away at his bench when he had a visit from the most important person in the land.

Tsar Mikhail walked into his little workshop without warning or entourage. He was smiling and looked very happy.

"Good morning, Evgeny," said the tsar. "I have a commission for you that will require all your talents to complete."

"Anything for Your Majesty," said Evgeny. "I'd be honoured to serve you."

"It will be the tsarina's twenty-first birthday shortly, and I want to give her a very special gift"

"What did you have in mind, Your Highness?"

The tsar produced a cloth drawstring bag and tipped a large handful of beautiful gemstones onto the jeweller's bench.

"I'd like you to take whatever gold you'll need from the treasury and make me a large crucifix set with these stones. Here is my authorisation," he said, handing him the document.

"It needs to be large enough for her to hold in her hand or to wear on a chain around her waist, as is the fashion. Most importantly, Evgeny, it has to be a master-piece."

"I shall take great pleasure in following Your Majesty's instructions," said Evgeny. "I promise you won't be disappointed."

"When you've finished it, I want you to engrave the Romanov crest and 'To Maria from Mikhail' on the back."

"Of course. It'll be just as you desire, Your Majesty."

The tsar took his leave, and Evgeny's friends in the workshops gathered round to congratulate him.

For nearly two weeks, night and day, Evgeny used every ounce of his considerable ability to produce his most incredible work of art yet. He was indeed an exceptional artist.

The tsar was more than impressed with the jeweller's work. "It's perfect, Evgeny. You have indeed produced a masterpiece. I shall pay you twice what we agreed. The workmanship is impeccable, and the result is even more than I hoped for."

"There's no need, Your Majesty. I'm so pleased it has met your expectations."

"I can't wait to see the reaction of the tsarina. I shall give it to her at the birthday ball I'm arranging for her."

On her birthday, the whole of the Russian nobility and visiting foreign nobles turned up in their finery for the grand ball. The tsar presented Maria with the cross wrapped in a paper-and-ribbon package, which, in her excitement, she tore to pieces.

"I've never seen anything so beautiful, Mikhail. I absolutely love it. Thank you, thank you, thank you." She kissed him in front of all those present.

"It *is* beautiful, my love, but it pales in comparison to you," said the tsar. "It will remind me of you always."

The party was a huge success. The tsarina lunched with friends during the day, and when she left, everything was normal in the palace. The minute she had gone, however, pandemonium broke out, and the whole place became a hive of activity. Everything that had been prepared came out as the ballroom was transformed, and the kitchens dispensed a delicious aroma of hot food. The tsar made an incredible job of keeping the whole enterprise from the tsarina. She was blissfully unaware that so many guests, friends and family had been billeted in houses and palaces nearby. When she was returned, early in the evening, she was absolutely amazed when she was welcomed by the tsar into an ante-chamber filled with those invited to the grand birthday ball in her honour.

After excitedly greeting them all, she retired to a side room, where the tsar had laid out a beautiful turquoise-and-gold gown for her. Her maids helped her dress, and then she entered the ballroom down a long, winding staircase to cheers and applause. The dress Mikhail had chosen complemented her considerable beauty and also managed to disguise her pregnancy, which was now becoming very evident. As the musicians played, she danced with the tsar, and the guests followed them onto the dance floor in a sweeping mass of silk, smiles and laughter.

Theo was glad he stayed. The women were as plentiful and as beautiful as the tsar had promised, and he ended up spending much of the evening with an exquisite beauty, whose English was as perfect as his Russian was not. When eventually the evening ended, he was sorry to have to say goodbye to her, but he needn't have worried. She was staying in the palace, and he had hardly settled for the night when he was awoken by a loud tapping at his door He grabbed a robe to cover his modesty and crossed the room to open the door.

"Ksenia! I thought you'd left."

"No need, Theo. I'm staying in the palace, and I thought, as you're also in the palace, that we might share a bed—just to keep warm on this frosty night." She smiled mischievously.

"Of course…just to keep warm." He grinned.

That was how the Earl of Lincoln met the woman who was destined to become his wife, the future Lady Clinton and one day, Countess of Lincoln.

For several blissful months, Theo courted Ksenia, and what began as a harmless flirtation developed into a deep, enduring love.

The birth of the tsar's child was approaching, and just four months after the wedding, the day arrived.

Theo stayed with the tsar as he paced up and down outside the tsarina's apartment. The activity in her room was constant throughout the day; the hot water and towels being taken into the room were enough to supply a regiment. While they waited, the tsar talked to Theo about his love for the tsarina.

"Why don't you go and tell her, Mikhail. Maybe it'll help."

"It's not the done thing in Russia for a father to be present at the birth."

"Mikhail, you're the tsar. Surely it's you who decides what is and isn't the done thing."

"You're right. I am the tsar, and I say it's right to be with my wife. Excuse me." He walked across the room and entered the tsarina's bedchamber.

Now it was Theo's turn to pace. He was happy for his friend and even happier for himself. He decided Ksenia was the woman whom he hoped might one day become his wife.

7

London, England: 2012

Dick had been in military intelligence since joining the army, aged eighteen. In later years, he was attached to the SAS. That didn't mean he was a trained killing machine like his pals in the regiment—although he had been on operations with them—but he was no easy mark, either. He was brought up in a rough area of London, and it left its mark and shaped his character. With his rock-hard body and being over six feet tall and built 'like a brick shithouse', as his pals used to say, he could hold his own in most situations. After his release at thirty-nine in one of the army cutbacks, he started to make his way in the world as a private investigator. Business was slow, the country was in the middle of a recession, and nothing pressing was going on when Sol Levy stumbled into him as he strolled down Regent Street.

He thought the shot he heard was a car backfiring until he saw blood spreading from a wound in Sol's shoulder. He ducked as two more shots were fired, splintering the stone wall behind him, but they were way off target if they were meant for Sol. Either way, they ended up uncomfortably close to Dick.

He dragged Sol into the safety of the nearest open doorway, out of sight of the gunman.

"What the fuck's going on?" he asked the dishevelled and bloody casualty.

"Nothing," said the little man.

"What do you mean 'nothing'? People don't normally get shot at in a London street in broad daylight."

"I'm sorry," said Sol, "but it's a long story and I need a doctor." That much was true. He was definitely losing his colour, and the bleeding showed no sign of abating. Checking that the shooter had gone, Dick stepped outside, hailed a taxi and then carried Sol and placed him gently in the back.

"Middlesex Hospital," he called to the driver.

"And step on it—this guy's hurt." He jumped in as well, closing the door behind him. His curiosity was eating at him, and he wanted to know why someone would want to kill an ordinary-looking little guy like Sol.

At the hospital, the doctors called the police. This was protocol when a patient presented with a gunshot wound. While the doctors were removing the bullet and patching Sol up, the police took a statement from Dick, in which he explained the turn of events as he remembered them. When Sol was stitched and bandaged, they then turned their attention to him. He gave them a cock-and-bull story, claiming he was a victim of an unprovoked 'drive-by' shooting, probably hoodlums on a drugged-up rampage. After several unsuccessful attempts to get more information from him, they made their excuses and left in disgust.

Sol was a rotund little guy, about five foot five, with greying wavy hair and cigarette-stained teeth. He wore a well-worn raincoat like the one worn by Columbo. He wore a checked open-necked shirt beneath the coat, a loosened tie and an ancient pair of olive-green cord trousers. His shoes were unpolished brown brogues. The general appearance was scruffy, but in contrast, he was clean-shaven and smelt of Aramis…strongly.

In comparison, Dick was smart in the extreme—something left over from his army days. He wore a French-blue blazer and grey slacks under a long, navy, woollen overcoat. His crisp white shirt sported a silk version of his regimental tie, tied in a small neat Windsor knot. His shiny black shoes were scuffed due to the incident, but clearly would have been immaculate. He had short-cropped dark hair, piercing black eyes, dark sallow skin and, unlike Sol, wore the fashionable dark shadow of a missed shave.

They were as different as chalk and cheese, yet Dick took an instant liking to the little man, who still managed to smile even after someone had put a hole in him.

After the doctors had finished with Sol, Dick shook his good hand and introduced himself. "Dick Brady—here's my card."

"Soloman Levy, but most people call me Sol," he said as he read the card. "A private investigator? That perhaps explains your quick reactions. You've obviously been shot at before."

"On army duty, yes, but not since I've been in this business," said Dick, pointing to the card. "This isn't America. Here, guns are the exception, not the norm. So, now that the police have gone, why don't you tell me what's going on? Don't even try to feed me the rubbish you gave them."

Sol looked enquiringly at Dick as if he was trying to assess if he could trust him. After what seemed an age, during which neither of them spoke, he seemed to come to a decision.

"Okay. Pull up that chair. I realise now I need help with this. I'll tell you the whole story, and if, after you've heard it, you decide to help me, I'll give you half of any reward. If you decide not to—and after today's events I wouldn't blame you—I want your word you won't repeat to a soul what I'm about to tell you."

"Okay," said Dick. "You have my word. Now don't keep me in suspense. Let's hear it."

For the next half hour, Dick listened with rapt attention as the little man told his tale.

Sol explained he was a professor at Cambridge University, where he researched English history with a colleague.

While looking through some old documents from the 1600s, they came across a letter from one of the original Pilgrim Fathers who sailed on the Mayflower to colonise the Americas. It was from a William Brewster and was addressed to John Cotton, the vicar of St Botolph's, Boston, England, at that time. It was sealed and appeared not to have been delivered, as the seal was intact.

"In the letter," said Sol, "William told John that prior to leaving England, he was one of those who had been imprisoned in the guildhall in Boston, Lincolnshire, for their religious beliefs. At that time in England, people who had a different view on how to worship God were being persecuted by the government. Before his arrest, the Earl of Lincoln, who was a supporter of their cause, entrusted him with a bag containing some gold pieces and a valuable artefact. The main item was a crucifix, encrusted with emeralds, diamonds and precious stones. It had been given to the earl by Mikhail Romanov, who ruled Russia from 1613 to 1645, for his help in fighting the Poles in the Polish-Muscovite war. This was to be used to help William and his followers set up a colony in the New World, where they could enjoy religious freedom. William went on to say that he hid the bag and its contents while imprisoned and hadn't had an opportunity to collect it before he was released and expelled from the town. He asked the vicar if he could retrieve it and take it with him to the New World when he himself crossed the ocean. He knew it was John's plan to follow on."

"And did he?" asked Dick.

"He did indeed. It's an acknowledged fact that John Cotton actually did so in 1620, along with around a thousand other Bostonians.

"There then followed a coded rhyme, which William said John would be able to decipher and so be led to the hiding place of the pilgrims' bounty. I've researched John Cotton—he was an educated man, having been a student at both Trinity and Emmanuel Colleges at Cambridge, where he became a fellow. After finishing his studies, he became a minister and served for many years as the vicar of St. Botolph's in Boston, Lincolnshire. He propounded his beliefs to his congregation, which grew in strength and number over the years.

"Unfortunately, his beliefs and opinions regarding hierarchy didn't sit well with the incumbent government. John was under constant scrutiny, and with the appointment of William Laud as archbishop of Canterbury, this scrutiny increased, and his position as vicar became untenable.

Within a year of this appointment, John and a large number of his congregation embarked on an ocean voyage to find a new life in a new land—a land where people weren't persecuted for their religious beliefs. It was to this clever and trustworthy man of conscience that William had entrusted details of the whereabouts of the bounty bestowed on them by the earl and now referred to by William as the pilgrims' bounty."

Dick discovered Sol grew up in Holloway in the Borough of Islington, London. He was the eldest son of Jewish parents. They lived in an area of London where many Jewish immigrants had gone to live to escape the ravages of Nazi Germany. Their own ancestors, however, had been in London for several centuries. Sol's father was a tailor who worked all hours to provide for his family, as did his mother, who worked on the buses and did extra shifts behind the bar in the local pub. They were good parents and enabled their gifted eldest son to study at Cambridge. No easy task in those days for a working-class family. Sol made the most of the opportunity and excelled in his studies to the extent that he was asked to stay on as a tutor after he graduated. This made his parents very proud, and he had many happy years in that capacity before moving into his research role.

It was during one of his lectures that he met Marios Savva. Marios left Cyprus after the Turkish invasion in 1974. The situation was unsettled, and his parents wanted him to be in a safe place. He was twenty-two years old and had been studying history in Nicosia.

His father insisted he continue his studies in England and obtain a recognised qualification. He was accepted at Cambridge, and that was where the two became friends. Unlike Sol, Marios was a hothead. Most of the friendship in those early years resulted in Sol extracting Marios from various scrapes. He drank too much, ate too much, smoked too much, womanised too much and gambled too much. He rode a motorbike but conveniently forgot, or chose not to get a licence or pass a driving test. It was as if he was reliving his teenage years and Sol was the big brother bailing him out. Their friendship survived all this, however, and his inborn talent saw him obtaining his qualifications on time. That Marios managed it so effortlessly irritated Sol, but he did it and with honours. As time went by, they were both seconded to the historical-manuscripts research department, where they worked together doing what they both loved.

Sol and Marios were very excited about their find, and all would have ended well had Marios not had a serious gambling problem. He was heavily in debt to a rather unsavoury character, and when pushed for payment, he mentioned the letter and that he would soon be in a position to repay in full. Not content with this, his creditor decided that the letter was his property and that if there was any treasure, it would be liquidated in full to clear the debt. Marios told Sol the guy would be calling at the university to collect the letter the next day. Sol was furious that Marios had got into this predicament. They had a loud argument, which culminated in Sol telling him to make himself scarce and go somewhere where he would be safe because there was no way Sol was going to allow a crook to get his hands on the letter. That was when Sol made the decision to take it to a place where he could work on the coded message, safe from the hands of Marios' creditor, Ben Scrud.

Scrud was an ugly man: bald, with cauliflower ears, a large bulbous nose and a permanent scowl. He had small, pitiless, spiteful eyes that revealed his true nature. He spent most of his youth as a small-time gangster and thug, and now, in his fifties, he plied the trade of bookmaker-moneylender with the help of several nasty enforcers.

Unfortunately for Sol, he anticipated there might be a problem collecting the letter and sent two of his men to ensure it would be made available. They overheard the row and not being able to cause a commotion at the university, followed Sol to the railway station with the intention of taking the letter from him at the first opportunity. Sol caught a busy train to London and then a cab to Piccadilly where he was going to meet a friend whom he thought could help him decipher the rhyme. As he got out of the cab, he spotted Scrud's two thugs, who were taking a rather too obvious interest in him, and he began to run down Regent Street.

Knowing the punishment they could expect from Scrud if they let him get away, the thugs obviously decided the use of a gun was justified.

"Well," said Dick, "that's some story, but if they were prepared to pull a gun in central London, they're not likely to give up now, so we'd better get you out of here and to somewhere safe. My place isn't too far from here. Let's get you there quickly."

"If you're sure," said Sol. "But I feel you've done enough already, and I don't want to put you in any danger."

"Listen, you've got me intrigued by this letter, and it'll be worth a little danger to be there when you solve the riddle."

Sol signed himself out of the hospital, and they left on foot, ensuring they weren't followed. They hailed a taxi, and ten minutes later, they were sitting in Dick's apartment in Baker Street. By this time, it was about eight in the evening. The recent events and Sol's injury, which was now beginning to niggle, had taken their toll, and he was more than ready to take a rest.

"Sol, I think after all the excitement, it would be a good idea for you to get an early night. I've put some fresh towels on the bed in the spare room, and you can use the en suite. We can decide on a plan of action in the morning. What do you think?"

Sol simply nodded.

8

Scrooby, England: Early 1600s

Richard Clifton was the rector at Babworth and John Robinson was the dean of Corpus Christi College, Cambridge. Both were dissatisfied with the governmental control of the Church of England and its insistence that only established clergy could preach. They felt that lay people should have been allowed to address the congregation and that women should have been allowed to participate in the services. This was frowned upon by government and church officials alike, and moves were underway to introduce more laws to curb it. Richard and John moved to Scrooby and took houses where their friend, William Brewster, owned the manor house. They knew he held meetings here for a congregation of like-minded people. William had written books about his beliefs, which were published and widely available. Explaining the difference between the established church and his ideas about the correct way to worship, they were becoming increasingly popular. The government soon took steps to curtail the publication of William's books. He was pursued in court by ecclesiastical and civil authorities, and to escape this persecution, he soon had to leave England with his followers. In the meantime, his ideas were gaining popularity, even amongst some of the nobility. The Earl of Lincoln was a notable supporter and became William's close friend after discussions with him on the subject.

The party of worshippers met in rotation at William's, John's and Richard's houses. One night, it was William's turn, and the happy little congregation turned up at his home, Scrooby Manor in Scrooby village.

"Thank God it's a warm night and we can use the garden," said William.

The garden was surrounded by a high stone wall and had beautifully tended flower borders and large lawns—ideal for accommodating a large crowd, and that evening, there were many worshippers.

The people gathered round, listening to William's sermon based on stories taken from the Bible and put into the context of everyday life. They listened to John and Richard in turn and in between, sang the songs and hymns they had grown to love. At the end of the evening, food was served while they discussed the evening's events amongst themselves. All in all, these were enjoyable events; those who attended were convinced their version of Christian worship was the version best suited to the god to whom they prayed. This, however, was not the view of the government of the time. They were determined to stamp out this wandering—as they saw it—from the true path of religious worship.

While the people were eating and chatting merrily, they heard a loud banging on the front door over the noise and babble. William, John and Richard exchanged worried glances.

"It might be nothing," said William. "Maybe someone's come late. I'll go and see."

He opened the door, and there stood a hot and dishevelled Martin Dalby, William's friend from the next village.

"Welcome, Martin. Come in and have a drink…you look worn out."

"Let me catch my breath and I'll explain why." They sat him down, took him a drink and waited in anticipation. When he had fully recovered, he explained the reason for his appearance.

"I've run all the way from the church in my village, William. The congregation was painfully small, and the vicar was very embarrassed because the bishop made an unexpected visit. He's so angry that he's left for Lincoln to obtain a warrant for your arrest. He has the blessing of the bishop, so they're bound to agree."

"How long do you think we've got?"

"No more than a couple of days, maybe less."

"We've no choice then," said William. "We must travel down to Boston and see if we can sail to Holland, where we should be able to live and worship in peace. Ask who among the congregation wants to join us, Richard. We leave at first light. We'll visit the earl on the way and apprise him of our situation."

The next morning they arrived at the earl's residence and were well received.

"I'm saddened to see you go, William. Are you sure it's really necessary?" said the earl.

"I think it is," said William. "The bishop isn't renowned for his forgiveness, unlike the saviour he's supposed to follow, and he was sorely embarrassed. I believe he'll obtain his warrant."

"Maybe you're right." The earl smiled. "He's a sour-faced individual at the best of times."

"Perhaps his nature will change after we've gone and no longer the thorn in his side he perceives us to be."

"I doubt that very much. I think he was born morose." They laughed heartily.

"Anyway, I must take my leave, or they may still thwart our escape."

"I understand. Before you go, I have a contribution to make to your adventure," said the earl. He whispered an order to a servant who returned with an oak box.

"In here," he said, "is a gift from a very good friend of mine. Unfortunately, it brought him no luck. Maybe it will do better for you." He took a leather pouch out of the box and passed it to William. Inside was an incredibly beautiful solid-gold cross encrusted with diamonds and precious stones.

"This must be worth a fortune," said William. "I can't accept it."

"You can and you will," said the earl. "My friend would be overjoyed that at last it's doing some good. You can sell it or break it down and sell the gold and gems. Either way, it should fetch a pretty penny, for you may well be in need of funds in this venture."

"You're too kind. How can I thank you?"

"Send me a copy of your next book, and don't get caught…that's thanks enough, William. I believe what you are doing is right, so good luck and get going—you've dallied long enough."

William left, and he and his little group travelled on to Boston. Leaving the women and children in Boston town, William and the men went down to the docks to find a captain who would agree to take them to Holland.

"What can you offer?" asked the captain of a well-made brig.

"This piece of gold should be a good reward for the short journey," said William, handing over a gold piece. The captain bit into the gold with his blackened teeth to ensure it was solid. He had the ruddy, weather-beaten look of a seafaring man and sported a full unkempt beard. He smelt of sweat and seawater, and his clothes looked like he had slept in them.

"You'd better get your people aboard within the hour to catch the tide then, Master Brewster." Exulted that they had at last secured passage, William and the men hurried back to the town.

They collected the women and children and returned in haste to the docks, where they boarded the brig, stowing their belongings where the captain and crew directed. As soon as they were travelling down the river that led to the open sea, they felt they were free at last. They started to sing their favourite hymns spontaneously, and an overflowing feeling of happiness abounded amongst them. That feeling was not to last.

But the captain of the brig betrayed them and reported them to the authorities. He obviously preferred the small reward offered rather than the North Sea crossing. Bailiffs from Boston boarded the vessel at Scotia Creek and after transferring them to open boats, took them back to the town. Word had spread, and they suffered a loud and unruly reception as they made their way from the docks to the Guildhall, under the bailiffs' arrest. The Guildhall was a tall building in the centre of town built in the reign of Elizabeth 1. It was arranged with a court on the upper floor and cells on the ground floor. The court also served as the council meeting room. They were arraigned in the court, and the leaders—William, Richard Clifton and John Robinson—were then imprisoned in the cells downstairs. The rest of the party were dispersed in the town.

The leaders languished in the Guildhall for several weeks, only being allowed out on Sundays to visit St Botolph's, the huge cathedral-like church just across the way. They were allowed to spend the day in contemplation while exploring the magnificent church and attending services. There were no guards inside the church. They swore on the bible that they wouldn't escape.

"This is a fine mess, William," said John. "What do you think they'll do with us?"

"Don't be scared. I think they'll just keep us until they feel they've broken our resolve and then send us back to our parishes. That won't please our vicar, but I think they'd rather keep a watch on us than imprison or execute us. They don't want to run the risk of making us martyrs to our cause. A more pressing problem is what to do with the earl's purse. If they decide to do a thorough search, it could be found, and that would be a huge blow to our future plans should we ever be able to escape this wretched island."

"I've been giving that some thought," said Richard. "Before I became a pastor I was a builder of some repute, and I have an idea."

9

Baker Street, London: 2012

Sol awoke to the smell of fried eggs and bacon drifting through the apartment. Dick had got up, showered at eight and by eight thirty had a full English breakfast complete with hot coffee dished up and on the kitchen table. Neither of them had eaten the night before, so they were both more than ready and made short work of it.

"Right," said Dick. "Can you tell me where you were going before the shooting?"

"Of course," said Sol. "I was going to see Brian Charity, who's an expert on the Pilgrim Fathers and the puritan period in general. I thought he'd be my best chance of deciphering the message in the letter. He works at the British Museum but has a flat above a shop on Regent Street, which was where I was heading when the shooting started."

"Since they followed you to that area, it might be wise to call him and arrange to meet elsewhere…just in case they're hanging around to see if you return. It's what I'd do if I were them. What about the champagne bar in Selfridges? It's only a short taxi ride up Oxford Street but far enough away to make it very unlikely we'd bump into them again."

"Sounds like a plan," said Sol. "I'll call him right away."

Brian agreed to the meeting, and they set off immediately.

"We might as well walk," said Dick. "It's not far, and by the time we get a taxi, we'll be there."

Less than fifteen minutes later, they walked through the ornate doors of the great department store and made their way across the floor and up the steps to the champagne bar. They took a table in the corner and had just settled when Sol stood up, smiling, and extended his hand to a jovial rotund man with curly blond hair, who went to join them. Brian had the look of an elderly schoolmaster and was wearing a tan sports jacket with leather-patched elbows. While the two old friends were catching up, Dick ordered champagne and smoked-salmon sandwiches for them all as they chatted.

Having just eaten breakfast, Dick and Sol were not that hungry; their host, however, tucked in with gusto. After he had finished, they got down to the business at hand.

"The letter's in old seventeenth-century English," explained Sol. "And being coded, the message is even more difficult to understand."

"Let's have a look at it and see if I can help." said Brian.

Sol pulled what looked like a piece of yellowed vellum paper with a broken wax seal from the inside pocket of his old raincoat. On the front of the letter, in a script penned by quill, were the words 'The Reverend John Cotton, Vicar of St Botolph's, Boston'. Brian opened it carefully. It was dated October 12th, 1619 and began, 'Good Morrow, John'.

William's explanation of his predicament regarding the earl's treasure followed, and like many similar letters of that time, there followed a coded message as a safeguard should it have fallen into the wrong hands. It read:

In God's own house within the town
In chapel fine as sun goes down
When thrice past the hour of noon
Third panel then lights up the gloom
And through a shadow by saint cast
Points the way to treasure vast
Revealed herein marked as the county
There lies beneath the kind earl's bounty

It was signed, 'Your humble servant and friend, Pray remember me, William Brewster'.

Brian read and re-read the letter with a puzzled look on his face.

"What do you make of it?" asked Sol.

Brian explained. "John Cotton was, as you can see, the vicar of Boston in the early 1600s, and St Botolph's was and still is the church in the middle of the town. In fact, I believe it's the largest church in England. It has one of the tallest towers in the country and is built of stone with carved reliefs and coloured-glass windows. The tower has no spire and is the reason the locals have nicknamed it The Stump. In fact, it's of such a size that I've never understood why it isn't classed as a cathedral. I can only think it must be due to the number of the surrounding population and not the dimensions of the building itself. There's a chapel in the church that's been there for centuries, which, funnily enough, is now called The Cotton Chapel, though I doubt it was in those days. As for the rest of it, I must confess I'm as confused as you, but I guess things might become clearer if you were to pay the church a visit. I can tell you, though, that there are several accounts of the Earl of Lincoln giving financial aid to the pilgrims and that he was a great supporter of the puritan cause."

Sol looked from Brian to Dick. "What do you think?"

"I think we'd better take a trip to Boston, don't you?" said Dick.

Before they parted company, Brian took a photo of the letter and promised to get back to them if he found any more information.

"Okay," said Dick. "Let's find you a change of clothes while we're here, and then I'll pick up a few things from the apartment and we'll head for Lincolnshire to see if we can solve this mystery."

"Let's do that," said Sol, and they said goodbye to Brian and headed off in the direction of the menswear department.

Armed with a few days' supply of shirts, underpants and socks for Sol, they left Selfridges and made their way back to Dick's. As they were exiting the lift, Dick saw that the door to the apartment was slightly ajar, and they could hear the sounds of banging and shuffling inside.

Putting his finger to his lips, he gestured to Sol to stay outside.

Gingerly, Dick pushed open the door and disappeared inside in an instant. Straining his ears, Sol heard muffled cries of surprise, followed by a loud bone-crushing thump and then silence. A minute later, Dick's head appeared round the door.

"Come in and see what I've found." Inside were two rough types sprawled out on the floor of the lounge.

"They're not dead, are they?" said Sol.

"No. I caught them unawares and just banged their heads together. They're just taking a nap."

The apartment was a mess. They had rifled every drawer, shelf and cupboard and just dumped the unwanted contents on the floor. Dick went into the kitchen and found some plastic handcuffs—souvenirs from his army days—in a pile the intruders had dumped on the floor. After cuffing their wrists behind their backs and their ankles together, he searched the pair of them. Both had the same model Berretta handgun. One in a shoulder holster and the other just tucked in his waistband.

"Nice people, Sol. I imagine it was one of these guns that put a hole in your shoulder." Dick dropped the guns into Sol's bag. "Never mind. What goes around comes around. Or to put it another way, don't you just love karma? Wait here, Sol." He pulled one of the intruders up and disappeared out the door.

Two minutes later, he reappeared and fetched the other one. When he returned, he packed some clothes and washing gear in a small holdall and then went into the bedroom and removed a panel in the floor of his wardrobe. He took out and unlocked a metal cabinet, from which he withdrew a well-oiled Smith & Wesson 41, complete with silencer. Then, along with some spare ammunition, he put both into the deep pockets of his overcoat.

Sol looked on wide-eyed, still clutching his Selfridges bag.

"Come on, Sol. Time to start fighting fire with fire, I think. I'll clear this mess up when we get back."

They took the lift and went down to the car park. When they emerged, Sol saw the two guys sitting up against the wall.

They were just coming around, a little groggy at first, but very soon spitting out threats of what they would do once they were free.

"Oh dear, gentlemen," said Dick. "How can you be so nasty after we'd almost forgiven you for shooting my friend?" He picked each one up and pushed them against the wall, still tied up. He took the gun from his pocket and began to screw on the silencer.

"First of all, I want the name and address of your boss, and if you refuse, I'll hurt you." This just provoked more verbal abuse.

"Look, I'm not a very patient man, so to save time, I'm going to demonstrate that I won't take no for an answer." In the blink of an eye, two loud metallic coughs echoed around the car park. Silenced guns were not as quiet as Sol thought. Dick had shot each of them in the right foot. Their initial yells soon became groans and then whimpers.

"Come on, gents. What you did to my friend was far more painful. Don't be cry-babies. Is it clear now that I'm serious?"

"Yes, yes," they both shouted out in unison.

"Okay then. The name and address, if you please. Write it down, Sol." Sol pulled the stub of a pencil out of his pocket and wrote the details on the inside of his Selfridges bag.

"If, gentlemen, you have given me in-correct details, or if either of you dare to follow my friend and me in the future, I *will* find you and you'll find our next en-counter far more painful. Do you under-stand?" They both nodded frantically.

"If I find you've forewarned your friend, Scrud, or if you mention our names to the police, the result will be the same. Is that understood?" They carried on nod-ding. "By the way, as a matter of interest, how did you get my address?"

"Scrud's got someone who accesses the police computer, and you left your address at the hospital," said one of the thugs.

"So much for the incorruptible British police," said Dick. "We'll leave you to make your own way home. Come on, Sol…we'll take my car."

When they reached the street, Sol, who had been very quiet, finally found his voice.

"You sh-shot them," he stammered.

"They shot *you,* Sol. This was just a little bit of retribution. In the movies, the good guys only get hurt at the finale. In real life, we get a turn along the way, especially when the crooks are as dumb as this lot." Dick came across many types similar to these roughnecks during his time in the army: men who had a cruel streak and enjoyed hurting people, usually at the instigation of another. Whether that other was their NCO or, if they were on the other side, a Taliban leader or Afghan warlord, the result was the same. People who obeyed these bullies were, invariably, cowards. He learned to react in kind with these types because that was all they understood. Although not a meek man, several tours of duty in Iraq and Afghanistan had honed his views about right and wrong. He would lose no sleep over their discomfort.

"Now, let's pay a visit to the leader of this band of miscreants before he interferes in our business any further."

They headed for the M11 and the North. First stop: Cambridge.

10

Moscow: 1620s

Theo knew something was wrong as soon as he saw his friend's face when he came from the room.

"I want to thank you, Theo," said the Tsar, his hand on Theo's shoulder for support. "If it hadn't been for you, I wouldn't have been there to say goodbye to my Maria."

The tears rolled down his face, hot and fast, into his beard, and his shoulders shook as he sobbed silently into his friend's shoulder.

"And the child?" said Theo.

"A son. Alive and well, but I feel no happiness."

"But, Mikhail," said Theo gently, "he will at least remind you of Maria."

"That's what I'm afraid of. I don't know how I can survive the pain, and a constant reminder will surely make it unbearable."

"Of course that's how you feel today, but Maria would have wanted you to love this child, and in time, you'll be grateful for a reminder of such a wonderful woman."

"Maybe in time but not today. Tell them I don't wish to see him today."

"Very well. Sit here and rest, and I'll talk to them for you."

Theo gave Mikhail's orders to the staff and the newborn tsarevich was taken away for the time being.

The next few days were miserable, with everyone in the country, as well as Mikhail, struggling to suppress their emotions. Maria had been well loved by the people, and they were finding her passing difficult to accept. Shutters and curtains were drawn in every house, and black crosses adorned every door.

The funeral was attended by representatives and nobility from nearly every country in the world. The cortège was a mile long, and the coffin was escorted by the Royal Horse Guards, who were all dressed in black uniforms, as were the many regiments who followed them to the Cathedral of the Archangel.

Those who were not in black wore black sashes across their chests. The tsarina's horse walked behind the coffin, now riderless, with her empty riding boots reversed in the stirrups.

The streets were lined with hundreds of thousands of the tsar's subjects, who all— including the poorest peasants—took flowers which they threw before the coffin as it passed by. When the cortège arrived at the cathedral, the crowds surged outside and joined in the service, singing with such strength that people said it could be heard over fifty miles away, carried by the wind.

Mikhail controlled his emotions well during the service, ignoring the one wayward tear that, for all his efforts, he could not prevent. The day finished with a dry thunderstorm, which somehow seemed an appropriate send-off for the much-loved tsarina.

With the service over, Mikhail returned to the palace and the people to their homes. Weeks of mourning drifted into months, and still he was morose and unhappy. Theo went hunting with him and tried to put some laughter back into his life, but to no avail. It seemed Mikhail had lost the ability to smile or take pleasure in anything.

One day, many months later, Theo decided to risk everything to get his friend back into the world and enable him to move on. He called on the lady who had been asked to mind the baby and asked her to return to the palace with him. He agreed to take full responsibility and deflect Mikhail's wrath if the decision was not well received.

"Your Highness, I wonder if you would do me the favour of taking a walk with me in the gardens? I'd like to show you something."

"Theo, I've learned to be wary when you use 'Your Highness' and not Mikhail. What are you up to this time?"

"If you join me, Your Highness, you'll find out." Theo smiled.

"Okay. My curiosity has got the better of me. Let's go."

They walked out of the palace and down the stone balustrade steps into the glorious gardens surrounding the Kremlin. As they turned down an avenue of poplar trees, they saw a wet nurse playing in the sunshine with her charge, a rosy-cheeked baby boy already the image of his mother. He beamed up at Mikhail. The recognition was instant.

"Once more, Theo, you've guided me on the right path," he said as he lifted his son into his arms. "It does feel good to have at least a little of her with me again." The baby giggled at that precise moment, and it was the first time Theo had seen his friend smile since his wife's demise many months earlier.

"From today," said Mikhail to the wet nurse, "my son will remain with me in my apartments. You can take a room there for yourself."

"I'd be honoured and very happy to do so, Your Highness."

And so it was decided, and Mikhail became, once again, the man whom Theo knew. Shortly after, Theo asked him for permission to return home.

"I shall miss you very much, Theo, but I realise you have to introduce Ksenia to your family. I'd like you, as part of my reward for your services, to take with you the cross I gave Maria for her birthday. I'd consider it a favour—just to look at it saddens me more than I can bear."

"I understand, Mikhail, and of course I will if you're sure it's what you want."

11

On the Road to Boston: 2012

After an hour on the M11, they reached the Cambridge turn-off, and Dick pulled into the car park of the Menzies Hotel.

"I don't know about you, but I'm ready for lunch. Come on, leave your bag, and let's see what they can offer us."

The brasserie in the Menzies was a lucky find. After a delicious meal, washed down with a glass of surprisingly good French white wine recommended by the waiter, they felt much more refreshed. They paid for their meal and set off for Mr. Scrud's address in the Arbury district of Cambridge.

"Do we have to see this man?" said Sol.

"We do if we don't want to be continually looking over our shoulders. I don't think he sounds like the sort to give up unless he's actively discouraged." Sol shrugged and they carried on following the coordinates on Dick's handheld GPS.

Scrud lived in a flat over a garage. The stairs to it were accessed through a small fenced yard, where there was a vicious-looking pit bull.

"Don't worry," said Dick. "I'll deal with it. Just stay behind me."

"Please tell me you're not going to hurt it," said Sol.

"I don't hurt dogs, just nasty people."

Sol discovered that Dick was a master at being prepared and that he had a way with dogs, almost like the horse whisperer. He took a package from his pocket: his napkin from the brasserie, wrapped around a juicy piece of pork loin.

"Just a precaution," said Dick. "People like Mr. Scrud often hide behind dogs." He started to feed the dog with small pieces of pork. The dog looked really happy and was obviously pleased to have found a friend. Dick put the last pieces on the floor and, with Sol close behind him, mounted the stairs and knocked on the steel door.

A muffled voice came from somewhere on the other side, and steps were heard approaching the spy hole. Dick pushed Sol up against the door and stood to one side, out of sight.

"Who is it?" said a gruff voice.

"I've been sent with some money from Marios Savva for Mr. Scrud," said Sol. They had rehearsed what to say during the journey. A few seconds elapsed while whoever was on the other side was checking Sol out through the spy hole, and then, obviously deciding he was no threat, he began drawing bolts back.

As the door opened, a voice said, "How did you get past the dog?"

Leaving no time to answer, Dick passed Sol and delivered a powerful punch to the guy's solar plexus. He went down like a dynamited building, and Dick kicked him in the head on his way down for good measure. He wasn't going anywhere any time soon, and so far, they had not made very much noise. Stepping over him, Dick walked down the corridor, which turned right and led to another door. He pulled out his Smith and Wesson and screwed on the silencer as he approached. The door opened when he turned the handle and revealed an unsuspecting character sitting behind an old wooden desk, counting money.

"Mr. Scrud, I presume," said Dick. Scrud grunted.

"What's it to you?" snarled the big lump of a man behind the desk, as he looked into the barrel of Dick's gun.

"Keep both your hands where I can see them and you might survive this meeting."

"What do you want?" said Scrud, complying with Dick's request.

"I believe we have some business to discuss, Mr. Scrud. Two of your employees attacked my companion here and shot him in the shoulder. This resulted in a painful injury requiring the use of a sling, as you can see. I'm here to give you the opportunity to make reparation to him for his pain and suffering."

"Fuck off," said Scrud, spittle flying from his mouth and his bloated face reddening from the neck up.

"Now, now, Mr. Scrud...let's not be hasty. Here's the deal. One out of your own book, you might say. I put my companion's claim at fifty thousand pounds. Today is Thursday the third. You have until Monday to deposit that amount in this account." He passed a slip of paper across the desk. "After that, the interest will cut in at a rate even you might find excessive. Then, if the total—including interest—still remains unpaid at the end of the month, I'll have to make an example of you."

"You'll get nothing from me, you clever bastard," screamed Scrud. Dick looked across at the man quivering with rage, his own eyes cold and calm, and his gun hand as steady as a rock. Scrud must have seen something in those eyes, too, because for the first time, Sol saw another expression on Scrud's face. It was fear.

"Have it your own way. We'll have to make do with an eye for an eye." Without further discussion, Dick shot him in the shoulder.

He made far more fuss than Sol had, screaming and crying like a scalded cat. Dick bent down and spoke into Scrud's ear.

"I'm feeling magnanimous today, so I'll consider this debt paid. However, if you or any of your thugs interfere in my and my companion's business again or cause us any distress, you'll be indebted to me once again. There will, therefore, only be one acceptable payment, and I promise you, Mr. Scrud, I *will* collect. Do I make myself clear?"

Scrud made a positive grunt in between groans and swearing.

They left the way they had entered, Dick making a fuss of the dog on the way out.

"Now, let's make our way to Boston and see if we can make some sense of your riddle."

12

Boston, England: 1620s

The jailer's keys clinked and bounced against his belt as he went down the stairs from the kitchens. He was accompanied as usual by Mary, the young scullery maid who was carrying the tray, and two armed guards, who made sure no attempt to escape was made. Since being held in the Guildhall, the pilgrims' leaders had not been unkindly treated. There was more than a little sympathy for their plight in the town. Many were of the opinion the state should not have interfered with matters of conscience, and almost all hated the 'Roman'-type church services. As the cook and the jailer were two of those who held these opinions, they had been more than well fed.

Mary had a loaf of bread for them, accompanied by a hunk of cheese, a large pitcher of water and some pickles. "Cook said this was left over from the Saturday-morning council meeting and it was better for you to have it than waste it," said Mary.

"Please thank Cook for her kindness, Mary, and tell her it's much appreciated," said William. They made a show of pouring the water and tearing at the bread until the jailer's party was climbing the stairs and safely out of sight.

"Right," said Richard. "Pull the crust off and break the bread into small pieces. I'll mix it with the water and some of the dirt we've swept from the cell and I should be able to get a consistency of something like mortar. If we keep it fairly wet, it should be usable for our plan tomorrow." Once the job was done, they tucked into the remains of the bread and the pickles and then settled down for the night to be rested for Sunday's exertions.

Soon after they heard the cock crow in the gardens of Fydell House next door, they awoke refreshed and made light work of the hearty breakfast Mary had taken them.

Later that morning, between services in St Botolph's, they set to work scraping at the mortar around a slab on the floor within the church, each taking a turn. John had worked so hard at it that day, it had caused blisters on his thumb and fingers.

With only a kitchen fork to aid them, it had taken three Sundays to loosen the slab enough to lift it. Then, all of a sudden, it was free. They looked behind them, but nobody seemed to have noticed. In such ventures, Lady Luck had to play a part, and this time she must have been smiling on them. Beneath the slab was a void, which was large enough to take the package entrusted to William by the earl. William quickly removed the package he had hidden down the front of his britches and surreptitiously laid it in the void beneath the slab. Richard then mixed the broken pieces of mortar and dust with the substance they had made from the bread and reset the slab. They scratched a small L (for Lincoln) in the stone for easier identification and stood back, pleased with their work. Once set, even a close inspection would have been unlikely to reveal the resting place of the treasure.

"A fine job, Richard," said William. "I doubt anyone will be able to tell it's been moved." Pleased with the result of their labour, they joined the guards outside and made their way back to the Guildhall.

The next day, word arrived that it had been decided to release them and return them into the custody of their own parish. The only stipulation was that they would return to the borough of Boston only on pain of instant imprisonment in Lincoln Prison, without further trial. They were summarily escorted from Boston by the town bailiffs and handed over to government agents to oversee their rehabilitation.

"What about the treasure, William?" whispered John.

"Don't worry. Richard's done a good job. Nobody's going to find it, and only we know where to look. If we can't get back ourselves, we'll get someone to collect it."

Sometime later, circumstances found the three friends together in Plymouth with the opportunity to leave with the tide on the Mayflower, a seaworthy ship bound for the New World.

"What about the earl's bounty, William?" said John. "It would be a great help in establishing our settlement."

"I have the ideal solution," said William. "You remember John Cotton, the vicar we met while we were in Boston?"

"I do," said John. "A very holy man I thought."

"He's one of our persuasion and is planning to follow us with a large contingent of his Boston congregation. I'll write to him explaining its whereabouts and ask him to bring it over when he comes."

"Is it safe to put it in writing?" said Richard.

"You leave that to me," said William. "I'll make sure only he understands where it rests."

13

Boston, England: 2012

Dick and Sol were on the Peterborough ring road, looking for the turn-off to Spalding and Boston. Thirty minutes later, they were approaching Boston itself. When still a few miles out, St Botolph's appeared in view like King Arthur's Excalibur being lifted from the lake.

"That's an amazing sight," said Dick.

"It is, isn't it?" said Sol. "Up until the nineteenth century, it was the tallest building in the world, and it's still one of the tallest non-cathedral churches in Great Britain."

"Where do you get all this information from?" said Dick.

"I suppose you could say it comes with my job," said Sol smiling. As they entered the town, the traffic was building up, and they used the GPS to find their way to the church. They ended up in the market place, where they parked, and made their way across the cobbled market to St Botolph's. It was late afternoon when they approached the main door, and they observed a man in a cassock locking the big black doors with a very large padlock.

"Good afternoon," said Dick. "When does the church open?"

"Not until tomorrow morning, I'm afraid." said the man in the cassock. "We've had problems with burglaries lately, so the church is locked up at night. It'll be open at six in the morning, though, and you're very welcome to come then."

"Thanks," said Dick. "Can you recommend somewhere to stay in the town?"

"Of course. Try the White Hart Hotel. It's just over the bridge to your right. You can walk to it in two minutes, but if you have a car, you'll have to go around the one-way system to get to the hotel car park. If you leave it in the market, you'll have to be up early to beat the traffic wardens." They thanked him and decided to take the car.

The White Hart Hotel was an old, white-painted, Georgian-looking building that leant and looked as if it was about to fall into the river.

The river Witham ran through Boston right alongside the hotel. The hotel did have spare rooms, so they booked a room each and arranged to meet in the bar ten minutes later, after taking their overnight gear to their rooms.

Dick made it down first and was sipping a large brandy when Sol joined him.

"What's your poison?" said Dick.

"Poison? Oh! I'll have a glass of red wine, please." said Sol. The waiter, who had been hovering, gave a curt bow and went off to fetch the wine.

"Right," said Dick. "Let's decide what we're going to do."

"What do you suggest?" said Sol.

"I hope that Brian's right and that the chapel in St Botolph's is the place to start. Otherwise it could take a lifetime to search a church that size. Doing it undetected over a long period would be no mean feat, either. Anyway, rightly or wrongly, there's no point in being there much before three. Remember 'thrice past the hour of noon'."

"Yes, you're right," said Sol. "Perhaps we could spend the earlier part of the day looking around the town, especially the Guildhall where it all began."

"Sounds like a good idea," said Dick. "Now let's see if we can order some dinner."

Dinner was first class, and it was several bottles of wine later when they made it to bed. They missed breakfast by a mile, as it was mid-morning before either of them surfaced.

"You look like I feel," was Dick's greeting to Sol.

"I think it's the change of water." Sol chuckled.

"Oh, nothing to do with the alcohol, then?" said Dick. They both laughed.

"Let's get some strong coffee before we hit the town," said Sol.

Their first port of call was the Guildhall, just across the bridge. An impressive and obviously ancient building, it was now being used as a museum.

They entered and were first shown the cells where the pilgrims had been held. They had black iron bars and a door secured by an ancient padlock. They were very basic, bare and uncomfortable by modern standards. Next, they were led upstairs to the chamber where the court that detained the Puritans for their dissenting beliefs was held.

"It's all much smaller than I imagined," said Dick.

"Ah, but then most things were in those days," said Sol. "Even the people."

"This from someone who stands all of five foot five." Dick laughed.

They left the Guildhall and followed their directions to the docks, which they found somewhat disappointing. Having been modernised over the years, they had none of the historic atmosphere they had both felt in the Guildhall. On the way back, they passed 'Doughty Quay'.

"This is more how I imagine the docks would have been in those days." said Sol.

A few cockle boats were moored up along-side the quay and gave the impression of being from another era. They spent the next few hours exploring the town before returning to the church at around two thirty.

If the outside of St Botolph's was im-pressive, the inside was nothing less than magnificent. Dick had never seen such a beautiful building and said so. Even Sol, who was used to the beautiful buildings of the university, was impressed. Awesome, towering, stone arches lined the stone-flagged aisle. They reached up to the dec-orated buttress ceiling, which was higher than any church in England. At one end was the most incredible stone font, en-crusted with carvings and raised on its own dais. At the other end was the most magnificent altar, surmounted by the carved figure of Jesus crucified, with fig-ures of saints on either side. To the left, the gilded pipes of the organ reached up ma-jestically, almost to the roof.

Once they had absorbed the atmosphere of this holy place, they looked around for

the chapel, and sure enough, there it was—
a little church within a church, accessed by
a small gate. There were quite a few people about: church people and tourists. Nobody seemed to be taking any notice of
them, so they made their way into the
chapel. Nothing stood out to give them a
clue what they were looking for. There
were many nooks and crannies and possible hiding places. With still a few minutes
to go until three, Dick went out to the
small tourist kiosk in the main church and
bought a paperback book about the 'Cotton Chapel', as it was called. He took it
back to Sol, who was still in the chapel,
looking thoughtful.

"Maybe there's a clue in here," said
Dick, offering Sol the book.

It held a wealth of information, but
nothing that gave them any clue or indica-
tion of any likely hiding places or secret
passages that might have led them to their
goal. The sheer size of the church made
their quest seem impossible. It was nearly
three, and they looked anxiously around
the huge building for any sign.

"Hold on." It was nearly three. "Look at how the light is falling through that window. The shadow of that saint looks like a pointing finger, and it's resting on that slab of stone flooring there," said Sol, pointing.

"You're right," said Dick. "And that's in the chapel. We can't do anything about it now, but we need to mark it."

Sol pulled out the stub of pencil he always seemed to carry. "Put a small cross on it with this."

Sitting outside the coffee shop next door to the church, they re-read the riddle.

"I'm sure we're right," said Sol. "The riddle mentioned the chapel, and that's where the slab is. It's too much of a coincidence to be wrong."

"I agree," said Dick. "So we need to decide our next move. While nobody seems to bother you in there, I'm sure they'd notice if you started lifting a paving stone."

"You're right," said Sol, "but I have an idea. Did you notice the steps on your left when we first went in?"

"I did. So what?"

"Well, my friend, they lead to the library. I doubt they lock the library at night, as they have such a large lock on the main door. That being the case, if we were to be in the library at closing time, we'd have all night to find what we're looking for. We could just emerge in the morning and mingle with the tourists, and nobody will be any the wiser."

"What if they search the library at closing time?" said Dick.

"We'd have to say our curiosity got the better of us and make our apologies."

With the plan settled, they left the church and walked into town, where Dick managed to purchase a small crowbar and a torch. They had an early meal at the White Hart and then headed back to the church.

14

Massachusetts, New World: around 1630

The wind blew fiercely as William waited for John Cotton to disembark. He had been notified that John's ship, along with several others, had dropped anchor in the bay, and he made his way down to the dock to be on hand to welcome John when he was ferried across. At last, he saw several boats laden with people and belongings making their way ashore.

He saw John on the first boat, waving, and knew his journey had not been in vain. As the boat touched the quay, John jumped off, stumbling a little as William caught him. The two friends embraced each other warmly.

"It's so good to see you," said John. "It's been a long time."

"You too," said William. "You're looking well. Did you have a good crossing?"

"I fared better than many," said John. "There was a lot of disease on the journey, and we lost some of our blessed brethren, I'm afraid. We set out with over nine hundred, nearly all from Boston. Is there somewhere we can talk where it's warmer? My teeth are chattering."

"Of course," said William. "What can I be thinking? Come on, there's a tavern here on the dock with a blazing fire and some hot toddy."

Once settled in front of the fire, they began to talk about old times and eventually got around to their time in Boston. "Now, John, did you understand my letter, and have you brought the pilgrims' bounty?" He could tell by John's face something was wrong.

"Letter? What letter? What bounty?" William proceeded to tell John what had transpired while in Boston and about his decision to hide the treasure in John's church for safety.

"It's been safe all right," said John. "I never got your letter. Who did you give it to?"

"I gave it to Mary, the scullery maid at the Guildhall," said William.

"Mary, Mary…" John thought back. "Yes. Mary got taken by a fever, suddenly. I remember I presided at her funeral. Poor thing—she was so young."

"What do you think happened to the letter?" said William.

"I imagine it would have been put with her belongings at the Guildhall, and after that, I really don't know."

"It's a sad story both for Mary and for us because we could have put the bounty to good use over here. However, we've survived and are making a good life here for our people. I think you're going to enjoy the New World. We can worship as we please without fear of reprisals."

"Sounds like a dream. Show me around, and let's find a place where these Bostonians can at last call home."

15

Boston, England: 2012

It was getting late and Dick and Sol had to hurry; they didn't want to get locked out again. It was almost empty inside the church. Would anyone spot them climbing the stairs to the library? They had to take the chance.

They climbed the stairs quickly, like two cats stalking a mouse. Nobody spotted them, and once inside, they gently closed the door. Now all they could do was hope they wouldn't be discovered before the church was locked up for the night.

An hour went by, then two, and nobody came to challenge them. Barely breathing, they opened the door and looked out into the darkened church. Straining their ears, they listened for the sounds of people, footsteps or voices. There were none. They crept gingerly down the steps, using the light from a small torch and made their way across the church to the chapel. They both jumped when Dick pushed the gate open and it squeaked loudly—something they had not noticed in the daytime, but then, sounds are always magnified at night. After crouching in the doorway for several minutes, they realised nobody but them had heard the noise, so they relaxed and entered the chapel.

"Over here," whispered Dick. "You hold the torch. I think it's one of these by this pew. Yes, there's our mark. Put some more light over here. Look, there's another mark scratched in the stone. Looks like an L."

Dick worked the end of the crowbar into the gap around the slab and lifted gently, a little at a time, until he could get a purchase with his fingers. Once he had a grip, the stone came up easily, too easily for a stone that had been sealed for hundreds of years. Inside was a void that was empty except for a folded piece of paper—modern paper.

It was a note:

Sorry Sol,

I guess this means you've worked the riddle out, too. I need to get away from Scrud and make a new life. With this, I've got a chance. I've handed in my notice at the university. I won't be coming back.

Be lucky, Sol...Marios.

"Fuck it," said Dick.

"Dick, remember where you are," said Sol.

"Sorry, but I can't believe we've come all this way to be shafted at the end," said Dick.

"Who says it's the end?" said Sol. "Marios has gone to start a new life. If you'd spent the last twenty years struggling in this overcast, cold, rainy country and then just came into a fortune, if you were from a beautiful sunshine island that you could never shut up about, where do you think you might go to start a new life?"

The light clicked on in Dick's brain. "Cyprus. Of course, he's gone to Cyprus."

"That's my guess," said Sol. "So that's where we're going next."

16

Cyprus: 2012

They returned to London to collect their passports and pack a bag each with extra clothing. Up until then, Sol still only had his Selfridges bag. They booked their flights to Cyprus online, which was due to leave at nine a.m. the next morning.

After an uneventful, if bumpy, five-hour flight, they touched down in Larnaca at four p.m. Cyprus time.

The detective work could begin. Sol was busy on the plane, making notes of all he could remember of conversations with Marios about his time in Cyprus. They agreed to get settled into a hotel and then meet to analyse the notes, before deciding on their next move.

They booked into the Sun Hall Hotel, located on the promenade in Larnaca, which had just been renovated. The rooms were therefore fresh and attractively decorated, each with its own marble bathroom. The views across Larnaca Bay were fantastic. The beach, with its myriad of coloured sunbeds, was full of people of all shades from white to pink and various degrees of brown. On the azure-blue sea, there was a range of shipping on the horizon, from tankers to small fishing boats nearer the shore.

All this was bathing in the glorious, late-afternoon, Cyprus sunshine. "I can take plenty of this," thought Dick as they sat on the balcony of Sol's room, enjoying the warmth of the sun, drinking coffee and eating cakes ordered from room service. Sol had laid his notes out on the table, and they were perusing these and making plans for the next day's hunting.

Marios was born in Cyprus, and according to Sol, he would go on and on about the good times when he was growing up in his village near Larnaca.

"That would be a good place to start," said Dick. "Where is it exactly?"

Sol spread out the map of Cyprus he had been given when they checked in. "It's not far from the airport but in the opposite direction to the way we came to Larnaca. Still, it can't be more than fifteen minutes from here by car. It's just a few kilometres away. There, look," said Sol pointing to the map. "Pervolia."

They decided to rent a car straightaway but delayed their visit to the village until first thing the following morning immediately after breakfast.

The next day blossomed with blue skies and warm sunshine as they drove to the village. The rental car was a Renault Mégane convertible—not quite the right car to travel incognito, but they didn't feel the need to hide.

Sol was right: in no more than fifteen minutes, they were approaching Pervolia. What a pretty little place it turned out to be, with a cobbled street running through the centre and little tavernas, cafés, ice-cream parlours and restaurants on each side. They stopped outside a café, went in and ordered two coffees.

"This is as good a place as any to make a start," said Dick. "When the waiter comes back with the coffees, you can show him your photo of Marios and ask if he knows him." The waiter returned full of smiles and placed the coffees on the table with a flourish.

"Is there anything else I can get you gentleman?" He spoke perfect English, with just a trace of an accent.

"Actually," said Sol, "we're looking for a friend of ours from the village, and we've lost his address. Perhaps you can help? I've got his photo here." The waiter looked at the photo, pensively at first, and then the smile returned.

"This is an old photo, my friend, but it's Marios, my father's cousin. When he's in Cyprus, he usually stays with Christos, another cousin. We're nearly all related, in some way, in the village."

"Where can we find this Christos?" said Dick.

"That's easy. He's in his restaurant over there, Christo's."

"Thanks," said Sol. "You've been a great help."

"No problem."

They finished their coffees then made their way across the road to Christo's. A young girl was wiping down the tables.

"Excuse me," said Dick. "Is Christos about?"

"Yes, he's in the kitchen. Who shall I say wants him?"

"Just some friends of Marios Savva."

"Okay."

Christos emerged moments later, and he turned out to be a real character. He was dressed in black from head to foot. He was about five foot eight, around forty-five years of age and a little overweight. He had a larger-than-life, bearded, jovial face, with a large nose above really thick lips. Despite the heat, he wore a black woolly hat, under which he almost certainly had a bald pate, although hair protruded at the sides and was tied in a ponytail at the back.

"Good morning. Friends of Marios?" he said while extending an overly large hand to shake.

"Yes. We've been told he's staying with you," said Dick.

"He is, but he's gone over the other side for a few days on business."

"The other side?" said Sol.

"Yes…the island has been split since the seventies. The north side, at present, is controlled by Turks and Turkish Cypriots, although we're hoping not forever."

"I'd like to see it," said Sol. "Perhaps we could meet up with Marios over there. Do you know where he's staying?"

"Yes, of course. He's staying at The White Pearl hotel in Kyrenia. He said he's going to meet with that rogue Ali Buccaraja. They've been friends for years. They're both interested in all things old…antiques, archaeology, you know Marios."

"Why do you say rogue?" said Dick.

"He's been in the papers a lot over the last few years, suspected of trading in religious icons, stolen when the Turks invaded the North. He's a wily old fox, though…nothing's been proven."

"How long does it take to get to the other side?" said Sol.

"Oh, an hour or less to Nicosia and then past the border checkpoint, and it's about thirty minutes to Kyrenia. You'll need your passports to cross over."

They made their excuses, thanked him for his help and left.

"You crafty bugger," said Dick. "*Perhaps we could meet up with Marios over there. Do you know where he's staying?*" he mimicked.

"It worked, didn't it?" They both laughed.

"Right," said Dick. "Let's get our gear from the hotel and head for The White Pearl. There's no time like the present."

"I'm with you," said Sol.

17

Northern Cyprus: 2012

A little over an hour later, they were at the border. They filled in a small white form which was stamped and then returned to them with their passports. Before they were allowed to cross over with the car, they had to purchase insurance, which was available from another booth at the checkpoint. Over the border, they noticed the immediate decline in the state of the roads and the properties in general. On the main road to Kyrenia, or Girne as the Turks called it, things improved, and they found themselves on a modern dual carriageway.

The White Pearl turned out to be a picturesque boutique hotel that overlooked the Venetian harbour of Kyrenia at the front and the Five Finger mountain range behind. Their luck was holding, as they actually had two rooms available. Considering the hotel only had ten rooms in total, it was most fortunate. The receptionist confirmed that Marios was staying in the hotel when Sol asked her but said he was not there then, indicating his key in the pigeonhole labelled Room Seven, behind her.

They dropped their bags off in their rooms and then made their way to the rooftop terrace and ordered lunch. The terrace was nearly full, the residents taking advantage of the clement weather.

Sol and Dick were seated at the last table available, which was a table for four and the only one with empty seats. It was why a stunningly good-looking woman approached them and asked if they minded if she shared their table. It was now Dick's turn to stutter.

"Of c-course not…please." He stood up and pulled a chair out for her.

"Yes, please, join us by all means," said Sol, rising.

As they all took their seats, she introduced herself as Ivana Feodorovna from

Moscow. She had long, shiny, black hair, high cheekbones, perfect white teeth and the most amazing green eyes. She was about five foot seven and had the body of a Greek goddess, although she was obviously of eastern European descent.

She wore a simple, black, all-in-one trouser suit and an elegant pair of high heels.

With the introductions over, they settled down to order, and eventually all three decided on a lunchtime meze—a selection of many small dishes, indigenous to the Greek and Turkish Cypriot communities. To Dick's surprise, Ivana joined them in ordering a bottle of Efe, a Turkish beer, which they all had to complement the meze. Lunchtime was turning out to be fun.

Ivana was vague about her reason for being in Cyprus. "I'm mixing business with pleasure," was all she ventured. Dick and Sol did not push the subject; they were enjoying her company.

"What about you two?" she asked.

"We're visiting a friend," volunteered Sol.

After a very pleasant afternoon, discussing the good and bad points of living in England and Russia respectively, they said their goodbyes and made their way back to their rooms. Except that Dick and Sol did not go back to their rooms; they made their way to room seven, hopefully to find Marios. When they got there, nobody answered their knock, so Dick produced a set of picks from an inside pocket and proceeded to pick the lock.

In less than a minute, they were in.

Someone had beaten them to it; the place had been turned upside down, literally.

"I wonder if they found what they were looking for?" said Sol.

"Somehow I doubt it," said Dick. "They've turned the whole place over. If they'd found what they wanted, they would have stopped searching, so there would have been an untouched area. That doesn't seem to be the case here."

"What the fuck's happened, and what are you doing here?"

A short fat man with sallow skin, glasses and an ill-fitting black wig appeared in the doorway.

"I'm here to see you don't throw away my share of the treasure," said Sol.

"Who's your friend?" said the fat man.

"Exactly that—a friend. Let me introduce you. Dick Brady, please meet Marios Savva." Sol's anger was boiling over. "So you decided to take it all for yourself then," he said, through clenched teeth. "Nearly twenty years we worked together. Friends, I thought. Almost like brothers, I thought. Then, when we make a joint discovery worth a fortune, you run off with it. How could you do that?"

Marios couldn't look Sol in the eyes. He was wringing his hands and staring at the floor. "I'm sorry, Sol. I just had to get away. What with Scrud on my back, it all just got too much for me."

"Too much for you? I took a bullet from Scrud for you," said Sol, pointing to the sling. "And yet you tried to run out on me.

You're not sorry...you're only sorry we found you." Sol was shaking with rage.

"Come on," said Dick. "You'll have a heart attack if you don't calm down. What's done is done. What we need to do is decide where we go from here. Where's the treasure now, Marios? And who do you think searched your room for it?"

"The only person I've told about it is Ali Buccaraja. The treasure consisted mainly of a beautiful jewel-encrusted cross I've ascertained to be the one given by Mikhail Romanov to his wife. After she died, he gifted it to the Earl of Lincoln for services rendered in a conflict at the time. I know Ali's sent pictures of it to several of his contacts. He has to do that to try and sell it, so I suppose there are several people who now know of its existence. As for where it is, it's here." He pulled the cross out of the large pocket on the side of the white cargo pants he was wearing.

Even in the indirect light of the room, the multitude of precious jewels glittered with a brilliance Dick could never have imagined. It was magnificent, covered in emeralds, rubies, sapphires and diamonds, along with many other jewels Dick did not recognise. It was a truly mouth-dropping work of art.

"Are you crazy?" said Dick. "Even that thug Scrud was prepared to use a gun to get hold of it. People have been killed for much less. It needs to be in a much safer place than your pocket."

"He's right," said Sol. "Let's put it in a safety deposit box for now and then pay a visit to Mr. Buccaraja to see if he can throw some light on who might have turned this room over. Do you agree now to share any proceeds with me, Marios? I'll take care of Dick."

"Of course," said Marios. "It's worth more than we could ever spend, anyway."

"Maybe more than I could ever spend, but with your gambling…who knows?" said Sol, scowling.

They tidied the room as well as they could and then set off for the bank and then Mr. Buccaraja.

Ali Buccaraja was a tall thin man with greying wavy hair and a matching thick moustache. His office was in an elegant parade of shops on a rise behind the harbour, with extensive views of the sea. The downstairs was given over to an art gallery, and his office was on the mezzanine accessed from within the gallery. He was wearing black silk trousers, a green velvet smoking jacket, a cravat and leather slippers embossed with a crown motif.

"Back again so soon," he said, smiling. "And who are your friends?"

"These are colleagues of mine, and the reason I'm back is because my hotel room has been wrecked. Only you know I'm here, so we're interested to know whom you might have contacted to organise such a search."

"I see," said Ali. "Most of them are people I've dealt with before. You know…collectors and dealers."

"You say 'most'," said Dick. "Which of those you haven't dealt with did you contact?"

Ali scratched his nose and turned on the laptop computer on his desk. "There was one new dealer who approached me last year, asking me to let him know whenever there were any Russian artefacts on offer, especially anything relating to the Romanov dynasty. Obviously, when Marios showed me the cross, I thought it was exactly what the dealer was looking for, so I emailed him a picture."

"Do you have the name of the dealer and the email?" said Dick.

"Of course, it's right here on the computer." He turned the computer around, and Dick made a note of the details:

Maxczart Fine Art,
215 Office 1, Profsoyuznaya Str, 117036 Moscow. Russia.
Email: art@maxczart.com
Office telephone: +7 (095) 220 88 90
Office Fax: +7 (095) 220 80 90

"I'll need some time to make some enquiries," said Dick."

"Is the cross still for sale?" said Ali.

"Of course," said Sol, "but we want to sell it, not have it stolen. I think, for the time being, just stick with the people you've already told. Don't do any more marketing."

"Have you any idea of its worth?" said Ali.

"Not to the penny," said Sol. "What's your estimate?"

"I think it could be as much as two million dollars, and just so you know, my commission is ten percent," said Ali.

Dick let out an involuntary whistle. "Two million dollars. No wonder they were so anxious to get hold of it. Maybe Scrud's not as daft as I thought."

"Why did you want that company's details?" asked Marios when they left.

"I've still got friends in the intelligence community," said Dick. "I'm just going to check it out. Obviously there's a fly in the ointment somewhere because genuine art dealers don't go around trashing rooms, no matter how much is at stake. And though it's a lot to you and me, it would almost certainly not be the first time a genuine dealer has dealt with items of this value."

"Sounds like a good idea," said Sol. "We don't want any more nasty surprises."

They decided to go back to the hotel and rest while Dick ran his checks. He didn't think whoever had searched Marios' room would return. After all, they knew there was nothing there for them.

Dick didn't get a reply to his request for information until the next day at breakfast, and when he got the phone call, the news was not good. He had asked an old friend—Oliver Masters, who had worked with him in military intelligence and was now the boss of a department in MI6—if he would check it out.

"Maxczart is a front for the Bratva," said Oliver. "That's the Russian version of the Mafia. We believe it's used by the 'Pakhan', who's their equivalent to the Godfather, in two ways. One is to be a vehicle for their funds because fine art increases in value at a rate far outstripping bank interest, or as a way to launder money when the item comes onto the open market. They then get one of their number to say the item has been in the family for maybe a hundred years, and if it's been obtained on the black market, it probably hasn't been seen for at least that long. When it sells at auction, it releases clean money. My people reckon this guy's got millions stashed from trading in valuable artefacts."

"How come he hasn't been arrested?" said Dick.

"These people are very clever and very well connected. Knowing what's going on isn't the same as proving it, and don't think it hasn't been tried. The last two agents who led investigations, as well as a government prosecutor, all met with violent deaths. That's another thing, Dick…if you've any dealings with these people, be very careful. They're absolutely ruthless."

"I'll keep it in mind and thanks for the heads up," said Dick.

When he relayed his conversation to Marios and Sol a cloud of gloom descended over the breakfast table.

"What have we got ourselves into?" said Marios.

"We?" said Sol. "What have you got us into, more like."

"Come on," said Dick. "Fighting amongst ourselves will get us nowhere. Let's look at the facts.

"Ali has sent out pictures of the Romanov cross to a guy who almost certainly would want it. By all accounts, even though he could easily afford to buy it, he's the sort of guy who would much prefer to steal it. He also has the resources to make that happen, so it's more than likely he's going to try it. I think, therefore, it's a safe bet he's responsible for the search of your room, Marios. Question is, what's his next move, and whom has he sent to steal the cross?"

"I've been thinking about that," said Sol. "It now seems a bit too much of a coincidence that Ivana, a Russian, chose to join our table for lunch, don't you think?"

"I don't know," said Dick. "She doesn't strike me as the sort to be working for the type of guy Oliver described."

"Talk of the devil," said Sol. "Here she comes."

Ivana was dressed for the beach; she was wearing a tiny yellow bikini and a matching see-through sarong. Her hair was piled high on her head, and she wore long dangly earrings. Her open-toe sandals were indeed summery, although the high heels would not have made for comfortable walking on the beach. In short, she was a real looker and oozed sex appeal. She wished them all good morning but fixed her beautiful green eyes on Dick.

Sensing they were surplus to requirements, Marios and Sol made their excuses and returned to their rooms, muttering their suspicions as they went.

"I can see you're going to enjoy the sun today," said Dick.

"Why not," she smiled. "I told you I like to mix business with pleasure."

"Talking about pleasure," said Dick. "I wonder if you'd care to have dinner with me this evening."

"I thought you'd never ask. Of course, I'd love to."

"It's a date," said Dick, grinning like the cat that got the cream. "Shall I pick you up at eight?"

"I'll look forward to it," she said, her eyes sparkling as she walked away, hips swinging provocatively.

"You've done what?" said Sol in disbelief when Dick got back to the room. "You've arranged to have dinner with her? What if she's the thief?"

"First of all, I don't think she is," said Dick. "Secondly, while we are at dinner, you and Marios are going to search her room and see what you can find out about her."

"How will we get in? I don't know how to use those picks."

"No need," said Dick. "She always leaves her key in the pigeonhole behind reception when she's out. One of you needs to distract the receptionist while the other gets the key. Just make sure you leave everything exactly as you find it. I don't want her to know her room's been searched."

"Okay," said Sol. "I'll do my best. Just don't come back early—my heart can't take surprises."

The day dragged for Dick. He spent some of it buying a new shirt and trousers for their evening out. For the rest, he read every newspaper and magazine he could find in the kiosk next door to the hotel. When at last it was tea time, he spent two hours bathing, showering and shaving before dressing in his new clothes, ready for his date with Ivana. Dinner was going to be special, he decided. He had booked a table at The Ambiance restaurant, which had tables on a boardwalk that stretched out over the sea. The food was purported to be excellent, and the setting was certainly very romantic.

18

A surprising discovery

When he knocked on her door, he was completely unprepared for the sultry vision that was Ivana. Her long black hair fell down over her shoulders onto her long, green, silk dress that matched her eyes. It was slashed to high thigh and had a plunging neckline and back.

She carried a small clutch bag that matched the stylish high heels she wore to complete her outfit.

"It's rude to stare," she said.

"I'm sorry," said Dick. "It's just that I don't think I've ever seen anything or anybody quite as beautiful."

"Flattery when the night is so young," she said, smiling. "And before you've had a drink—I'm impressed." They both laughed, and Dick offered up his arm, which she took as she closed the door.

Sol and Marios went down early that evening and took seats in the lounge with a good view of the door. They had changed from their T-shirt and shorts into smart shirts, trousers and light jackets. Sol had a camera on a strap hanging from his neck. They watched and waved as Dick and Ivana went to reception, where Ivana left her key as Dick had said she would.

Once they were out of sight, Sol approached reception casually and asked the young girl on duty if she would mind taking a picture of Marios in the lounge as he 'struggled with cameras'. She agreed, of course, and while she obliged, Sol collected Ivana's key from its resting place.

Sol gave the all-clear signal to Marios who thanked the girl for her help and rejoined Sol by reception.

"Okay," said Sol. "Let's do it."

They made their way upstairs to her room and let themselves in. The room was tidy—they had to be very careful if they were to leave no trace.

"You take that side and I'll take this," whispered Sol, "but make sure you put everything back as you find it."

"Okay," said Marios, "but why are we whispering?"

"Just get on with it," said Sol, still whispering.

"What are we looking for exactly?" said Marios.

"Anything that might give us a clue about whom she works for and what she's doing here, if she's not just on holiday."

They worked methodically from the dressing table to the wardrobe and then the bedside tables. They found her passport, which showed her name. As she had said, it was Ivana Feodorovna.

"It could be false, of course, if she really is the thief," said Sol.

"I don't think so," said Marios. "Look at this."

From the same drawer in which they had found her passport, Marios pulled out a black calfskin wallet that contained further IDs and, most notably, a card with a picture identifying her as a member of the

DRRA, a department of the Russian government. Sol took a picture of it to show Dick, and then they carefully replaced everything, locked the room and made their way back downstairs.

It was easy to repeat the photo act, this time quoting Marios' same disability with cameras. Now Sol was the subject of the photo while Marios returned the key.

"I think we've earned this," said Marios as they both ordered large brandies at the bar.

"Yes, I think you can definitely say mission accomplished," said Sol. "I wonder what Dick's going to make of it?"

"I don't think he'll be too interested tonight, lucky bugger," said Marios. "I think we might as well have dinner and save our findings for him until the morning."

Sol nodded in agreement and they carried their brandies into the dining room.

The ambiance was everything Dick hoped it would be. The food was exquisite, the wine exceptional, the service attentive and the atmosphere perfect. They ate mussels cooked in wine while the sea lapped at the boards beneath their feet. The conversation never lagged as they followed on with pan-fried veal steaks washed down with a light red burgundy.

Ivana asked Dick about his life, and he told her about losing his parents in a road crash early on in life.

"I was taken in by my father's two unmarried sisters, who doted on me and spoilt me dreadfully. When they could bear to be parted from me, they sent me to a boarding school nearby so that they could have me home at weekends. Luckily for me, I found studying easy, so the years at school were happy ones. For most of my young life I planned to join the army. I studied hard and applied early to attend the military academy at Sandhurst. With my grades and my references, I got accepted, and then I progressed in the vocation I loved. I served all over the world, and all was going according to plan until the government cutbacks and my unwanted early retirement. Out of the army, I had to find a new career, and I was just embarking on that when I met Sol. And the rest you know. What about you?"

"My life hasn't been so exciting," said Ivana. "I grew up in a privileged family who lost much, but not all, of its assets despite the revolution. I'm not ashamed to admit that, being the youngest of four siblings, one brother and two sisters, I was my father's favourite. It's funny the things that prompt your memories. Did you notice the kitten playing in the sand with a napkin that had blown off a table?"

Dick nodded.

"It reminded me of when I was a little more than eight years old and a callous man on a bike dropped a canvas bag containing several meowing kittens in the middle of the main road. I remember my heart pounding, fit to burst, as I ran into the road to scoop them up just before a snow plough thundered by.

"It would have smashed their innocent little bodies and extinguished their tiny lives in an instant. My father then took me to a house that took in orphan children, and I can still see delight on the faces of those children when we gave them a kitten each to care for. The people who cared for the children were kind and did their best, but resources were limited. I realised then how lucky I was, and ever since, it's been my dream to open an orphanage for those less fortunate one day. When I was sixteen, my father arranged a marriage for me with a young man from a good family. Although it was an arranged marriage, I grew to love him, and it was the saddest day of my life when I lost that beautiful man to cancer. Since then, I've immersed myself in my work and until now had no interest in men. I was as surprised as you when such strong feelings surfaced."

"Let's hope the next part of your life will be filled with happiness," said Dick.

"It certainly seems to be improving. I just love it here, Dick…you've chosen well."

All in all, it was a magical evening, and they were sorry when it was time to leave. They thanked the restaurant manager for a wonderful evening and walked arm in arm back to the hotel.

"Shall we have a nightcap in the bar?" said Dick.

She gave him a smouldering look. "Let's take it upstairs," she said.

In her room, she pulled him toward her, crushing her sensuous body up against him. As she kissed him, her tongue darted in and out of his mouth, brushing over his teeth and driving him mad with desire. Still locked together, they fell on the bed and started pulling off each other's clothes in wild abandon. She wore no bra, and he cupped her breast and gently but firmly grazed the nipple with his teeth.

She groaned and shuddered as he pushed her dress further down until she was naked. She wore no panties, and all she was left wearing were her shoes and earrings. Their breaths were hot and heavy.

She had ripped the buttons on his new shirt in her eagerness to get him naked and had pushed his trousers to his ankles with her feet.

He felt his heart pounding as she pulled him hungrily down on top of her hot body, and without guidance, he plunged deep into her. They both groaned in pleasure as their bodies slammed against each other in frenzied unison. After several wonderful minutes, she screamed; he could hold on no longer and exploded inside her like an erupting volcano. They fell back on the bed, bathed in their own sweat, fully sated and exhausted.

"Wow, that was special," she whispered.

"It sure was," said Dick. She laid her head on his chest, and they fell into a deep, untroubled sleep.

Dick rose with the dawn, kissed the still-sleeping Ivana and made his way back to his room to shower and get dressed for the day ahead. He would send some flowers to her room and invite her to lunch, he decided. While he was still singing in the shower, Sol let himself into the room.

"What's making you so happy this morning, or can I guess?" said Sol.

Dick came out in a hotel dressing gown, towel-drying his hair. "I had a great night. How about you?"

"It was quite informative, I'll tell you that."

"Come on, Sol. Don't keep me in suspense—what did you find?"

"It turns out she's almost certainly here for the Romanov cross," said Sol.

Dick winced. "Oh no. I was praying we'd got it wrong."

"We did in a way," said Sol. "Turns out she's from the DRRA."

"What's that when it's at home?"

"It's the Department for the Return of Russian Artefacts. They're tasked with locating Russian art around the world and attempting to oversee its repatriation to Russia."

"So where do we stand with that?" said Dick.

"It depends what they're prepared to pay. Remember this wasn't a stolen item but a gift from the tsar, so they have no rights to it. That said, it's part of their history, so if they want it back and are prepared to pay the going rate, I say why not."

"How come she hasn't approached us about it," said Dick.

"I imagine she's been dealing with Ali, and he'd be hardly likely to put us together to safeguard his commission. I doubt she knows we have it."

"Perhaps we should enlighten her. I'm meeting her for lunch."

"Can't do any harm," said Sol.

19

A disappearance

They made their way down to breakfast and ordered for themselves and Marios. When they were on their second coffee and Marios had still not appeared, Sol sent Dick to fetch him. Dick returned five minutes later looking worried. "He's not in his room. The bed's not been slept in, and there are signs of a scuffle."

"What do you think's happened?" said Sol.

"Nothing good. Come on, we'd better get over to the bank."

"Why the bank?"

"Because if somebody who wants the cross has got him, they'll make him tell them where it is," said Dick.

They were outside the bank as it opened and went straight to their safety-deposit box and checked its contents. It was still there.

"We can't risk leaving it here," said Dick. "We'll have to find somewhere safe Marios doesn't know about."

"I think it's time we went back over the other side," said Sol. "Let's pack our bags and go. If Marios reappears, it's where he'd go anyway."

"I think you're right," said Dick. "I'll tell Ivana who we are and exchange contact numbers. Other than that, let's not tell anyone where we're going. We can contact Ali by phone when we need to."

Dick knocked on Ivana's door, holding flowers he bought from a nearby florist. A sleepy voice answered his knock. "It's me," he said.

"I thought you were still here," said the sleepy voice.

"I need to speak to you."

The door opened and a dishevelled, but still beautiful Ivana beckoned him inside.

"What beautiful flowers. It's very sweet of you."

"Ivana, let me make you a coffee. We need to talk and I haven't much time."

"There's a coffee maker on the dresser. I'll take it black. Now, what's so urgent?" She yawned as Dick set about making the coffee.

"Ivana, I've found out by chance I may be the person you're looking for."

"Oh, don't worry. I'd already come to that conclusion," said Ivana.

"No, I mean with regards to business. I have the Romanov cross, and I know of your interest. Ali Buccaraja is handling the sale for me."

Ivana was wide awake now. "You have the cross?"

"I do, and I see no reason why you shouldn't be the buyer, but I must warn you there's danger from your Russian Bratva. They also want it. Marios has disappeared, and I think they might have him."

"My god! What will you do?"

"There's not much we *can* do at present. We don't know for sure they have him, and we don't have any idea where else he might be. All I do know is that his room hasn't been slept in and he's left no message for me or Sol. Right now, we'll head over to the other side of the island, and I think you should join us. If it *is* them and they find out you're interested in the cross, you could be in danger. Let's exchange phone numbers and I'll call you when we're settled." They quickly exchanged numbers and Dick prepared to leave.

"Tell me…how did you come to own the cross?" said Ivana.

"It's actually Sol and Marios' property, but it's a long story, so I'll tell you when we've got more time."

They kissed, said goodbye, and Dick ran down to reception to meet Sol. Sol had their bags and the cross, of course, so they paid the bill and left for the border.

20

Back across the border

"I think we should find somewhere to stay a little less conspicuous than the Sun Hall, Sol. We don't want to be easy to find," said Dick.

"You're right. Let's ask that Christos if he knows of anywhere and to tell us if Marios shows up."

"Okay, Pervolia here we come."

Within an hour, they arrived in Pervolia and went straight to see Christos. He recommended a small basic hotel on the outskirts of the village: the Sokoriky. Blending in amongst a large settlement of housing near the beach, it was unremarkable and unlikely to attract attention from the casual passer-by, which was exactly what they wanted.

As soon as they had checked in, Dick phoned Ivana and told her to meet him at the airport roundabout, where he would pick her up and guide her back to the hotel. She agreed to call him when she had arrived.

"I'll be in a red Mini," she said. Sure enough, an hour and fifteen minutes later, Dick's phone rang.

"I'm here. How long will you be?" said Ivana.

"Ten minutes, max," said Dick. Then to Sol, he said, "Book a room for her. I'll bring her straight back."

"Isn't that a waste? The way you two are performing?" said Sol, grinning.

"Funny man…just book the room."

Dick flashed his lights when he saw Ivana's car on the roundabout, and she followed him back to the hotel.

After depositing her suitcase in her room, they went down to join Sol in the bar.

"Perhaps now you can tell me how you came by the cross?" said Ivana.

"Seems as good a time as any," said Dick. "I'll let Sol tell you the story from the beginning."

"Well," said Sol. "It was like this…" He related how they found the letter and worked out the whereabouts of the earl's bounty, leaving nothing out. Ivana was shocked when he came to the part about being shot.

"You were right, Dick," she said. "These people are dangerous."

"The people who shot Sol are pussies compared to the bunch I believe are after the cross now," said Dick. "The Russian Bratva is in an entirely different league."

"Why are you so sure it's really them who are after it?" said Ivana.

"Because Ali gave me the name of a fine-art company to which he had sent details of the cross, and when I had it checked out, that's what my informant came up with."

"Your informant?" she said, eyeing him quizzically.

"I told you at dinner I was with Military Intelligence. I've still got contacts, and believe me when I say there's no room for doubt."

Sol continued with his story, bringing her right up to date with their visit to Marios' room and finding it empty, but omitting their search of her room the previous night.

"So that's how you came to be in possession of the Romanov cross. A very interesting story. Would you care to know a little of the history of the cross before the tsar gave it to your earl?"

"I would," said Sol eagerly. "What can you tell us?"

"The tsar had the cross made for his wife by the best jeweller in all Russia at that time, a Jew called Evgeny Telepnev. The tsar was madly in love with the tsarina and had it made as a gift for her twenty-first birthday. Unfortunately, soon after, she had difficulties during the birth of her child and died with the cross in her hand. After her death, the tsar was inconsolable and couldn't look at the cross without being reminded of his loss.

"At this time the Polish-Muscovite war had just ended. Your earl had been invaluable to the tsar in the campaign, so he decided to dispose of the cross by gifting it to your earl. The earl had helped the tsar throughout the campaign and stood by him right up until the Treaty of Deulino, which marked the end of hostilities. That was as much as we knew, and now, of course, you've told me the rest of the story. You can see why we'd want it back in Russia. It's such a romantic story, and what with Mikhail being the first Romanov tsar, we think it's an important part of Russian history."

"I don't see any problem with that, Ivana. It's just a matter of you and Sol coming to an agreement on price. That's right isn't it, Sol?" said Dick.

"Of course, although I'd like to discuss it with Marios, if possible, as it was a joint find."

"Personally, I'd like to get it sorted as soon as we can and get it winging its way back to Russia before anyone gets hurt over it," said Dick.

"Ali Buccaraja is sending pictures and a description to both Christie's and Sotheby's. They should be able to give us some idea of its value in today's market," said Sol.

"Okay, but make sure he doesn't know where we're staying," said Dick. "I think the less people know about the whereabouts of the cross at present, the better."

They went upstairs and freshened up before lunch. "Where do you fancy?" said Sol. "My treat."

"What about the Christos' restaurant?" said Dick. "Then we'd be on hand if Marios appears or sends a message to his cousin."

"That sounds fine," said Sol.

"I agree," said Ivana. "I'm curious to meet this Christos—he sounds interesting."

They climbed into the Mégane and set off down into the village to lunch at Christo's. They were made very welcome.

"Where's Marios?" asked Christos.

"We were hoping you could tell us. We met him and then he disappeared again," said Dick.

"He'll turn up. He's like a bad penny, as you English say."

The food was fresh and moreish. There were bowls of delicious salads with new potatoes and locally caught fish, a selection of meats and cheeses. Several bottles of Aphrodite white wine were downed by the trio before the platter of cakes and deserts hit the table as well. All this was finished off with a demitasse of Cyprus coffee and chocolates.

The afternoon passed quickly, and by the time they were ready to leave, it was getting dark. Sol asked for the bill, which Christos brought but reduced drastically.

"A bottle of wine with me, the sweets with me and the coffee with me," he said, scratching out items on the bill. They made up for his generosity by leaving a hefty tip.

"Thanks for a wonderful afternoon," said Ivana.

"Yes," echoed the others.

"Lunch was great," said Dick.

They shook hands, got into the Mégane and drove back to the Sokoriky.

"I don't think I'm going to make dinner tonight, guys. I'm so full, but it was wonderful. Thanks very much, Sol," said Ivana. "I think I'm going to have an early night. Hope you don't mind?"

"Of course not," they chorused, and after cheek kissing, they bade her goodnight.

"It's a bit early for me, Sol. Do you fancy a drink in the bar?"

"Why not. I can sleep when I'm dead."

They headed for the bar and started the evening with two very large brandies.

They spent the rest of the evening going over all that had happened since they first met on Regent Street, which seemed like a lifetime away. Eventually, they got around to talking about Marios and where he might have been.

"We know he hasn't got the cross, so he hasn't run off again," said Dick. "He'd hardly go off without getting his share."

"So you think he's been kidnapped?" said Sol.

"I'm beginning to think that's a definite possibility. What other explanation can there be?"

"Should we go to the police?" said Sol.

"In my experience, it's best to leave involving the police as a last resort," said Dick. "However, if he doesn't show up by tomorrow, I think we might have to."

On that sombre note, they said goodnight and made their way to bed.

21

Previously: a surprise for Marios

arios couldn't sleep. He paced up and down the room, turning over in his mind all that had happened. The fact that Ivana worked for the DRRA was very interesting. If they were to buy the cross, it would be put on show to the public. That made Marios feel much better.

He felt guilty about trying to make a clandestine sale, which would probably put it in the hands of a private collector and wouldn't see the light of day. He was also feeling guilty about leaving Sol out. They had, after all, found the letter and re-alised its significance together. They had been at the university for many years and researched thousands of old documents between them. It was something they both enjoyed, and it was more than just a job to them. Of course, he told himself, he had no option with a thug like Scrud on his tail. He realised, though, that he could have handled it differently. Sol knew of his gambling problem and would have helped with the dilemma of Scrud. It would not have been the first time Sol had bailed him out over the years. He felt he owed his old friend big time. How was he going to re-pay him? It would not be easy, but losing sleep was not going to help anyone. He phoned down to the bar and ordered a large brandy nightcap. Ten minutes later, there was a knock on the door. It was not room service.

"Good evening, Mr. Savva," said the huge waiter, carrying the drink on a tray. "I believe you ordered a brandy. Please feel free to try this one with our compli-ments."

As Marios picked up the glass a shovel-sized hand closed over his and crushed the glass into jagged shards. Blood dripped from his raw ripped flesh onto the tiled floor, and he winced in pain. "Now, Mr. Savva, we need to have a little talk, but first..." The huge waiter punched Marios on the jaw, and he fell to the floor into oblivion.

When he came round, he was bound to a chair with duct tape. He was unable to move, and there was a piece of duct tape over his mouth as well. Blood was still dripping from his fingers, although it had congealed. His head ached from the blow, and he was struggling to think.

Who was this animal? Surely Scrud hadn't tracked him over three thousand miles, but as his vision cleared and his attacker came into view, he realised it wasn't Scrud.

"Right, Marios. I see you're back with us," said a voice from beyond his line of sight. "You've met Mr. Yakovlev, I see. He's going to ask you a few questions while I go downstairs to the bar for a drink. I suggest you be open and honest with him because the man has such a low tolerance for liars and such a bad temper."

"But how did you find me?" wheezed Marios.

"You're too free and easy with your credit cards. Very easy to track if you know whom to ask at the police-computer section. Such helpful people the police, if you pay them well. Bye for now." He left the room, and Yakovlev returned into view, looming over his helpless victim.

"I'm going to remove the tape over your mouth. If you start shouting or screaming, I shall punish you with much pain. If, however, you tell me what I want to know, this will be a much more pleasant experience for you. Do you understand?"

Marios nodded furiously, his eyes wide with fear. The tape came off painfully, taking the stubble surrounding his mouth with it and leaving a red sore where it had been. He took large gasps of breath. It wasn't easy breathing with the tape on.

"Let's make a start. First, who are your companions, and what's their interest in the cross?"

"Cross, what cross?" Marios dared.

For this, he received a blow to the chest that cracked his sternum; the pain was excruciating. "Now, do I have to repeat the question, or will you tell me what I want to know?"

"They're just f-friends," stammered Marios. "They have no knowledge of any cross"

"So they wouldn't know of its whereabouts then, but obviously you would."

"I left it with a dealer on the other side of the island," Marios risked.

"Would that dealer be Ali Buccaraja?"

Marios nodded and was repaid with a combination of blows that left his head ringing and swelling.

"It might interest you to know that I've spoken with Mr. Buccaraja, and he says you're in possession of it. I've searched your room, and I'm sure it's not there. So where is it?"

Marios couldn't take any more beatings. He could hardly talk through his very swollen lips, but he managed to whisper. "The bank…it's in the bank."

"Shit," said his torturer. "And there's no way you can collect it looking like this." He rained more blows down on his helpless victim in frustration.

22

A gruesome end

The next morning, Dick was roused by a loud knocking on his door. It was Ivana.

"Get dressed and come downstairs. Christos wants to see you in the bar. I'll wake Sol up," she said.

Full of sleep and trying to get his head together, Dick stumbled down the stairs, pulling his shirt on as he went and bumping into Sol on the way.

"What do you think he wants?" said Sol.

"I don't think he's here to complain about the size of your tip," said Dick. "We'll know soon enough."

As they entered reception, Christos was there talking agitatedly to Ivana. He turned when he saw them.

"Have you seen the news this morning?" he said, looking frantic.

"No, we've only just woken up," said Dick.

"Come into the bar," said Christos.

The three of them followed him into the bar, and he switched on the TV. He flicked through the channels to the news and translated from Greek.

"*In the early hours of the morning, a patrol boat from Northern Cyprus discovered a body of a man in Kyrenia Bay,*" said the stern-faced newsreader. "*He had been badly beaten, and items found on the body identify him as a Marios Savva. If anyone has any information concerning this man, they are urged to contact the police. This will be a joint investigation with both forces on the island.*"

When Christos finished the translation there was a shocked silence as they all took it in.

Dick was the first to recover.

"I think you'd better take us down to the police station, Christos. It seems we haven't taken the information I received seriously enough. We should bring the police up to speed with the situation."

"Who would do this to Marios?" said Christos.

"I have my suspicions," said Dick. "I'll explain on the way to the police station."

Turning to Ivana, he said, "There's no point dragging you down there, Ivana. You only know what we've told you, anyway."

"Okay," she said. "I'll wait here until you get back."

They jumped into Christos' car and set off for the police station in Larnaca. Marios had not given Christos any idea about why he was in Cyprus other than that he had a little business to transact and that he then intended to retire. Dick and Sol told him the whole story, and by the time they got to the police station, they had brought him up to speed.

The police took down their statements in detail and said they would send copies to the other force in the north of the island. They could not do anything else, as the body had been found outside their jurisdiction. They apologised that they could not offer protection, but they did agree to send regular patrols to their hotel while they were staying there.

As the trio approached Dick and Sol's hotel, there was a call from Ali.

"I've been trying your mobile, but it was switched off," said Ali.

"We were being interviewed at the police station. I had to switch it off," said Dick.

"So you know about Marios?" said Ali.

"Of course. That was why we were there."

"Right, well, two things then. First, I've heard back from my contacts at Christie's and Sotheby's, and they're both of the opinion that, if the item is genuine, its value at auction would be around two million dollars. That's the good news. Second, and not so good, is that I had a visit from a 'colleague'—that's how he described himself—of Mr. Alexander Noskcaj of Maxczart. He said Mr. Noskcaj wants to talk to you directly, and would I pass on your mobile number. You know normally I wouldn't countenance such a thing—client confidentiality and all that."

"The 'all that' being worried about losing your commission," said Dick.

Ali ignored the sarcasm. "Fact of the matter is, I was more worried about what he might do if I refused, so I handed it over, which you'll understand if you meet the guy," said Ali.

"Don't worry about it. I'm quite interested to hear what he's got to say. Let's agree to keep each other up to date on any developments," said Dick. He hung up.

Ivana met them when they returned and was told about the phone conversation.

"What a cold-hearted, greedy bastard that Ali is," said Dick.

"Do you think it was the Bratva who killed Marios?" said Sol.

"I think it's highly likely, but we can't be sure yet. How do those valuations affect your position, Ivana?"

"I'll have to contact my superiors and take instructions. Normally, in a situation like this, they'll want confirmation of authenticity. That involves taking it to an expert they know on the island or, if they don't have anybody here whom they consider capable, waiting until they send someone of their own," said Ivana. "Once authenticity is confirmed, they'll make an offer."

"That can't come soon enough," said Sol. "I can't wait to see the back of it. Being shot once is quite enough, thank you."

It was during breakfast, half an hour later, when Dick got the phone call.

"Good morning, Mr. Brady. My name is Noskcaj…Alexander Noskcaj. I wonder if it's convenient to discuss some business that might benefit both of us?"

"And what business might that be, Mr. Noskcaj?"

"Let's start as we mean to go on, Mr. Brady, and not play games with each other. I'm interested in the Romanov cross, and Mr. Buccaraja informs me you and your colleague are looking to dispose of it. Seems like a match made in heaven."

"Has Mr. Buccaraja informed you of its value?"

"I wasn't aware a valuation had been obtained," said Noskcaj.

"Ah. Perhaps because it was only confirmed this morning. The value is two million dollars, and there's an offer on the table for that amount." He half-lied.

"I see. I was hoping we'd be able to come to a more reasonable compromise and save us all a lot of trouble," said Noskcaj threateningly.

"Can't see why we would consider compromising when we have a firm offer already," said Dick.

"Unfortunately," said Noskcaj. "I can't be in Cyprus at present, but perhaps we could discuss it again after you have spoken with my representative on the island. He'll be in touch." He rang off.

"What a nice man," said Dick sarcastically.

"You'd be wise not to take him too lightly," said Ivana. "He didn't get to be boss of the Bratva by being a fool, and as an organisation, they're known to be quite ruthless."

"Are you saying we should sell to him rather than you?"

"Most definitely not. All I'm saying is, be careful because until you've disposed of the cross, you'll be in danger. These are evil people who will stop at nothing to get their way. Remember Marios."

"I am remembering Marios," said Sol. "And if these bastards are responsible for his death, no amount of money would tempt me to sell to them."

"I'm with you, Sol," said Dick. "So let's make plans. Priority is to put the cross somewhere safe. It would be really unforgivable if these people were able to just steal it."

Dick and Sol took their leave and arranged to meet with Ivana for dinner that evening.

23

A strange meeting

The three of them shared an Indian meal at the Coast of India, a restaurant in the village whose owner had also known Marios well. People were very subdued; it appeared Marios was well liked, and there was genuine sorrow for his passing.

"Did you manage to find a safe place?" said Ivana.

"We did. Sol had a brilliant idea," said Dick.

"Let's try and forget about it for a while and enjoy this dinner," said Sol.

"Yes, let's," said Ivana.

Dinner was a mouth-watering selection of Indian dishes, accompanied by a delicious rosé wine from a vineyard in India. When it was time to pay the bill, they got their first surprise of the evening.

"It's been paid," said Dave, the owner. "By that big guy at that table outside." He pointed.

They looked to where he was pointing, and there sat what could easily have been Arnold Schwarzenegger's brother. Slavic in colouring and with a Neanderthal heavy brow, he was easily as big as Dick. He saw them looking and raised a shovel-sized hand in a wave.

"If you two are as curious as I am why this stranger should pay for our meal, wait until I get back," said Dick. He got up from the table and went outside to meet their benefactor.

"Mr...?" he asked.

"Yakovlev," offered the man.

"Mr. Yakovlev, thanks for dinner, but why?"

"It's not me you have to thank but my employer, Mr. Noskcaj, who wishes you good health and would like to do business with you. It's a gesture of goodwill, you might say."

Yakovlev was dressed in a camouflage T-shirt and jeans with black combat boots.

He looked like a soldier on leave from the army.

"That's very kind of him, and we have no problem in doing business with him. We're just waiting for his offer," said Dick.

"I'm so glad to hear that because Mr. Noskcaj relies on me to remove any problems in the way of his business interests," said Yakovlev smiling and revealing a mouthful of gold teeth.

"Just remind him the offer we have at present is two million dollars," said Dick.

"Just remember what I said about problems, Mr. Brady. I'm sure we'll be in touch again." He got up, and scowling, with one final 'goodnight', he left.

Dick returned to the others and relayed his conversation with Yakovlev.

"I think there's no doubt this is our initial warning, equivalent to a shot across the bow," he said.

"Why did you say we had no problem doing business with him?" said Sol.

"Because while he thinks there's a chance of getting what he wants the easy way, he's less likely to set guys like Ya-kovlev on us."

"He looked mean," said Ivana. "I'd hate to be on the receiving end of someone like that." She shuddered.

"It's not you they're interested in at present," said Dick, "but it might be a good precaution if you were to return to Russia until the cross is disposed of. If they find out who you're working for and realise you could be a competitor in bargaining for the cross, I believe you'd be in grave danger."

"He's right," said Sol. "Any agreement can still be made by phone, subject to our delivering the cross to your embassy on the island. There's no need for you to be here."

"However important this cross is to you," said Dick, "it's not worth risking your life for it."

"I'll think about it and maybe talk to my superiors tomorrow," said Ivana.

They made their way back to their hotel, and Sol said goodnight and went to bed, leaving the other two sipping a nightcap in the bar.

"That man's really unnerved me," said Ivana. "He looked so mean and cold. I really don't want to be on my own tonight, Dick."

"If that's an invitation, I'd like nothing better than to spend another night with you. As I remember, last time was a lot of fun." He smiled playfully.

She realised she was blushing and chided herself for it, but it was uncontrollable, so she just smiled with him. They finished their drinks, making small talk, keeping off the subject of the cross and then went upstairs arm in arm.

The next morning, they went down to breakfast together to find Sol sitting at the table, reading an English-language Cypriot newspaper.

"The police have made no progress in finding the killer," said Sol.

"Perhaps we should point them in the direction of Mr. Yakovlev," said Dick.

"I'd be very surprised if he wasn't involved. In fact, if I was a gambling man, I'd bet on him being the killer."

"I think we should," said Sol. "While he's fending off the police he'll have less time to bother us."

"Makes sense. We'll go right after breakfast, and hopefully, Ivana, we can get you on a plane out of here today," said Dick.

"I called my people before breakfast, and I'm awaiting instructions," said Ivana.

While they were still eating, Christos arrived at the hotel with a package for Dick. "After what you told me, I think you need this," he said.

Inside the package was a Sig Saur P226 handgun with a holster and extra ammunition. Dick had not been able to take a gun into Cyprus and had no contacts there to obtain one. He had explained this to Christos during their visit to the police station.

"Thanks. How much do I owe you?" said Dick.

"There's no charge," said Christos. "Let's just hope you don't need to use it."

Just then, Ivana got the call she had been waiting for from her superiors in Moscow. She was to be on the midday flight to Moscow. The head of her department had also contacted a friend of his in the FSB (Russian Security Services), who offered assistance if required and to this end had given Ivana an emergency phone number in Cyprus to hand over to Dick and Sol. They had also organised an expert to verify the authenticity of the cross, who was due to arrive on the same plane that would take Ivana back to Moscow.

For the hour that followed, Dick helped Ivana pack and enjoyed a passionate last encounter in her room before she had to leave for the airport.

Dick and Sol drove her to the airport, and Dick carried her bag to the check-in desk. Saying goodbye did not come easily to him. They had become lovers, yes, but there was something else there: something more enduring. At Departures, they clung to each other, Ivana with tears streaming down her face and Dick with a sense of loss, which felt like he had been kicked in the stomach. He was surprised when he felt a hot tear well up in the corner of his eye. It was years since he had felt this close to a woman, if indeed he ever had.

He held her at arm's length and said, "When this is over I'll come to Moscow, I promise." They had one last hug, and then she pulled away from him and almost ran through the door to Departures.

24

An expert decision

Dick and Sol made their way down to arrivals to await the appearance of Mr. Valentino Bortnikov, the expert sent by Ivana's department. They had written his name on a piece of cardboard, and a man answering the description they had been given was walking towards them.

"Mr. Brady and Mr. Levy, I presume?" he said in heavily accented English.

"Of course," said Sol. "Mr. Bortnikov?"

"The very same."

"We have a car outside," said Dick. "Can I take your case?"

"That would be most helpful," said Bortnikov.

He carried a shoulder bag, not unlike a doctor's bag, in addition to his suitcase. Around sixty years of age, he had long white hair parted in the middle and a pair of gold bifocals perched precariously on his rather large nose. He had curious, inquisitive, blue eyes that were taking in everything around him, and he wore a long dark coat which seemed unnecessary in the Cypriot heat. He soon took it off to carry it over his arm, revealing beneath what looked like the black suit of an undertaker. He was obviously dressed for the weather in Moscow, right down to a pair of black ankle boots. They took him back to the hotel, where he checked into what had been Ivana's room.

When he went to meet them in the bar, he had changed into an old-fashioned beige safari suit and a pair of leather sandals. He wore no socks and looked not unlike a relic of the 1960s.

"Right then," he said. "Is it possible to view the item in question so that I can make my report?"

"It is," said Dick. "If you'd like to make yourself comfortable with a drink here in the bar, I'll go and get it. It'll probably take me about twenty minutes."

Mr. Bortnikov sat down at a table with Sol, and they ordered beers and got acquainted while Dick went to get the cross from its hiding place.

"Good afternoon, Father. I've come for my package. I need to show it to someone and then return it, if that's okay."

"Of course, my son. Wait there, and I'll fetch it for you." He disappeared into the priests' private area and after several minutes, returned with Dick's locked box.

Dick had taken a leaf out of William Brewster's book and, with a slight variation, left it in the village church for safekeeping. Definitely one of Sol's better ideas.

He took the box and made his way back to the hotel. Sol and Mr. Bortnikov were still in the bar.

"Here it is." He placed the box and the key on the table.

"Let's take it to a table outside in the light," said Mr. Bortnikov. He had his bag with him and took out various tools, magnifiers and vials of liquids. He opened the box and unfolded the protective chamois-leather cover from around the cross and exposed it to the bright sunlight.

"It is certainly beautiful," he said. "Let's see if it's what it's claimed to be." After around twenty minutes of tests and scrutiny, Mr. Bortnikov came to a decision.

"I have no doubt, gentlemen, that this is the genuine article. The design and workmanship is in keeping with the era, the stones are cut as they were then, the metal is of the right age with the right marks, so a forgery is out of the question. As for being the Romanov cross, I have a copy of the jeweller's working design and a photograph of a painting of the tsarina with the cross. It is, gentlemen, identical. This is indeed the Romanov cross, and I shall report this fact to the DRRA immediately."

Dick and Sol were not surprised. They knew by how they had found it and by Brewster's letter that it was the real thing. And yet they were still relieved to hear it from an expert.

"This calls for a celebration," said Dick. "Let's go down to the village. I can return the cross to its place of safety, and then we can all have a drink."

Mr. Bortnikov made his report, and they were all in high spirits as Dick drove them down to the village. Dick left them with Christos while he returned the cross to its hiding place, and then he joined them as they toasted the Romanovs, William Brewster, Mr. Bortnikov and finally absent friends.

"It's sad Marios isn't here," said Sol. "Even though he pulled a stroke on me, we were friends for many years, and he deserved to share in all this."

"It just wasn't meant to be," said Dick. "But after this is over, I think we should see if there's any way we can bring his murderer to justice."

"If it's whom you suspect, it'll be no easy task," said Mr. Bortnikov.

"We don't need it to be easy, just possible," said Dick.

Just then Mr. Bortnikov's phone rang. Looking puzzled, he handed the phone to Dick. "It's for you," he said.

"Dick Brady here," said Dick. He listened intently for some time then hung up, looking shaken.

"What's up," said Sol. "You've gone deathly pale."

"That was Ivana's boss. They sent a car to the airport for her. She went through passport control but never arrived at the car. They've listed her as officially missing."

25

Changing fates

Dick's first instinct was to fly to Moscow, but Ivana's boss told him to sit tight and that they would inform him as soon as they had any leads. They contacted the FSB, who agreed to instigate surveillance on Noskcaj and his known associates. They also advised Dick to make contact with the FSB people in Cyprus using the contact numbers he had been given.

Dick couldn't sleep that night. He got fed up with tossing and turning in bed, so he dressed and went down to the bar. As it was after one a.m., it was closed, but he helped himself to a brandy and had just sat down when his mobile rang.

"Mr. Brady. I thought you might still be up." It was Yakovlev. "I understand you have something missing, and Mr. Noskcaj suggests we may be able to assist in its recovery."

"I'm only surprised it took you so long to call," said Dick.

"Better late than never, as they say. Now, about the cross. Mr. Noskcaj realises you'll have incurred expenses and is prepared to pay five hundred thousand dollars for safe delivery of the cross. In return, he can guarantee to be successful in assisting in the recovery of your missing friend. I'm authorised to make payment to you in cash here in Cyprus once I have the cross in my possession."

"I'll have to consult my colleague, but if I were to agree," said Dick, "Ivana would have to be present at the exchange."

"That could be arranged. Now consult all you like. You have twenty-four hours to make a decision." The phone went dead.

Dick woke Sol and relayed the conversation with Yakovlev.

"We've no choice," said Sol. "There's no way anyone else is going to get hurt over this."

"I was hoping you'd see it that way, but before we cave in to these rats, I'm going to see if the FSB has any advice."

As soon as the embassy opened, Dick made the call, and within an hour two FSB agents turned up at the hotel. Introductions were brisk. The senior officer was around forty, five foot eight, with thinning blond hair, blue eyes and a freshly shaven plump face. The other had dark cropped hair with a short-trimmed beard, dark eyes and was about six foot tall with pronounced cheekbones. They smiled stiffly as they shook hands.

"I am Agent Fedor Berzin, and this is Agent Dimitri Dimichev. We have some news I'm sure will surprise you."

"Good news or bad?" said Dick.

"Very good news, Mr. Brady," said Fedor.

"Let's not be formal. Call me Dick."

"Okay, Dick. The good news is that Miss Feodorovna is in the custody of the FSB in Moscow."

"But how? Last night she was definitely in the hands of Noskcaj and co. I had a phone call in the early hours, and they were using her as a bargaining chip."

"From what she has told our officers, she was kidnapped at the airport, a hood was thrown over her head, and she was bundled into a vehicle. She was taken to an old disused railway station just a few miles from the airport. When the hood came off, she was in a room with no windows and just a bed. She heard the car drive off and thought they might have left her alone, but a guard went into the room carrying a coffee pot and cups. It appears she managed to seduce the guy, and when his trousers were around his ankles, she smashed the coffee pot over his head and knocked him out cold."

"Well I'll be," said Dick.

Sol just clapped and said, "Good for her. What a woman."

"Can I speak with her?" said Dick.

"She's still being interviewed at present, but they said she'll call you as soon as they've finished. In the meantime, we'd like to discuss tactics and be involved in any further dealings between you and these criminals.

"That sounds fine to me," said Dick. "I could use some back-up."

26

An unfortunate loss

It was midday before Dick got another call, and this time Fedor and Dimitri listened in. It was Noskcaj.

"This is getting very tiresome," said Noskcaj. "I made you a cash offer, which should more than compensate you for your trouble."

"You did, but I understood that the reason it was reduced was because you had something else to offer...the safe return of a friend. That offer, I believe, is no longer in your hands."

"Ah, yes," said Noskcaj. "Such a resourceful lady. We really should have taken more care, and believe me, the punishment of the person concerned will be severe."

"That's not my problem," said Dick. "However, the price has now gone up. That's your punishment."

"It won't pay to be flippant with me, Mr. Brady. You have other friends in Cyprus, and my reach is long."

"Then I suggest you use it to reach deep into your pockets. The price is two and a half million dollars." Dick hung up.

"Did you get enough to make a case?" said Dick.

"I don't know," said Fedor. "Whether it's enough to prove he organised the kidnapping will be up to our prosecutors. As for me, I'm convinced."

"Me too," said Dimitri.

A short time later, Ivana called, and Dick felt as if his heart was going to burst out of his chest. "Are you sure they didn't hurt you?" he asked.

"They didn't really have time. I heard them say they were going to send a few guards back within the hour so that they could do shifts, but I'd gone before they got back."

"You really are quick with that seduction technique."

"To which one do you refer, kind sir?" They both laughed.

"When do you think the DRRA will make an offer for the cross?"

"It could take a few more days. They have to get the government to authorise the treasury to make payment. You know, the usual red tape."

"Okay. We're all really happy you're unharmed, especially me. I'll call you again tonight."

"Right, speak to you later then. Bye."

Fedor and Dimitri were told that Ivana was being kept in a safe house and that they were authorised to offer protection to Dick and Sol. They checked into the Sokoriky.

There had not been any more phone calls for two days, and just when Dick was beginning to think that Noskcaj had perhaps lost interest, they received a visit.

Dick and Sol were sitting outside the Sokoriky, when a courier pulled up with a package addressed to them both. Inside was a DVD. Dick stuck it in his laptop and pressed play. Yakovlev's face filled the screen, gold teeth and all. His gravelly voice began...

"Mr. Brady, while you were worrying about Miss What's-her-name, I was wondering why I'd spotted you twice, visiting the church. Never on a Sunday, and you don't really look like a churchgoing man to me. So I thought to myself, if I was going to hide a cross, where would I choose? And then it came to me. Of course, the best hiding places are always those in plain sight, so a church would be the best place for a cross, wouldn't it? I went and looked in the church, expecting to see it displayed, but nothing. And then I had a hunch. I told the priest I'd been asked to pick up a package left for safekeeping by my friend, Dick. Lo and behold, he had just such a package and was only too pleased to be rid of it. So you see, my friends, I've solved yet another problem for Mr. Noskcaj, and this time without resorting to violence. Maybe I'm getting old. Don't bother reaching for the phone. By the time you get this, I'll be long gone, so goodbye, my friends, and have a happy life." The screen went blank.

Fedor and Dimitri checked and found that Yakovlev had caught the Moscow flight the day before. They had no reason to have anybody watching the airport, and he had not turned up at any of Noskcaj's addresses, which were all under surveillance. He had disappeared into the large metropolis that was Moscow.

Dick turned to Fedor. "There's nothing more we can do here now. Can you let them know in Moscow we're going to be on the next flight?"

"Of course," said Fedor, "but Moscow's a big place, and you'll be on his home ground, so I hope I don't have to tell you to be careful."

"Is there any way you can get me a weapon in Moscow?" said Dick.

"Not officially, but Dimitri is registered as our cultural attaché here, and he has to go back to make our report on the matter. He could take your gun in his diplomatic bag, which, of course, he'll deny knowing about if asked."

"Thanks. From what I know about Noskcaj, I think I might well need it. Right, let's check out the next flight."

There were two flights a day to Moscow, but the early one was full, so they couldn't leave until three p.m. the next afternoon, arriving in Moscow four and a half hours later. That night and the next morning dragged for Dick, the only bright part being his call to Ivana. She was devastated to hear Noskcaj had got his hands on the cross, but thrilled that Dick would be visiting Moscow.

"They won't let me leave the safe house at present, so you and Sol can use my apartment. I don't want you going near Noskcaj alone, though. It would be far too dangerous."

"I'm meeting with some FSB agents when I arrive, and they've promised to help."

27

Moscow, Russia: 2012

Their plane landed at Sheremetyevo Airport just eighteen miles northwest of the centre of Moscow itself. It had been an uneventful flight, during which Sol slept almost the whole way.

Dick availed himself of a couple of the complimentary drinks. Neither of them chose to eat on the plane. Once they had collected their baggage and cleared customs, Dimitri met with Dick in the men's room and gave him the pistol. "I'd keep that holstered and out of sight, if I were you, Dick. I'm not sure how the other agents might react."

"Okay," said Dick. "I'll keep it hidden." Once it was in place and out of sight, Dimitri guided them out to the waiting Lada Priora sedan and introduced them to the agents who had gone to meet them.

"This is Mr. Dick Brady and Mr. Sol Levy," said Dimitri. "And these are agents Andrei Gromyko and Bogdan Vasin."

"We've been instructed to take you to your accommodation," said Andrei. "Miss Feodorovna has given us the keys and the address. As it is late evening now, we'll pick you up at eight a.m. tomorrow. Then we'll take you to headquarters, where we can decide how to proceed."

"Sounds sensible," said Sol. Dick just grunted.

"I can understand your eagerness to get on, Mr. Brady," said Andrei, "but it would be better to start with all resources at hand. Sadly, at this time of night, except in cases of national emergency, this isn't possible."

"He's right," said Sol. "Anyway, you'll be thinking more clearly after a good night's sleep."

It did not take long to reach Ivana's apartment, which was very central and very comfortable.

"I'll take the couch," said Sol, who settled down with a spare blanket. Dick lay down on Ivana's bed and called her on the phone.

"Guess where I am…"

The next morning, as they promised, the agents arrived at eight a.m. sharp. Dick and Sol were already up and breakfasted, so they joined them in the car for the short drive to FSB headquarters, a large, impressive, stone building left over from the communist era and still very much in use. They took the lift to the fourth floor and were introduced to Gregor Ivanovich, the agents' boss.

He began, "Mr. Noskcaj has been a person of interest for some time, but until now he hasn't left any evidence of committing the crimes of which we believe he's guilty. That has now changed with the kidnapping of a government officer, and we'll make every endeavour to bring him to justice. However, even our department in this day and age has certain restrictions on what we may and may not do. That is, in my opinion, why these criminals get away with so much. They know the law, unfortunately often better than we do. That's where a man with your background and abilities could be most useful, Mr. Brady. You may be able to cross a line we shouldn't. I say 'shouldn't' because we've been known on occasion to bend the rules when we feel we can. I'm sure by now you'll have realised I've received a file on you from our London office, so I'm fully aware of your capabilities."

"Yes, I guessed as much. Can you bring me up to date on what you know about Noskcaj? His addresses, business activities, likes, dislikes and movements, since you say he's under surveillance."

"I can do better than that," said Gregor. "If you would take a seat at that desk, I'll have our file brought to you and you can take the information you need."

"That would be more than useful," said Dick. "And I hate to ask more of your hospitality, but would it be possible for Sol to stay with Ivana in the safe house until we have things under control?"

Sol immediately remonstrated. "I'm in this for the long haul, Dick. I want to be with you."

"I know that, Sol, but this is almost certainly going to be dangerous, and you've already been shot once."

"I think you should listen to Mr. Brady," said Gregor. "These people are hardened criminals and will kill without a second thought."

"Okay," said Sol. "I suppose being locked up with a beautiful Russian woman can't be all bad."

"That's settled then," said Dick. He turned to Gregor and the others. "Can we drop the 'Mr. Brady'? Dick will be just fine."

"Of course, no problem," said Gregor.

For the next two hours, Dick immersed himself in the Noskcaj file while the others took Sol to the safe house and tackled their own paperwork at desks in the adjoining office. After he had finished, he poked his head around the door.

"Can we go and look at where this piece of shit lives?"

"Of course," said Andrei. "I'll call the guys on surveillance and let them know we're coming over. It's only fifteen minutes from here. Bogdan will fetch the car."

After ten minutes in the car, the surroundings began to change from typical inner city to residential and then very upmarket, mainly walled properties. Of these, Noskcaj's house stood out as one of the most imposing.

It was set behind eight-foot-high white walls topped with black wrought-iron spikes. You could not see it through the gates, but the roof and the top floor could just be seen from the road. There did not appear to be another entrance, and at the gates there was a camera entry system. Dick pulled out a copy of an aerial photo he had taken from the file, which gave him an idea of the layout of the grounds. What he did not know was how many guards were on duty and where they were placed, but he made an educated guess.

The surveillance team had seen Noskcaj arriving at about six p.m., his normal time. He left every morning at seven a.m. and drove to his office at an old wine warehouse down near the docks, except on Sundays when he usually stayed at home.

"I've seen enough," said Dick. "Now let's go back and work out a plan."

Back in the office, they went through the file again and set up storyboards with various strategies and pictures of Noskcaj's known associates including Yakovlev, who had not yet been seen.

"I think our best opportunity," said Dick, "would be to get the electricity company to cut power to the house after Noskcaj has left in the morning. Then we turn up at the gate in a power-company van, dressed in the appropriate overalls to 'repair a faulty cable connection at the mains'. If we can't gain access this way, a night-time raid is the only alternative."

Dick turned to Gregor. "I think there's very little chance of making a success of this if I go alone. Is it possible for Andrei and Bogdan to accompany me? If not, I have two friends, now retired from the SAS, who I know would be prepared to come over if I asked."

"Well," said Gregor. "I doubt very much if I could get permission to use members of your special forces on Russian soil, retired or not, and I couldn't order my people on an unauthorised raid. If, however, they chose to volunteer, that would be their decision and out of my hands."

"If then," continued Gregor, "you discovered anything on this raid that pointed to illegal activity on behalf of Noskcaj and his friends, I'd be quite within my remit to send in a back-up team. That they would be on standby would simply be a coincidence."

"I'm in," said Andrei.

"Me too," said Bogdan.

"Right, gentlemen," said Gregor. "I'll leave you to make your arrangements. Contact me when you have something to report. I'll be ready."

They made a call to the power company and spoke to the senior manager. They told him they needed his cooperation in a serious matter of concern to the FSB. He agreed to help, and it was arranged for Andrei to go over immediately and explain what they needed, face to face. Meanwhile, Bogdan and Dick made a visit to the armoury in the basement of the building, and Bogdan got three sets of body armour and two Glock pistols with ammunition. Bogdan looked uncomfortable.

"I don't think I'll be able to issue you with a government weapon, Dick."

"Don't worry. I have my own back at Ivana's—we can pick it up from there." Bogdan was puzzled but shrugged his shoulders with relief.

Not long after they got back upstairs, Andrei returned with three power-company overalls.

"I've parked the van in the basement car park. We can pick it up when we like."

"I've been thinking things through," said Dick. "I think we should wait until tomorrow for the raid, for two reasons. First, if we go in as soon as he leaves, it's likely we'll have more time before he knows what we're up to. Second, it'll give you time to make the same deal with the telephone and mobile-phone companies. It would be a great help if they weren't able to contact him from the house once we're in."

"That can be done," said Andrei. "But once the electricity is off, what about the gate entrance system?"

"That'll have a battery back-up for power failure, so it will work even without mains," said Dick.

"Sounds like we've covered all the angles we can. I imagine the rest will be down to luck." said Bogdan.

"Let's go over it all again," said Dick. "I believe in giving luck a helping hand by being thorough." After two more hours of discussing what-if scenarios, they decided to call it a day and meet in the morning at six a.m.

"Why don't we all go out for a drink tonight and we'll show you the Moscow night life," said Bogdan.

"Tempting as that is, fellas," said Dick, "I've got a date with a friend tonight I don't want to miss, and I was hoping you'd drop me off at the safe house and pick me up from there tomorrow."

"Oh, so you're going to visit Sol?" Andrei smirked.

"Yeah, let's say it's Sol." Dick laughed.

Ivana fell into his arms as soon as he walked in the room. "I've so been looking forward to seeing you."

"Me too," said Sol. "How have you got on?"

"I'll tell you what…let me have a shower and freshen up, and then I'll tell you both all about it," replied Dick.

"Okay," said Ivana. "When they rang and said you were coming, I put some food on the stove. Should be ready in twenty minutes."

"Sounds perfect. I'll see you at dinner then."

"Don't be long," said Sol. "I'm dying to know what you're planning."

Dick lingered under a hot shower. It helped him relax and drain some of the strain from his body. It had been an interesting but stressful day. Afterwards, he shaved quickly, using the razor provided by the FSB, having left his own at Ivana's. Feeling much more refreshed, he dressed and walked back into the main room, where Ivana and Sol were just setting the table.

"Something smells nice," he said.

"It's fresh vegetable soup with fresh bread," said Ivana. "They have a trusted housekeeper here who brought the bread and vegetables in earlier, and they have a pressure cooker."

The meal was warm and tasty, accompanied by some good wine. Dick recounted much of the day's events, and Sol, his curiosity satisfied, took half a bottle of wine with him to bed.

"Alone at last," said Dick. "I've been dreaming of this moment since you left Cyprus."

"Funny," said Ivana. "I didn't have you down as a dreamer...I saw you as more of a doer."

She pulled him towards her by his belt and kissed him with a passion that made his blood pound in his ears and his penis twitch and stir uncontrollably. Rock hard, he ached for her embrace. Taking him by the hand, she led him into her bedroom and locked the door. They took longer about their love-making this time, savouring every moment. He kissed her in every private part of her body, and she reciprocated in kind. Taking pleasure in each other's bodies before penetration had no diminishing impact on the ultimate result. Quite the reverse. Her long, low, whimpering moan signalled their simultaneous orgasm, which was longer and even more intense and mind-shattering than before.

"You're something else," said Dick, after he had finally stopped panting and was able to talk.

"I hope that's a good thing." She sighed dreamily.

"Oh, you can bank on that. I can't believe you're still single."

"Probably because I'm very choosy. At least, that's what my mother says."

"So why me?" said Dick.

"I don't really know. I just felt an irresistible attraction the moment we first met."

"So it wasn't my rugged good looks?"

"That might have helped." They both laughed.

He held her in his arms as if he could never let go, and that was how they woke up the next morning. Dick got up at five a.m. and washed and dressed without disturbing her, but when he kissed her gently to say goodbye, she opened her eyes sleepily.

"Please be careful, Dick. I've only just found you, and I don't want to lose you."

"I'll be all right, don't you fret. I'll call you later and let you know how we got on." He kissed her again, said goodbye and closed the door behind him.

Sol was waiting in the lounge already up and dressed. "What are you doing up?" said Dick.

"I wanted to see you off and wish you luck," said Sol. "I've made you tea and a bacon sandwich."

"Thanks, I'm ready for that. I'm absolutely starving. No sign of Andrei and Bogdan?"

"No, but you said they were coming at six and it's only a quarter to."

Sure enough, at six a.m., Andrei and Bogdan turned up as agreed. They had with them the overalls, some power-company IDs and some tool bags. In the bases of the bags were compartments in which they had hidden their weapons.

"I can't imagine getting in that place without being searched," said Andrei. "And if they find our pistols, we'll be finished before we start."

"Good thinking," said Dick. "I'm sure you're right."

They all wore their armoured vests like body warmers, over their shirts, and then dressed in the overalls. Andrei had stuck power-company logos on the vests to help with the subterfuge. With their fake IDs clipped to their breast pockets, they looked just like any other power workers.

"Okay, we've got just under an hour before he leaves. Let's use it by going over the plan of the house and checking where the fuse boxes are. It'll arouse suspicion straightaway if we look as if we don't know what we're doing."

They did this and checked, cleaned and packed away their weapons. At seven a.m., they left in the power-company van for the Noskcaj house.

28

A plan comes together

They parked outside Noskcaj's house and checked with the power and telephone companies that all signals were down. This was confirmed by seven fifteen a.m. At seven thirty, they drove up to the gate and pressed the buzzer. A gruff voice asked, "Who is it?"

"Good morning, sir. It's Moscow Electric. There's been a power surge in the area that's caused a blackout, and we need to check and replace your fuses to get you back online," said Andrei into the voice-box of the entry system.

"Please drive straight up to the house," said the voice.

They parked outside the front door, and two men dressed in suits came out to greet them. Their suit jackets hardly concealed the tell-tale bumps of shoulder-holstered pistols. These were obviously guards, which was confirmed when the elder of the two said, "This is the home of a very important man, gentlemen, so I hope you won't object to a swift search before entering the house."

Andrei looked round at Dick and Bogdan. "I've got no problem with that. Have you two?"

They shook their heads and then submitted to the search. After a body search, the guards had a cursory look in the tool bags and, satisfied, led them into the house.

"I think there are two fuse banks," said the guard. "One in the cellar here." He pointed to a door. "And one in the laundry room here on the ground floor. When you've finished, we'll be in this room by the entrance and will open the gates for you to leave."

"Those are the details we have too," said Andrei. "We'll get on and be out of your way as soon as possible."

The guard grunted and walked back in the direction of the room he had indicated.

"Right," said Dick, once he was out of earshot. "Here's the plan. I don't think for one minute there are only two guards here, so we'll have to deal with these two quietly if we can. We'll go down in the cellar and take out all the fuses.

"Then we'll tell them that we can repair them but that we've discovered a problem they'll have to get their electrician to sort. We'll offer to show them the problem so that they can explain it to their electrician. Hopefully, only one of them will come to look and we'll overpower him and secure him in the cellar."

The plan went like clockwork. The older man sent the younger one to check out the problem, and Bogdan floored him with a blow from a wrench. They took his pistol, gagged him and tied him securely, hands and feet. The next stage was also easy. The three of them walked into the room with guns drawn. The older man was completely taken by surprise and though angry, had to admit defeat. They gagged and secured him and carried him down into the cellar, where they left him with his friend.

So far so good. They checked all the rooms, and the ground floor was clear. Moving as silently as they could, they climbed the stairs to the next floor, and there, sitting on a chair outside a room, was another guard, who appeared to be sleeping. Just as they were congratulating themselves on their luck, he opened his eyes, and in a lightning move, he pulled his gun and fired two shots. One hit the wall behind Dick's head, and the other made a hole in Bogdan's left arm. If there were any other guards in the house, every opportunity for surprise had now gone, so Dick raised his Sig Saur and shot him in the chest. After all the noise of the shooting, it was eerily quiet.

They bandaged Bogdan's arm with a field dressing. Luckily, the bullet had gone right through and spent itself in the wall. All of a sudden, they could hear scuffling and what sounded like weeping. It was coming from behind the door where the guard had been sitting.

They checked all the other rooms on the landing and they were clear. Dick stood tall to one side of the door, and Andrei knelt beneath him and raised an arm to turn the door knob. If anybody fired from within, they would have been unlikely to hit either of them. The door was unlocked and opened with a creak. The weeping increased in volume, but nobody fired. They entered the room warily, guns at the ready, and were amazed at the sight within. There were five double beds crammed into the room and probably twice as many young women. Most of them showed signs of beatings, and several were crying and shaking. Dick carried on checking the house for guards but found none. The girls told him there were five guards, but two of them accompanied Noskcaj each day. They had been told that they were there to be softened up, which meant they would be systematically raped and beaten, until they learned to do exactly what they were told without question. They were then going to be sold at an auction organised by Noskcaj. Some had answered ads offering big money for modelling. Others had just been snatched from the streets.

"At last, we've got something we can act on," said Andrei. Bogdan went down to the van to fetch a two-way radio, which he used to call Gregor with an update. Within ten minutes of the call, the electricity and phones were back on, and ambulances and a back-up team were on their way. Bogdan waited with the girls while Andrei and Dick did a systematic search of the house. They found a computer, which they took, but very little else.

"It's strange," said Dick. "There isn't even a safe, unless we've missed it. If it hadn't been for the girls, there'd have been nothing here to incriminate him."

"And according to the girls," said Andrei, "the auction was set for tomorrow, so if we'd left it another couple of days, we'd have had nothing against him again."

"There's got to be more somewhere," said Dick. "There's got to be records, and he must have a stash. You don't become head of the Bratva and have nothing to show for it."

"Perhaps it's all at the warehouse," said Andrei. "That would make sense."

"That's our next port of call, then," said Dick. "And this time, Gregor should be able to make it official."

Sure enough, Gregor followed the ambulances up the drive.

"Well done," he said. "We've now got authorisation for a full-scale investigation into Noskcaj's activities and a warrant to search all his premises. In thirty minutes' time, we'll have two SWAT teams ready for a raid on his warehouse, and I'd be happy if you gentlemen would join us."

"Try and keep us away," said Dick.

They joined Gregor in his car, and he drove them to the warehouse. The Swat team consisted of about sixty men and were carrying every possible vicious weapon from the standard AK47 to the modern PP2000 man-stopper. Dressed in black combat kit and wearing German-style helmets, they looked like they meant business. Their commanding officer, Kapitan Igor Asimov, answered to Gregor.

When Gregor informed him that Dick and Andrei were going to join his troops in the operation, he issued each of them with a yellow band worn like a bandolier. These, he said, would ensure they did not get hit by friendly fire from his troops in the heat of battle.

29

A different situation

The warehouse was a completely different situation to the one at Noskcaj's house. The advance scouts of the SWAT team had spotted around twenty guards, and those were the ones they could see. All of them appeared to be well armed with high-powered automatics. There was a yard in front of the warehouse, accessed by large industrial gates. The kapitan had sent one of his men, who had managed to crawl up without being seen and had placed an explosive charge on them. He then ordered half a dozen snipers into place before the start of the assault. When they were in position, he gave an order on his helmet mic, and the snipers began to take out targets at will, using silenced Dragunov sniper rifles with thermal scopes. Silenced or not, their presence was soon detected, and as soon as he observed return fire, he ordered the gates to be blown, and the three trucks of men, including Dick and Andrei, thundered into the compound. The men spilled out of the trucks and lay down a vicious barrage of deadly accurate fire. While they were methodical in clearing each building as they went, Andrei and Dick headed for the main block, where they thought Noskcaj was most likely to have had his office.

It was hard fighting all the way. "I don't know what he's paying these guys," said Dick to Andrei, "but it must be a lot, considering the fight they're putting up." Smoke was beginning to float in drifts, filling their nostrils with the acrid smell of gunpowder. They eventually fought their way to the main entrance and kicked through the doors, firing as they went. Inside, they realised there was nothing to fire at. It was obvious these offices had been recently occupied, from the smoking cigarette stubs and the still-warm coffee cups. Whoever had been there, though, had managed to escape.

"Damn." Dick cursed.

There was no doubt the raid had been a success for the FSB. They found all manner of contraband in the warehouses, including a drug-packing factory and a printing machine set up to forge Russian banknotes. They killed eleven guards and captured a further seven, but the casualties had been horrendous.

Of the sixty men deployed, seven were dead and eleven badly injured. Noskcaj's ex-Spetsnaz guards were an aggressive enemy and no easy target. As for Noskcaj, there was no sign of him.

"All the records we've found show the profits from these illegal operations going to 'My Friendly Friend'. What the hell does that mean?" said Dick.

"Bit of a mystery," said Andrei.

The only good thing from Dick's point of view was that Noskcaj was now a wanted man—a man who would be indicted as a criminal and would spend the rest of his life in prison if the Russian government ever caught up with him. However, they found no trace of the cross.

Dick didn't go back to the safe house. With Noskcaj on the loose, he didn't want to risk putting Sol and Ivana in danger. He thought he would know if he was being followed, but one could never be sure, and he didn't want to take the chance. He decided to stay at Ivana's, and he rang them from there and recounted the details of the day's operation. They were disappointed the cross had not been recovered but relieved Dick had come through it unscathed. Gregor's people were still trying to break the encryption on the computer they found in the house. Dick arranged for Andrei to pick him up in the morning and take him to headquarters so that he could see first-hand what progress, if any, had been made.

30

An unexpected visitor

The doorbell rang at seven thirty a.m. Dick had dressed and was making himself breakfast.

"You're bloody early," he said as he opened the door.

A totally unexpected blow to the chest sent him crashing to the floor.

"Well, the early bird catches the worm. Even more appropriate in your case. Mr. Noskcaj sends his regards."

It was Yakovlev. Although Dick was taller, Yakovlev was as strong as an ox, and he picked up the startled Dick and threw him across the room.

"I think this is going to be fun, Mr. Brady. Now get up and fight like a man."

That was Yakovlev's first mistake because giving a fighting man like Dick Brady time to recover was a bad idea. He feigned a stagger, and as Yakovlev stepped in to take a punch, he sidestepped and landed a powerhouse blow to the gut that would have felled most men. Yakovlev realised this was not going to be as easy as he thought, but he did not go down. Instead, he retaliated by swinging his ham-sized fists and landed some powerful blows. As he prepared to repeat the combination, Dick head-butted him so hard, it knocked him over onto his back. Instead of staying down, he just shook his head and climbed back up.

"I can continue like this all day," he said. "Eventually, you'll get tired, Mr. Brady, and then I'll break your neck."

"Do you know I think that, just maybe, you could," said Dick. "Sod this!" He pulled his Sig from its holster in the small of his back and shot Yakovlev in the chest. At such short range the damage was serious.

"I thought you would fight man to man," panted Yakovlev.

"What on earth gave you that idea?" said Dick. "Now look…that's quite a serious wound, and if it's not treated soon, you'll most certainly die."

"So get me an ambulance," said Yakovlev irritably and obviously in pain.

"First things first," said Dick. "I want some information, and I just hope for your sake you have it, otherwise I'm going to shoot you again and leave you here to bleed to death."

"What information?"

"Wait just a minute." Dick left and returned with a shower curtain, which he laid on the floor. "Now just roll over onto that and stop bleeding on my friend's floor."

"You're a hard man, Mr. Brady."

"Call me Dick, and yes, I know. It comes from a lifetime of dealing with people like you. Now, information."

"What do you want to know...Dick?"

"I want to know who Noskcaj's 'Friendly Friend' is. All the records we found show the proceeds of his nefarious lifestyle going to his 'Friendly Friend'. I want you to tell me who that is." Yakovlev laughed, and it made him cough up blood.

"That looks bad," said Dick. "I wouldn't take too long with your answer. What's so funny?"

"What's funny is that it's not a who but a what. Just near the warehouse in the dock is an old, out-of-commission warship. Noskcaj owns it, and it's called the Druzhny. How's your Russian, Dick? Do you know what that means?"

"Druzhny? Haven't a clue. Enlighten me."

"It means friendly, and on that ship, in the captain's cabin, he's built a huge strong room, where he keeps all his valuables. He has a team of ex-Spetsnaz on guard there at all times."

"So that's why we found nothing in his warehouse." Dick's eyes widened with the revelation. Just then Andrei walked through the open door.

"What's going on?"

"Mr. Yakovlev and I have just made a deal," said Dick. "And as he's kept his side of the bargain, I'd like you to call an ambulance."

Andrei took a look at Yakovlev and telephoned for an ambulance.

"Right," said Dick. "We've got a ship to storm. Can you call up the SWAT team? I'll explain everything on our way to the docks."

31

The Ghost Ship

It was two hours before Kapitan Igor turned up at the docks with the SWAT Team, closely followed by Gregor.

"What's the situation?" said Igor.

"I'm not sure," said Dick "I've been told that, other than the bank assets, the tangible proceeds of Noskcaj's criminal ventures are stored on that ship." He pointed to the Druzhny. She rose from the frozen water like a ghost ship. Though early spring, the weather in Cyprus was warm, but in Moscow the thaw had not yet set in. The frost clung to the old twentieth-century warship, still sporting her disused deck guns draped with icicles hanging from their rusted barrels. Against the cold, grey sky, it was a sad sight to see.

"I was told she was guarded by more Spetsnaz," said Dick. "But we've been here two hours, and we've seen no movement."

"Either they're very careful not to show themselves," said Andrei, "or our information is wrong."

"Somehow I don't think he was lying, but something's not right," said Dick. "Let me go aboard alone first, and if you hear firing, then send in the cavalry."

"That's a dangerous game," said Gregor. "At least put on some body armour."

Igor fitted Dick out with full SWAT-team kit and ordered snipers into position as back-up. They did a radio check, and Dick cautiously made his way to the ship's gangway while they watched from hidden positions. The gangway was in surprisingly good condition compared to the rest of the ship, and Dick crept up quietly and carefully, watching for trip wires or any other warning systems. There were none. On board, he went below deck, listening for any sounds or movements and worked his way to where he was most likely to find the captain's cabin. When he found it and radioed them, there was disappointment in his voice.

"Gentlemen, our information was correct, but unfortunately the bird has flown." The SWAT team swarmed aboard and confirmed the ship was indeed unmanned.

Gregor and Andrei joined Dick in the captain's cabin, where he was leaning dejectedly against the wall of a room that looked more like a bank vault. The open doors were made of twenty-inch-thick solid steel. There were shelves along two walls, all empty like the rest of the room. In contrast to the rest of the ship, this room was in pristine condition. Down below, the SWAT team found the crew quarters had also been kept up to date, and there were signs of recent use.

It looked as though Yakovlev's information had been accurate.

"He beat us to it," said Dick. "He must have had contingency plans in place to react so quickly."

"He's a professional criminal and no fool," said Gregor. "I think we need to accept we're dealing with an intelligent adversary and try to anticipate what his next move might be. Try to put ourselves in his place and think like him. Let's go back to headquarters and review the situation."

"Sounds like a good idea," said Dick.

The atmosphere in the car on the way back to headquarters was subdued. Each of the men was lost in his own thoughts. This was soon to change because, when they arrived, there was a pleasant surprise waiting for them.

Peter Eltsov, the head of the IT department at the FSB, was there to greet them, along with Bogdan.

"There have been developments, gentlemen," he said. "If you would be seated, I'll explain."

"We have some new highly classified computer processors which allow us to decipher encrypted information at previously unheard-of speeds. Encryptions that would have taken months or maybe years to break can, with these processors, be broken within a few hours. As I said, this kit is highly classified, so your Mr.

Noskcaj wouldn't be aware of it. Information he considered a hundred percent safe on the computer you found at his house is being deciphered as we speak."

They followed Peter to the IT department and watched in wonder as the information began building on the large computer monitors before their eyes.

"He's obviously a man who plans ahead," said Dick. "Now that he's been compromised in Russia, we need to know where he would be likely to head next."

"I have access to a computer that could estimate his most likely destination, based on all this information," said Peter.

"Let us know as soon as you have a result," said Gregor.

Feeling a lot happier and more optimistic than they had when they left the docks, they decided to go for lunch and unwind after the tensions of the morning. Gregor insisted it would be his treat.

"I'll take you all to the Central House of Writers restaurant in what we call Old Moscow," he said.

32

To track a criminal

Dick updated Ivana and Sol by phone and asked them to make their way to the restaurant Gregor had suggested. He felt that, with Yakovlev out of action and Noskcaj on the run, they would be safe now. The others drove about ten minutes from headquarters on Arbat Street, parked the car and then walked through a labyrinth of lanes, passing many stunning mansions. A few minutes later, they came across the beautiful, white, stuccoed building that was the restaurant. Ivana and Sol had arrived before them and were waiting outside.

How this building had survived in the austerity of communism was a mystery. It looked like a small white castle out of a fairy tale. Inside the restaurant, it was like stepping back in time to another more glamorous, era. The lighting was from crystal chandeliers. There were carved fireplaces, rich wood panelling and antique balustrades. The windows were of coloured glass, and the interior décor and carpets were in red and cream. The overall feeling was of opulence. The food and service was a perfect match. The elegantly dressed waiters, in tail-coats and white gloves, served a choice of Russian or French food, and Dick let Gregor order for him. They dined on mushroom soup served with fried mushrooms and cheese sippets, followed by grilled venison. Andrei ordered the wine, a Russian Myskhako organic red cabernet from Kuban, Russia's warmest wine-producing area. It was delicious.

It was a much more relaxed and happy crew that returned to headquarters a couple of hours later.

"Right, Peter," said Gregor. "What have you got for us?"

Peter Eltsov was a tall thin man with an old-fashioned monocle, slicked-back grey hair and a long grey moustache. He wore a pink shirt with white collar and cuffs and a navy-blue blazer. As he divulged the information he had obtained, he stuck out his chest with pride.

"The information has revealed he has several residences around the world, but according to the computer, he's most likely to head for a private villa he owns in Barbados.

"His second retreat is likely to be a small estate next to the Oberoi Hotel in Agra, India."

"Looks as if we're likely to get a tan either way, fellas." Dick grinned. "That's assuming Gregor will allow you to accompany me?"

"Now that there's a Russian warrant out for his arrest, I see no problem with that," said Gregor. "But what about Bogdan's arm?"

"It's okay, sir," said Bogdan. "The bullet went straight through. It will soon be on the mend."

"All right. I'll get you the authorisation, but be sure to keep me advised of your progress. I'll leave you now to make your travel arrangements, as I've got other matters to attend to." He shook Dick's hand and said goodbye.

"Where are you and Sol going to stay while we're in Barbados?" said Dick, turning to Ivana.

"If you think, Mr. Brady, that you're going to leave me behind, you're very much mistaken," she said, her eyes flashing.

"Or me," said Sol.

"It might still be dangerous. We don't know what protection he'll have if he's there. I doubt Yakovlev's the only thug on his payroll," said Dick.

"We'll take our chances," said Ivana. "Being stuck in that safe house is like being under house arrest."

"And we've had enough of it," chimed in Sol.

"Blimey, you two are a formidable team when you work together. I'll have to remember that," he grinned. "Okay, you know the risks, and you're grown-ups, so I'll accept your decision."

"Good," said Andrei. "I'll get the flights booked. I suggest you get your things together, and I'll try and get us on the first flight out tomorrow."

They left Andrei to arrange the bookings and caught a taxi back to Ivana's and packed for the journey. Sol and Dick packed their small holdalls, and Ivana had a large expensive-looking suitcase.

"That can't be all you're taking, surely?" She laughed.

"We'll buy anything we need at the airport or when we get there," said Dick.

"What about weapons?" said Sol. "How will you get them on the plane?"

"Andrei and Bogdan are organising that, so we'll be going in clean."

"That's a relief. I always feel guilty going through baggage check, even when I've got nothing to hide," said Sol.

The phone rang. It was Andrei with good and bad news. The good news was he had booked the flights. The bad news was that there were no direct flights to Barbados. They had to stopover in London and then change airports. It was going to be a long journey.

They caught their first flight at five fifty the next morning on a flight to London Heathrow. They then made their way to London Gatwick to catch the connecting flight to Barbados. They caught a transfer bus from Heathrow and spent several hours in the first-class lounge at Gatwick before boarding. They slept for most of the flight. Andrei had booked them in first class, and their seats turned into six-foot-six beds.

A meal was served about an hour before landing, and the plane touched down, on time, at nine p.m. After going through customs, they met up with Andrei and Bogdan, who had once again taken advantage of diplomatic status and made their way straight out of the airport. A limousine took them swiftly to the embassy in Bridgetown, where Andrei had arranged for them to stay for the first night.

33

Just Outside Bridgetown, Barbados

The embassy was situated on the top of a hill just outside Bridgetown and was accessed by a long winding drive lined with palm trees. Built in colonial times, it was once owned by a Dutch millionaire, who had made a fortune out of bananas in the years after the Second World War. It was painted pale pink and had white window frames and balustrades. The ceilings were fourteen feet high, and a breeze through open windows, in addition to the ceiling fans, kept the rooms reasonably cool. They were welcomed by an efficient butler, who gave orders to several uniformed boys and soon had their luggage dispersed to their rooms.

"Perhaps, gentlemen, you'd like a light supper and a nightcap before you retire?" he said.

"That would be very much appreciated," said Andrei. The butler asked them to wait in a lounge where a maid served them drinks while their meal was being prepared. They could hear the sound of crickets clearly from the surrounding grounds. It was very peaceful as they relaxed in this beautiful mansion.

They agreed to leave planning their next move until the morning and spent the remainder of the evening enjoying the excellent supper that had been provided. Dick and Ivana were given a room together, courtesy of Andrei making a request of the butler. There was a large double bed in their room, placed under a ceiling fan. There were mosquito nets on the windows and a back-up net hung from the fan and covered the bed entirely. The bed was a bit of an antique, and Ivana giggled when it squeaked as they made love. Lying there naked together, Dick could think of nowhere he would rather have been. The smells of exotic flowers drifted in from outside, and that and the sounds of the crickets lulled them softly to sleep.

The next morning, they awoke as warm sunshine flooded the room and reflected off the white-painted wood-panelled walls. They could smell the sea as they stretched and rubbed the sleep from their eyes. They quickly showered and dressed for the day, Ivana in a light floral summer dress and sandals, and Dick in a T-shirt and shorts he bought at the airport.

Sol had beaten them down to breakfast, and Andrei and Bogdan arrived as they were taking their seats at the table.

"Did everybody sleep well?" asked Andrei. There were nods all round.

"Right. I've had a message from the ambassador, and he says that we're welcome to stay here, as he's in Moscow for a fortnight."

"That's really kind of him," said Dick. "It'll save us some time. Now let's decide what we need to do today. I think our first job is to find out if Noskcaj is here and if so then do some surveillance on his villa to see what we're up against."

"Our people have checked with immigration and he is here," said Andrei. "The problem with surveillance is that the villa is at the end of an unmade private road surrounded by tropical jungle. That means it can't be done by just sitting comfortably in a car. We've got to penetrate the vegetation to get a view of the house without being seen."

"Not a nice job with all the creepy crawlies they have here. There are insects and snakes," said Dick, screwing up his face with distaste.

The others nodded in agreement with the exception of Ivana. "You men," she said. "Such a lot of fuss over a few spiders."

"Spiders!" Dick feigned fear. "I hadn't thought about the spiders." They all laughed.

"Right," said Bogdan. "The villa's situated up in the hills near Sandy Lane Bay. I've prepared some equipment—binoculars, cameras, etc. Let's have a drive up there."

At Sandy Lane, they dropped Sol and Ivana off at the beach and then turned right off the main highway up into the hills. The first thing they noticed was that tiny brightly coloured huts had replaced the more elegant dwellings along the highway. Locals were sitting out on verandas, sipping cold drinks, smiling and waving at passers-by. The people on the island were a friendly bunch. The road soon deteriorated into little more than a track, overgrown with vegetation on both sides and hardly wide enough for two cars to pass each other. When they were half a mile away, they parked the car in the entrance to a maize field and continued on foot. Bogdan had a map and had marked the unmade road that led to the villa. They were soon there. The problem was that they would have no excuse for being on this road. There was a rotting painted sign, which still said quite clearly NO TRES-PASSERS, and they didn't want to show their hand this early on. To avoid being seen, their only alternative was to go past the road and then make their way through the vegetation alongside it. To this end, Bogdan had brought along three wicked-looking machetes to aid their progress if the going got tough. After what seemed like an age, but was actually only about thirty minutes, they reached a spot where they could overlook the villa. Through their binoculars, they could see several people moving around, and three Range Rovers were parked outside. They settled in for a long day of surveillance, taking turns with the binoculars and making notes of the comings and goings.

One of the Range Rovers left on two occasions with three occupants, none of them Noskcaj. They had studied the FSB surveillance pictures of him and were unlikely to make a mistake.

Andrei took note of the times of the excursions to see if they would be repeated the next day and so form a routine. If they could make their move when at least three of them were out of the way, so much the better. At the end of the day, they drove back to the embassy, collecting Ivana and Sol on the way.

"You lot look rough," said Ivana. "How did you get on?"

"It's not much fun hacking your way through undergrowth then lying on the ground thinking about spiders. Yuk!" said Dick. Ivana laughed.

"We got a fair bit of information today," said Andrei. "I'd just like to check on where they disappear to when that Range Rover leaves. I wouldn't be surprised if there's a favourite restaurant nearby. If it's a regular watering hole for them, we might be able to get some more information from there."

"I'll stay with the car tomorrow," said Bogdan. "I'll follow them when they leave."

They got an early start the following day and were in place by seven a.m. Andrei started making detailed notes. This time, they spotted Noskcaj and three others leaving in the Range Rover at about ten thirty a.m. They returned at eleven thirty. At one thirty p.m., the car left again without Noskcaj but carrying the same three guards. This time they did not return until four p.m. like the day before.

"It looks like they enjoy long lunches," said Andrei.

"That's good for us," said Dick. "It gives us a better window of opportunity. Let's see if Bogdan can tell us where they've been."

Bogdan had done a really good job. He followed them to St. James, where they spent the afternoon lunching at the Lone Star restaurant. After they had left, he managed to strike up a conversation with the owner, and it turned out he was none too happy about their visits. It appeared that Noskcaj enforced a protection arrangement on him and other restaurants in the area. Apart from paying Noskcaj a monthly fee, the agreement also included free food and refreshment for him and his minions whenever required.

"He was so angry about it that he couldn't hide his resentment," said Bogdan. "He says they're there every day at lunch and visit other places in the evenings. They always dine on the finest foods and order the most expensive wines and champagne, which they drink in copious amounts but never pay for. He said it's not always the same ones who come, and he thinks there are about eight in total. I'm sure it would be easy to get him on our side so that he could give us a warning phone call when they're leaving."

"Do you think he'd dare to go further and maybe spike their drinks?" said Dick. "That way we'd have more time to secure and search the villa."

"Why don't we go there for dinner tonight? You could ask him yourself," said Bogdan.

"Sounds like Ivana's motto, mixing business with pleasure. Great idea," said Dick.

They collected Sol and Ivana from the beach again and answered their barrage of questions.

"You two must be so bored on that beach all day to be so interested in what we've been up to," said Dick.

"I can live with that kind of boredom," said Sol. "Take as long as you like. This tan's coming along nicely, and I've acquired a taste for the local rum and coke."

"Me too," said Ivana. "I'm feeling so rested, and I always feel better with a tan."

Back at the embassy, they changed for dinner.

"Stop looking at my white bits," said Ivana as Dick joined her in the shower.

"You show me yours and I'll show you mine," said Dick, laughing

"That's not fair. You don't have any white bits. You're white all over. Except for that red nose."

After they had finished horsing around in the shower, they dressed for dinner, Dick in white shorts and a colourful Hawaiian shirt and Ivana in a pink, cotton, skin-tight dress. It was strapless and very, very short.

"They'll certainly see you coming," said Ivana, smiling.

"And if that dress covered any less of you, I could use it for a napkin." He grinned.

Sol, Andrei and Bogdan were waiting for them, dressed a little more conservatively but still able to pass as tourists. Andrei had hired an open Jeep rather than using the embassy car, and he drove them to St. James and the Lone Star.

The restaurant was built right on the beach. It was slightly raised, with tables set on a wooden dais that overlooked the glorious moonlit Caribbean Sea. A lamp hung over each table giving enough light for them to read the exotic menu, and blazing torches were placed where the restaurant met the beach. The tables were covered in white linen and the chairs in sea blue. The atmosphere was fresh and exotic at the same time. Bogdan introduced them to Isaac, the owner, and they agreed to meet later in the bar.

They asked the waiter to recommend a meal and chose his suggestions. The food was exquisite and the wines no less so. They kept off the subject of Noskcaj at dinner and had enjoyed themselves. But as they sat at a table in the bar with their brandy and coffees, his name drifted back into the conversation. Bogdan took Isaac over to their table and asked him to repeat his story. He didn't need much prompting.

The anger Bogdan had described was still evident in the vehemence with which Isaac described Noskcaj and his henchmen.

"I can see you're pissed that he's taking your leg up," said Dick. "Are you prepared to do something about it?"

"Like what? What do you have in mind?"

"We need to get inside his place to search for something he's stolen from us," said Dick. "If you could slip something in their drinks when they come down for lunch, something that would knock them out for several hours, it would leave us with fewer of his cronies to deal with at the villa and save us looking over our shoulders for the return of those lunching."

"And where would I get this 'something'?" said Isaac.

"Don't worry about that," said Bogdan. "Our people will sort that out, no problem."

"What about when they come round?" said Isaac. "They'll know something's up."

"They'll have memory loss with what we'll give them," said Bogdan. "We'll put them in their car with an empty canister of nerve gas. They'll think their car's been rigged, so no suspicion will fall on you."

"Anyway, by the time they come round, their main interest will be getting back to the villa," said Dick.

"Okay," said Isaac. "I'm in. Just let me know when."

They left the restaurant and headed back to Bridgetown. "Listen, fellas," said Dick. "I've been thinking. Even if Isaac can take three or four of them out for us, there's still going to be at least four left and maybe more if Isaac's got it wrong. I've called a couple of old pals in for back-up. I hope you don't mind."

"We've got no problem with evening up the odds," said Andrei. "We're not in Russia now, so there are no rules to comply with."

"Good. That's settled then. They'll be here tomorrow morning."

34

Friends reunited

The next morning after breakfast, Dick, Andrei and Bogdan's first port of call was the airport, where they collected Spud and Danny.

"Now then, me old mucca," said Spud. "Missing us, was yer?"

"You know the little fucker can't manage without us when there's a real job on," said Danny.

Spud was a Cockney, born and bred in the docks area in the East End of London. He remembered holding his grandma's coat as a child while she took on all and sundry when the pub turned out. He had a rough upbringing but had turned out to be a lovable character—unless you were the enemy. Danny was just as tough, from a family of no-nonsense coalminers outside Cardiff. Both of them carried the accents they were born and brought up with. Since joining the army in their early teens, the two were inseparable. Now on Civvy Street, nothing had changed. If one wanted to use their services, they came as a pair.

They looked like fair and dark versions of the incredible hulk. For all their bulk, they were light on their feet, as big people often are. They were skilled marksmen and experts in martial arts. The army recognised their natural talents early on, and they had swiftly been channelled into the SAS. Promotion came almost as swiftly and simultaneously. They were the youngest sergeant instructors on record. They were used to working under fire in war zones and had quite a few undiscussed black ops under their belts. They were two guys whom you would definitely want to be on your side in any action. And they were obviously delighted to see Dick, as there was much hugging and banter as they renewed their acquaintance in the arrivals section of the airport.

"We'll need to get you kitted out with weapons," said Dick. "Any favourites?"

"No need, mate," said Spud. "We've got our own contacts on the island. You tell us about the job and our local friends will get us what we want."

"You've got contacts here in Barbados?" said Dick incredulously.

"We've got contacts nearly everywhere, pal," said Danny. "We're now what you might call an 'International Concern.'" They all laughed.

"Okay," said Dick. "We'll get you settled in, and then I'll bring you up to date. Andrei here says our invitation extends to you, so we'll all be staying together at the Russian embassy.

"Sounds posh," said Spud. "Don't think I've ever stayed in an embassy before. Stormed one or two but stayed...nah." Spud and Danny were nearly in hysterics. Dick got the joke, but Andrei and Bogdan looked bewildered. Dick realised that perhaps they were not aware the SAS was famous for storming the Iranian embassy in London.

"Take no notice of these two," said Dick to Andrei and Bogdan. "If the army hadn't taken them in, they'd have been on the stage in stand-up comedy."

Still in a merry mood, they drove back to the embassy along the palm-fringed highway. Dick contacted Isaac and told him the earliest they would make the attempt would be the next day. He wanted to give Spud and Danny time to get over any jet lag and time to obtain what they needed for the job. They had a working lunch so that Dick could explain the plan and show the boys the layout of the villa. Afterwards, he gave them time to collect whatever weapons they needed and then let them rest.

Sol and Ivana joined them for lunch. After the introductions, Dick had to suffer the usual barrack-room banter.

"Bloody hell, Captain, you kept that one quiet," grinned Spud.

"I hope you've laid on something as tasty for the enlisted men," whispered Danny.

"Come on you two," said Dick, smiling. "Let's get down to business.

His plan was a simple one. They would use a rented van and have stickers made for the sides and the bonnet, saying 'Lone Star Takeaway'. Two of them would arrive at the villa in the van and tell the guards their guys lunching at the restaurant had sent them a takeaway. They would then pull out some pizza boxes and offer them to the guards. As the guards reached for the boxes, the delivery team would pull out their guns. While this distraction was taking place, the rest of the team would have stealthily approached the rear of the villa and started to clear it room by room. If all went according to plan, nobody needed to die, but then in the real world, things rarely went to plan.

"We've got a bit of a bonus for you," said Spud.

"What's that?" said Dick.

"You've heard of the spy drones the yanks use?" They all nodded.

"We've brought you a junior version. We'll be able to fly it over the villa, and with its infrared heat detection, it'll show us exactly which rooms they're in."

"How on earth did you get that through customs?" said Dick.

"I told them I was a model-aeroplane enthusiast and wanted to fly my plane while on my holiday in Barbados. They clapped me on the back and wished me well."

"I'll be buggered," said Dick.

35

An efficient assault

It was in fact two days later when they embarked on the assault. It had taken longer to get the van prepared than Dick had expected. Spud and Danny were kitted out with stun grenades, smoke bombs and a matching pair of Gen 4 Glock handguns with laser sights. They wore these in chest holsters and also carried back-up Berettas. Their body armour was the latest state-of-the-art and could withstand most attacks, short of a rifle grenade. Dick and Andrei's were less conspicuous because they would be masquerading as the restaurant's delivery boys. All of them shared Bluetooth, two-way, radio headsets, and Danny had a jamming device that would disrupt mobile phone communication without interfering with their two-way radios.

Geared up and ready to go, they drove to the villa without incident. A mile from the entrance, Dick found a field with enough foliage to conceal the van and parked well out of sight from the road. They made the rest of the way on foot. When they arrived, they found their last surveillance site and settled down to wait for the lunch crew to leave. Sure enough at one thirty p.m., one of the Range Rovers loaded up and drove away in the direction of the restaurant. When they were out of sight, Danny stepped several yards back to ensure he couldn't be seen from the villa and launched the drone. Spud immediately started manoeuvring the drone while watching its progress on a laptop screen, which picked up signals from the on-board camera. It was soon soaring over the villa rooftop.

"There you go," said Spud pointing at the screen. "There are two in the back room that looks out over the pool and two in what looks like the lounge just inside the front door."

"Right," said Dick. "You, Bogdan and Danny start making your way around back to that room. Me and Andrei will go and pick up the van and make our approach in, let's say, thirty minutes. Let us know when you're in place."

"No prob, Captain," said Spud. The three of them moved off into the undergrowth. Thirty minutes later, Danny's voice came over the two-way.

"We're in place, Captain."

"Okay. Switch on that jammer. We'll be at the front door in two minutes."

Dick pressed the buzzer on the entry phone. He heard the whirring of a video camera that was zooming in on him.

"Who is it and what do you want?" said a voice with an eastern-European accent.

"I'm from the Lone Star with a takeaway your friends have sent for you," said Dick.

"We didn't order any takeaway," said the voice suspiciously.

"You're friends said they felt sorry for you being left behind and ordered us to bring you a takeaway. We're only doing as we're told."

"Wait there." Dick and Andrei waited with food cartons in their hands, their guns drawn and concealed in the boxes. Even so, the man behind the voice was no fool, and he approached the door with a partner whose gun was also drawn.

"Put the cartons down on the steps," he ordered.

Dick and Andrei had anticipated this scenario, and they moved as if complying. Then suddenly, without warning, they fired on the two men.

In the split second they appeared to be putting the boxes down on the steps, one of the men had lowered his gun. That man went down with the first shot. The second man, the owner of the voice, was sharper. He had not relaxed his vigilance and fired almost simultaneously. His shot hit Andrei in the chest, and it was Dick's second shot that took the man out. At the time of the first shots, there was a sound of a stun grenade. Spud and Danny were also on the move, and the noise of the grenade was followed by a single shot.

Dick's first concern was Andrei. Although the wound was nasty, the impact had been reduced, though not stopped, by his vest. Miraculously, it failed to penetrate any vital organs. The biggest danger was loss of blood and shock.

Spud, Danny and Bogdan managed to avoid being hit. The stun grenade had done its job, and the single shot had been a warning to the disorientated pair in the back room. They were quickly secured with plastic cuffs, hand and foot. All in all, apart from Andrei's injury, it was surprisingly easy, but then four were always going to be easier than eight.

They helped Andrei into the van and sent him back to the embassy with Bogdan for medical treatment. The two bodies were put in the back to be disposed of by the embassy clean-up squad. Danny switched off the jammer, and Dick put in a call to Isaac at the restaurant.

"They haven't been here long," said Isaac, "but they've all had Bogdan's drink.

I don't think it'll be long before the sand-man comes calling." He chuckled.

"Okay. We'll search the house and then get down to you and put them in their vehicle, ready for their wake-up call." Dick wondered why they had taken so long to get to the restaurant.

They turned the house upside down. They emptied every drawer and cupboard and ripped up floorboards; all to no avail. Eventually, after a little gentle persuasion, one of the captives revealed that he had seen Noskcaj go to a safe in his bedroom. It was concealed behind the mirror above the wash basin in the en-suite bathroom. Once they had found it, however, no amount of persuasion would get the guard to reveal the combination. He was obviously telling the truth and simply did not have it.

Spud came to the rescue. A little Semtex and a detonator, and the combination became irrelevant.

"You must have been a boy scout," said Dick. "Talk about being prepared."

"That's me," said Spud. "Always ready for the unexpected".

After a shout of 'fire in the hole', the door to the safe hung open, revealing a few thousand dollars in cash, a file of what looked like household accounts, a dozen packets of white powder (probably cocaine) but no sign of the cross.

"Fuck it!" said Dick. "I was sure it would be here."

"Well, Noskcaj isn't here," said Danny. "He must be down at the restaurant. Let's go and pick him up, and when he comes round, we'll ask the bugger what he's done with it."

"And he's going to tell us just like that," said Dick. His sarcasm was a product of frustration.

"Maybe not just like that." Danny grinned. "But Spud's got a way of encouraging a man to get things off his chest, if you get my drift."

"Looks like that's our best option," said Dick. "I'd like to see Mr. Noskcaj squirm a bit, anyway."

There was disappointment at the restaurant. Only three men were there and Noskcaj wasn't one of them. They looked like a group of passed-out drunks.

"I don't fucking believe it," said Dick. "I saw him get into that car with my own eyes. How the fuck has he pulled this off?" He paused for a second. "Change of plan. Let's load them into their car and take them back to the villa. We can't question them here, and I definitely want to ask them how Mr. fucking Houdini Noskcaj managed this."

They loaded the three comatose bodies into their own car and drove back up to the villa. There, they secured them to chairs in the lounge and then poured buckets of water over them until all three were awake and aware of their predicament.

"Now then, gentlemen," said Dick. "I'd like you to enlighten me with the whereabouts of your Mr. Noskcaj."

It did not take long for Noskcaj's itinerary to be revealed. Spud's skills were not needed. It seemed that Noskcaj was not paying them enough to secure loyalty in this situation. Just the threat of Spud's intervention was enough to solicit, in detail, answers to all Dick's questions.

It appeared Dick was right. Noskcaj had been in the vehicle with them, but they dropped him off at the airport before returning to the restaurant. Mr. Noskcaj was booked on a flight to London, where he was joining a connecting flight to New Delhi in India. He was heading for his estate, where, he had told them, he had an important meeting. He was carrying a small leather case which he never let out of his sight. In fact, he became abusive when one of them offered to carry it for him. The dimensions of the case were perfect for the transportation of something the size of the cross. It appeared he was one jump ahead of them again.

"Isaac has reported these arseholes to the local police for extortion, so that should keep them out of circulation for a while." said Dick. "Let's pick Isaac up and drop him off with these at the local nick and then go back to the embassy and plan our next move."

"There he goes again," said Spud. "Can't wait to get back to his Russian filly."

"And no thought for his pals," said Danny, shaking his head in mock sadness.

"Ha bloody ha," said Dick. "Actually, I want to get back to update Sol on the location of the cross."

"Course you do," they said in unison.

"Come on, let's go. I forgot what piss-takers you two could be."

Ivana and Sol were waiting for them.

"God, it's been a long day," said Ivana. "We knew you were all right when Bogdan and Andrei got back, but I was still worried."

"Still no cross then?" said Sol.

"Afraid not," said Dick. "The wily old bastard's managed to elude us again although more by luck than judgement."

"Where do we go from here?" said Sol.

"If we're going to 'follow the money', as they say—although in this case it's the cross—it looks like we're off to India."

"I've never been to India," said Ivana. "I've heard it's very beautiful."

"Is that your way of telling me you intend to come?" said Dick.

"Why wouldn't I?"

"How about because, once again, it will almost certainly be dangerous," said Dick.

"You know what they say," said Ivana grinning. "Danger is the spice of life."

"My god," said Danny. "How does he do it, Spud? Getting a woman like that."

"And he ain't even good-looking," said Spud.

"And with such cheesy lines," said Sol.

"Hey, don't you start joining in," said Dick. "They're bad enough without help from you."

"I think he's sweet," said Ivana.

"Oh my God. She calls him sweet, Spud," said Danny, and they both collapsed laughing.

"That's quite enough from you two," said Dick. "Now let's go and freshen up and then meet in the lounge to discuss the next move."

"Okay. See you there in an hour," said Spud, still grinning.

Later, they were all back down and seated around a table in the lounge.

"Right," said Dick. "I'm going to book the flight to New Delhi and an indefinite stay at the Hotel Oberoi in Agra. We know the Oberoi is very near Noskcaj's estate. Bogdan and Andrei are going to sit this one out. Andrei needs to recover from his wound, and Bogdan's arm's playing up, so a little convalescence seems right for these two. Problem is that will leave us two men down for any action we might want to take in Agra."

"Don't worry about that, old son," said Spud. "Just call us the three musketeers. We'll be more than a match for old Noskcaj and his cronies."

"And if he has got a small army," said Danny, "two can play at that game. We've got a bunch from the old reg just itching for someone to fight with."

"It'd only take a phone call," said Spud. "There'd have to be an awful lot of them, though, to be more than we three can handle."

"Right then," said Dick. "We'll get over there on the next available flight and take a look at exactly what we're up against." Dick and Ivana left them drinking with Bogdan and Andrei, who had joined them in a wheelchair. He looked surprisingly well and, against doctor's orders, joined in with the drinking.

Dick and Ivana took a Jeep from the embassy car pool and drove down to a secluded beach.

The evening was warm and balmy with a soft breeze floating in from the ocean. At first, they walked along the water's edge, allowing the surf to reach up to their knees. Then as the sun went down, they clung together and kissed passionately.

Dick couldn't remember how they came to be naked, but in just a short while, they were. They lay on the sand with their feet just cooling in the water's edge as their passion reached boiling point. Dick kissed her under her chin and moved down to her breasts, taking her hard nipples in his mouth on his way down across her quivering stomach until he buried his searching tongue into her hot and hungry mound. Her back arched as his tongue dashed back and forth across her now hard and erect clitoris, and she moaned in pleasure. When he felt she was at bursting point, he ran his tongue up her body until his lips met hers, and as they kissed with hot passion, he drove deep into her. Thrusting and bucking in the sand as if in a panic they finally groaned together as the world seemed to explode in their loins. After several heavenly seconds, panting and breathless, they uncoupled and lay back on the sand, exhausted.

"You just keep getting better," whispered Ivana. "I've never had sex like that before. You're full of surprises."

"They say that you're only as good as the one you're with," said Dick. "So it must all be due to you." He held her gently in his arms, her head upon his chest, and they drifted into a dreamless slumber, lulled by the sound of the waves lapping at their feet.

36

New Delhi, India

"They what? They've been arrested for extortion? What the fuck's going on?"

Noskcaj was seething. The phone call he had just received was the last thing he needed. "Someone will pay for this, and if it's that Dick Brady, *I'll make him sorry he was ever born,*" he screamed into the phone, seconds before he smashed it down on the receiver.

Noskcaj's brain was racing. He had arranged to meet a buyer for the cross in India and could not afford mistakes. This buyer, he knew, could easily raise the two million he was asking for. To a Saudi sheikh with a hobby of collecting medieval artefacts, two million was just pocket change. He was, however, extremely security conscious and might easily have pulled out if he felt his security was at risk.

Noskcaj had to be sure that this would never happen.

He dialled furiously, tapping his fingers on the phone while he waited to connect. "Yuri, where's Yakovlev? Convalescing? Shit! I need you to fetch your team here on the next flight out. I'm not bothered about money. I'll double your fee if you get here by tomorrow."

He felt his blood pressure lower as he replaced the receiver. Yuri's team of eight ex-Spetsnaz Russian Special Forces would be with him sometime the next day. Once they were in place, his residence would be impregnable. The deal with the sheikh would go through. He filled a large brandy balloon glass and savoured the Champagne brandy he loved. Noskcaj's hideaway in India was built like a Mexican hacienda, a large bungalow with outbuildings in a plot surrounded by an eight-foot wall with just one entrance. There was nothing inside between the white-painted wall and the buildings. Outside were open fields from the road up until the hacienda gate. It had in fact been built by a Mexican drug baron, who intended it to be easy to defend and hard to attack. He had succeeded for the most part. It did not, however, save him from getting his head blown off on one of his rare visits to his distributor in California.

How Noskcaj had come to own it was unknown by the FSB, but there were almost certainly some ties between the Russian Bratva and the international drug dealer. Noskcaj felt confident and safe behind his high walls in a building that was soon going to be protected by some of the fiercest warriors on the planet.

The Spetsnaz, the outfit these guys had come from, were almost as renowned as the Navy Seals or the SAS. They were highly trained in all aspects of combat and handpicked from the best recruits available in the Russian military. Like their American and British contemporaries, they had to undergo months of extra training, which was deliberately hard and which painfully few managed to complete. Training was ongoing and relentless for those who did survive. Once accepted into the ranks, they were only sent on the most dangerous missions. By the very nature of these missions, many, despite their training, never returned. The body count was exceptionally high in their branch of the military. It was fair to say that those who were still alive at the end of their terms of service could be considered the best of the best. These men after such intense service in the military found it hard to settle into civilian life and invariably found their way into the various organisations supplying mercenaries to the world's trouble spots.

This time, though, they would be working for far more than soldier's pay. At least now, when they risked their lives, the pay would more accurately justify the risk. For many of them, though, the pay was not what drew them back into the business of war. It was the adrenaline rush they experienced going into battle and the respect they received for their expertise, doing the only job they knew and doing it well. Of course the huge fee Noskcaj was prepared to pay for protection was a factor in their decision to return, but in truth, some of them learned to enjoy killing.

Dick's plane touched down in New Delhi, and within a short while, they had cleared customs and were picked up by a minibus sent by the hotel.

"Welcome to India." Their turbaned and uniformed driver beamed. "Please let me help with your cases, madam," he said to Ivana while the rest of the team placed their belongings in the opened back of the minibus. "We have a two-hour drive to the hotel, so please sit back and relax, gentlemen and madam. I shall stop on the way for refreshments."

The bus then took off on one of the most horrific journeys any one of them had ever been on. Traffic converged on what must have been the main road from all directions and at mind-blowing speeds. Nobody gave way, and traffic entered the main road from side roads without warning and without slowing down. Intermingled with all this were cows, ox carts and elephants. Chaos was the only word to describe what was happening on the road before them, and the driver had asked them to 'sit back and relax'.

"No chance, bloody hell," said Spud. "I'd rather be fighting a squad of the Taliban than this." Danny looked pale and Sol was very quiet. Ivana, on the other hand, was grinning from ear to ear, her eyes sparkling.

"How come you're not bothered?" said Dick, not entirely comfortable with the ride himself.

"I find it quite exciting," she said. "I was always the one to be first on the frightening rides at the fairground. It must be something in my genes."

"And there'll be something in my jeans soon if he don't slow down," said Spud.

After a couple of hours of this and miraculously without witnessing any accidents or being involved in any, they stopped for a break.

By this time, although they weren't used to it, they accepted this was how travel was in India and were not constantly panicking, although still far from relaxed. The break was, therefore, welcome, and they stopped at what looked like an old fort—something one would expect to see on a movie set, complete with medieval turrets and brightly dressed turbaned staff serving cold drinks in tall glasses from beaten-brass trays.

They had changed their money at the airport and received huge wads of notes in return for a comparatively small amount of cash. They were surprised at how little they needed to settle the bill for the drinks.

They were soon on their way again, and the second part of the journey seemed somehow less frantic.

Just under two hours later, they arrived at the Oberoi Hotel in Agra. Two guards at the entrance saluted and the minibus continued up the elegant driveway to stop at the main entrance. It was like something out of a Victorian novel. The hotel staff—from the manager down to the daily house-maids—lined up to greet them. There must have been around fourteen people in the welcome party.

"I feel like I've just stepped back in time and arrived at a country house for the weekend," said Danny.

"This is quite a reception," said Spud. "I think you've picked the right hotel, Dicky boy."

The manager quickly checked them in, and they were shown to their rooms, which, at Dick's request, were located on the top floor to give them clearer views of their surroundings and their intended target.

"I picked it because it's near Noskcaj's place," Dick explained. "In fact, aside from the Taj Mahal, which you can see from your balcony, I think if you look to the left, you'll be able to see Noskcaj's hideaway too. Remember that when you're organising the ordinance, Spud. A pair of good binoculars or a telescope could come in very handy."

Dinner that evening was a dream. In a gloriously decorated dining room full of gold and crystal, they were served a delicious selection of Indian food. It far surpassed anything they had encountered outside India that purported to be genuine Indian cuisine. The food was served by very competent girls, beautifully dressed in silk saris, and the wine was served by an immaculately uniformed and knowledgeable waiter.

Sated and relaxed, they retired to a small adjoining room where Dick produced a print-out of the plan of Noskcaj's hacienda. He had received them by email from Bogdan and Andrei, who seemed to want to continue contributing to the operation from afar.

The layout showed a large, rambling, main building with two lounge areas, a large kitchen and seven bedrooms. Every bedroom had en-suite facilities, and there was further guest accommodation in the various outbuildings. The plan was also accompanied by a recent aerial photo, which emphasised just how difficult an assault would be.

"Looks like he likes to entertain with all that accommodation," said Spud.

"Somehow he doesn't come across as a very sociable man," said Dick.

"I think if I had a choice, I'd prefer to be the guy defending this place rather than the one attacking," said Danny morosely.

"I see what you mean," said Dick. "This one's going to take some thinking about."

"That's the problem as I see it," said Sol. "How much thinking time do we have? He could be disposing of the cross tomorrow."

"He could be," said Dick. "If he does, though, the cross will have to be moved either by him or the buyer. It might, in fact, make our job easier to recover it outside the complex because, to be honest, I see no easy way of getting in there without casualties."

"My guy will be arriving here tonight with my weapons order, and I've asked him to bring along the binoculars you wanted," said Spud. "Maybe we should look at it again after we've done a bit of surveillance?"

"Good idea," said Dick. "Let's do a weapons check first thing in the morning and then set up the binoculars on my balcony. We might see something that doesn't show up on a flat plan or a photograph. As with most things, there's nothing like the real thing."

"Sounds like it's time to hit the bar," said Ivana.

"A girl after my own heart," said Danny. "Please tell me she's got a sister going spare."

"She would be going spare or going nuts if she had anything to do with you," said Spud.

"Oooh! That hurts," said Danny. "You can be so spiteful at times."

"Well, you silly sod, what would a lovely girl like that want with a big roughneck like you?"

"There you see," said Danny. "You don't realise I've got a gentle and generous side to my nature."

"If you have I've never seen it, but if you're so bloody generous, get to the bar and get the drinks in."

Everybody laughed, and Danny, looking sheepish, did just that. He bought everyone a drink.

"Don't worry," said Ivana. "I think my sister would love you, Danny."

"Oh my gawd, I'll never hear the last of it now," said Spud. "Why did you have to encourage him?"

"Because she knows class when she sees it," said Danny, grinning like a Cheshire cat.

37

A dangerous opposition

Spud spared no expense on the binoculars. They were a pair of Sunagor 30-160x70 Mega Zoom, and he had taken a tripod with him. It was just after dawn, and Spud and Danny set them up on the balcony. The degree of magnification was almost shocking. They could see every aspect of the buildings in Noskcaj's compound clearly.

"Okay," said Danny, "I'll take the first watch while you lot get breakfast."

"Sounds like a plan," said Spud. "My stomach is already starting to rumble."

"Ivana is still in the shower," said Dick. "You lot go on and we'll follow you down."

Breakfast was served as scheduled by the Oberoi, so by the time Ivana and Dick got to the dining room, everybody was already tucking in.

They had only just got their breakfasts in front of them, when Danny barrelled into the room. "You're not going to believe what I've just seen."

"I told you those binoculars are not for looking in hotel bedroom windows," joked Spud.

"I'm not kidding, you dickhead. An eight-man squad has just arrived at Noskcaj's, and by the way they're dressed and tooled up, I think it a safe bet to say they're Spetsnaz."

"Shit," said Spud. Dick was quiet and thoughtful, and Ivana had turned pale.

"You'll have to call it off, Dick," said Ivana. "It's not worth risking your lives for."

"I think," said Dick, calmly, "we've come too far to give up at the last hurdle."

"But Dick, the Spetsnaz. My God, you'll never beat them," said Ivana.

"That's you thinking and talking like a Russian," said Spud. "Now, me thinking as an Englishman would say they're no match for the SAS."

"On that note, Spud," said Dick, "I think this might be a good time to call for those reinforcements you said might be available."

"I'll get onto it right away," said Spud. He got up and left the table.

"I feel so useless in all this," said Sol.

"No need for that," said Dick. "You can relieve Danny from the binoculars and write down everything you see, whether you think it's important or not. Take Ivana with you. I'm going to talk tactics with Spud and Danny. We'll join you shortly."

Spud was outside the hotel with Danny, talking rapidly on his cell phone. He finished the conversation as Dick joined him. "They say it's better to be born lucky than rich," said Spud, and you must be bloody poverty-stricken because you're so bleedin' lucky."

"How come?" said Dick.

"I've just spoken to Badger from the old mob, and their last job was a black op in Afghanistan over two months ago. Since then, they've been cooling their heels in the UK, and they're bored out of their minds. When I told them about our little problem, they were fighting for the phone to sign on. Looks like all ten of them will be joining us ASAP."

"How are they going to get here?" said Dick.

"They're calling in a favour from an RAF mate, who's going to organise passage on a jet leaving for New Delhi in three hours, and my contact here will bring them to us by helicopter."

"Pity you couldn't have organised a helicopter for us. Would have saved us from that nightmare drive," said Danny.

"See what I have to put up with," said Spud to Dick. "He's such a bleedin' pussy."

"Oh, like you loved that trip," said Danny. "Come on let's check out our weapons."

Now that they had help on the way, they needed more weapons.

Spud was not sure how much the SAS lads could take with them, if anything, so he asked his contact to ensure what they needed would be on the helicopter. What was eventually provided was awesome. Dick checked over two L115A3 sniper rifles, three Diemaco machine guns with UGL grenade launchers, three Law 66mm one-shot rocket launchers, two MP5SD machine pistols with silencers and one Welrod silenced pistol, which was known to be extremely quiet. There was ample ammunition for all the arms and several extra handguns along with stun grenades and tear gas. The most unusual item was a Barnett Predator AVI compound crossbow with telescopic sights, which was capable of sending a bolt at three hundred and seventy-five feet per second and, of course, was even quieter than a silenced gun.

"Looks like we'll be spoilt for choice," said Dick.

"You never know what you are going to need on this sort of escapade," said Spud.

"He's right," said Danny. "Better to have too much than not enough and overkill's a word we don't use in our business...for obvious reasons," he added as Dick raised an eyebrow.

"Okay," said Dick. "Let's make sure they're all in good working order and then put them away for now. We need to see what Sol's come up with on the surveillance, if anything."

After two or three hours of oiling, greasing and checking the ordinance, they joined Sol on the balcony of Dick's room.

"Anything to report?" said Dick.

"Lots of action since these new guys arrived," said Sol. "They've set up sentry points around the buildings and there's a guy with a rifle on the roof. I've draped a cloth over the binoculars because he's got a scope on that rifle and I'm not sure if his range of sight extends this far. I just thought it prudent to take precautions."

"Good thinking," said Spud. "You should never underestimate any special forces."

"Looks like they're digging in," said Dick. "It's not going to be easy to get around those defences."

"If it was gonna be easy, we wouldn't be here," said Spud. "But I know you'll think of something."

Ivana emerged, holding the phone. "It's for you, Dick, Andrei says he may have some useful information for you." Dick took the phone.

"Hello, Andrei. How are you feeling?"

"Don't worry, I'm on the mend, and I've got some intel that might be of use to you."

"Let's have it. We need all the help we can get."

"We have it from a very good source that Noskcaj has a buyer for the cross, and he's on his way to India. His name is Ibrahim bin Haman al Racour, and he's mega rich. He collects mediaeval artefacts from all religions, not just Islamic. He's paranoid about security and is accompanied at all times by two highly skilled bodyguards. He rules over a region with immensely rich oil and gas deposits and is friends with Russia and the West, so try to ensure no harm comes to him."

"Does he realise the cross is stolen property?"

"I doubt that very much," said Andrei. "He doesn't need to buy stolen goods. He can afford to pay the going rate for whatever he wants."

"Right then. I might have a plan," said Dick. "Thanks for the heads up. I'll call you back later." The next few hours were spent scouring the internet for images of Ibrahim bin Haman al Racour. There were none. He was indeed security-conscious and also had a hatred of publicity of any kind. There was precious little to read anything about him on the net. Dick decided this might just have given them the edge over their adversary and his team of hired killers. He called Andrei back.

"Can you find out if Noskcaj has ever met this guy face to face? Does he know him well or is he just an unknown buyer with lots of cash?"

"Give me half an hour." The phone went dead.

38

A wealthy Arab

Precisely twenty-eight minutes later, the phone rang. It was Andrei.

"I can guarantee he's never met him, and as for knowing what he looks like, even we can't find a current picture of the sheikh. The deal was set up, would you believe, by your old friend, Ali Buccaraja, as the go-between. He's one of Ali's contacts, not Noskcaj's."

"Thanks, Andrei. That might just be the break we need. Can you let me know when the sheikh's arriving and how?"

"I can tell you now he'll come on his private jet as far as New Delhi and from there on a chartered helicopter to Noskcaj's place."

"Okay. Find out the name of the charter service and check out what day and time they expect him to arrive."

"Consider it done. I'll give you the details as soon as I've got them."

Spud had been listening, "What devious plan have you got up your sleeve now?"

"Just a little surprise for our Mr. Noskcaj and his band of merry men. Come on, we've got lots to do."

They took a car from the hotel car pool that came with a chauffeur and headed into Agra. The chauffeur directed them to a small shopping arcade where they were able to purchase what was required for Dick's scheme.

Things were hotting up. Dick and Spud managed to buy an Arab thawb, a long over-garment worn by Arab men, and several ghutra: Arab men's headwear. These together with sandals for Dick and a curve-bladed dagger and sash completed the disguise. Dick needed no make-up— his complexion was dark. He planned to wear sunglasses to complete the transformation, and his 'guards' would wear black combat uniforms with the ghutra.

When they got back to the hotel, there was mixed news. Sol had spotted a machine gun nest being set up in Noskcaj's compound, and Danny had received a call from Badger and his crew. They were due to arrive before dawn. The plan was to land on the other side of Agra so that Noskcaj's men were not forewarned of their presence.

They would then make their way to the hotel in small groups, dressed as tourists, so they didn't arouse interest.

Dick had taken the suites on either side of him to temporarily house Badger's crew. Then, Dick, Spud, Danny and Badger met in Dick's room to organise the operation.

They arranged that Dick would take Badger's helicopter back to New Delhi to intercept the sheikh. The plan was to warn him that this was a bogus deal and that it was, in fact, a planned kidnap attempt. He would be asked to make no contact with Ali Buccaraja or any intermediaries so that the authorities had an opportunity to apprehend the kidnappers.

Dick felt quite confident the sheikh would very quickly return to his jet and on to his Arab sheikhdom. Dick would then assume the sheikh's identity and arrive at the Noskcaj property by the very same helicopter ordered by the sheikh.

Dick, along with two guards, would enter Noskcaj's property. Dick would refuse to disarm his guards, and this, he felt, would be expected. He was also fairly confident Noskcaj would not allow the sheikh to be searched. When the opportunity presented itself, Dick would draw his weapons and begin firing. This would be the signal for Spud and Badger to start their assault. First, the regimental champion sniper would take out the guy on the roof and his team would take out the remaining sentries. Danny would destroy the machine-gun nest with a Law 66m rocket launcher, with which he was deadly accurate. The team would then use ropes with grappling hooks to scale the walls of the enclosure and swarm into the building clearing it room by room.

It would not be an easy task. The Spetsnaz were a formidable enemy. They did, however, have surprise on their side along with tear gas and stun grenades.

Dick rode the helicopter to New Delhi with the twins Johnny and Davy Wiggins. Apart from winning every hand-to-hand fighting competition in the regiment, they were expert marksmen and had taken to cage fighting like ducks to water whenever they were between jobs. They had large bald heads with protruding foreheads and were fun to be with, providing you were on the same side. Dick and the twins waited in the helicopter charter office for the sheikh's arrival.

"As Salaam Alaykum, Your Highness," said Dick bowing to the visitor.

"Wa Alaykum Salaam, my friend," said the sheikh. In perfect English, he added, "To whom do I have the pleasure of addressing?" The sheikh's guards were already checking Dick for weapons.

"My name is Dick Brady, Your Highness, and I have some rather unpleasant information for you. Mr. Noskcaj, the man you were to meet, is a criminal wanted in several countries—especially his own, where he runs part of the Bratva, the Russian Mafia, and his intention is to kidnap you for ransom."

A temporary look of shock crossed the sheikh's face, but it was gone almost as soon as it arrived.

"I see, Mr. Brady, and what would your interest be in this matter?" he said, completely calm.

Dick decided to stretch the truth a little more.

"Sir, I've been seconded by British Intelligence to see that you come to no harm. Obviously, you have friends in high places."

"And how do you intend to keep me safe?" asked the sheikh.

"I do know, Your Highness, he has a small army based at his property, and I'd prefer that you were out of the way when an arrest is attempted."

"I see," said the sheikh, turning to his guards. "It would appear, gentlemen, that we have had a wasted journey. Take me back to my plane." He turned back to Dick. "Thank you, Mr. Brady, for your concern. If there's ever anything I can do to repay you, please ask."

"Just one thing, Your Highness. Could you be sure not to contact Ali Buccaraja or any other intermediaries there may be to this deal, as we don't want to alert him to his imminent arrest."

"Will you inform me when you have this accomplished?" said the sheikh.

"Of course, Your Highness, immediately."

"Very well. I bid you goodbye and wish you luck, Mr. Brady."

The sheikh flounced out of the office, followed closely by his guards.

Dick called over the twins. "That's stage one completed. Now let's get our outfits sorted."

Ten minutes later, Dick had made the final adjustments to the twins' headgear and was checking out his reflection in the gents' toilet mirror. He was now fully dressed as an Arab sheikh. When he walked out into the office, the twins ex-claimed in unison, "Blimey, it's like déjà vu."

"I'm sure I've seen this guy before, Davy."

"You're right, Johnny. Me too."

"Okay, boys. Let's hope Noskcaj goes for it, too…long enough for us to get the upper hand."

They made their way over to the heli-copter for their journey back to Noskcaj's compound. Dick radioed Spud and told him what had happened and that they were on their way back, ETA about an hour and twenty minutes. Spud had everything or-ganised. The snipers were in place and the rest of the team ready to deploy at a mo-ment's notice. Danny had set up his rocket launcher, aimed directly at the machine-gun nest, and he had a second prepared just in case. Even the best can sometimes make mistakes, was his motto. In this case, a mistake would almost certainly have cost lives, and it was not a risk he was pre-pared to take.

Badger was the first one to hear the thump-thump of the helicopter approaching. "Condition red," he whispered into his headset. "Chopper's on its way."

Dick saw the compound as he approached and observed several armed men emerging to meet them.

"Okay, looks like we're on. Follow my lead," said Dick. "Wait for me to make a move."

"Okay, Captain. We're ready when you are."

As the helicopter touched down, Johnny and Davy opened the door and lowered the steps, jumping down to help Dick as he descended.

"Good morning, Sheikh Ibrahim." It was Noskcaj's voice. "Welcome to my humble home." He held out a hand as if to escort the sheikh inside.

Two of his men stepped forward. "Weapons," they said. They pointed at Johnny and Davy, who tensed and gripped their guns.

"My men will not give up their weapons, and as yours have theirs, I see no need," said Dick, dressed as the sheikh.

"Of course," said Noskcaj. "Old habits die hard. Please come in."

Noskcaj waved off his disgruntled men, but, as Dick said, they still had their weapons.

Noskcaj showed them into a large room with a heavily beamed ceiling and a huge open fireplace, which seemed redundant in the Indian heat. The air conditioning was very discreet. Dick could feel it but not see it, and there were several large fans hanging from the ceiling recirculating the air. In the centre of the room there was a small black velvet dais with a spotlight above it set up. Lying on top of this was the Romanov cross, sparkling and resplendent in all its glory.

"Here, Your Highness, is the reason for your visit. Please feel free to examine it while I organise some refreshments," said Noskcaj and left the room as he spoke. The Spetsnaz he left behind did not take their eyes off Dick and his guards for a second.

They had been well trained. When Noskcaj returned, he was carrying a tray with tea and biscuits. He looked over at Dick and his eyes hardened.

Noskcaj dropped the tray as he levelled a pistol, and Dick felt the splash of warm blood from Davy's shoulder wound. Because everything happened so fast, the Spetsnaz in the room were confused, giving Dick and the lads the few precious seconds they needed to find cover. Dick tipped over the large oak table, and he and Brian sheltered behind it. Davy was lucky, as the impact of the bullet threw him back behind a large iron fire screen. He was purposefully engaged in applying a field dressing to his shoulder wound. Dick pulled out the two machine pistols from under his robe and prepared himself for battle.

"You'll never get out of here alive," screamed Noskcaj. "You didn't expect Yakovlev to be here, did you? He spotted you on the room's closed-circuit TV."

"I'm pleased he's made such a swift re-covery," shouted Dick. "Let's hope you can do the same."

The room was filled with a cacophony of fire from both sides, with neither doing much damage. Then there was an al-mighty explosion from outside. The rocket launcher took out the machine-gun nest, and he didn't need a second try.

The dais had been penetrated by bullets and fell behind the table shielding Dick and Johnny. The cross lay on the floor be-tween them. Dick picked it up and mo-tioned to Johnny to put it in his pocket, as the thawb he was wearing had none. Davy sorted himself out and joined in the fray with gusto. Of the five Spetsnaz who were in the room, three had been shot, and the two remaining were only firing single shots, so were low on ammunition. Noskcaj, however, was still blasting away but, thankfully, hitting nothing of im-portance. Dick thought the first shot must have been a lucky one for Noskcaj.

The sounds of battle resounded throughout the house and were moving inexorably nearer, and with the occasional glimpses Dick got of Noskcaj when firing, he appeared nowhere near as confident as he had been. Suddenly, there was an explosion, and everything went black. Dick felt half conscious and could hear gunfire close by but was powerless to do anything about it. Spud had arrived in the room with Danny and, seeing the stand-off, made a decision. He threw in a stun grenade and quickly disarmed the two remaining Spetsnaz and cuffed and secured Noskcaj.

As Dick came to his senses, he was being treated along with Johnny and Davy by the regiment medics. There was no lasting damage, just a temporary ringing in the ears. They had taken the compound, but four of Badger's crew had been seriously injured and one killed. The Spetsnaz had suffered even more casualties. The two in the room and three others were the only survivors. If the element of surprise had not been in Dick's favour, he thought, things might have ended even worse. Yakovlev was not among the prisoners. He had somehow evaded capture.

Noskcaj was not happy when two officers of the FSB turned up to escort him back to Mother Russia. He was taken by helicopter to New Delhi and then put on a diplomatic jet bound for home. There were no customs or formalities. He was marked on the paperwork at the airport as a returning attaché.

"I doubt he'll ever see the outside of a prison again," said Spud. "And some of those Russian prisons in Siberia are not fun places."

"It's a shame his sidekick's not going with him," said Dick. "Yakovlev isn't among the prisoners. Somehow he evaded capture. He seems to have a charmed life."

Dick was relieved all had been accomplished without more loss of life, although he mourned the one man they lost.

As for the Spetsnaz, he felt for them, even though they had been on the opposing side, and it made him feel better to let the survivors go, taking with them a portion of Noskcaj's cash.

He gave Spud, Danny and the boys most of the remainder of the cash they found in Noskcaj's bulging safe and sent them on their way to bury their dead.

That just left Sol, Ivana and him.

Back at the hotel, Ivana was thrilled and relieved he had returned safely and with the cross. They made love for hours in the huge bed in the Oberoi, from which they could see the Taj Mahal through the windows. Later, exhausted, he fell into a deep sleep. The tensions of the preceding few days finally caught up with him.

He slept right through until nearly lunchtime of the following day. By the time he surfaced, Ivana had gone out, probably doing more shopping. It seemed to be one of her favourite pastimes. He had a long leisurely shower, shaved and then dressed in fresh linen shorts and a T-shirt. He wore the sandals he bought for 'the sheikh' and went down for lunch.

"I wondered when you'd show up," said Sol. "Boy can you sleep."

"Guess I must have needed it," said Dick. "Have you seen Ivana?"

"Not since you two disappeared into your room yesterday."

"Strange to go out without leaving a message or a note," said Dick.

"Maybe she's gone shopping and forgotten the time," said Sol.

"I'll ask the concierge if she's taken a car, after we've had lunch."

"She'll probably be back by then, anyway," said Sol. "There's only so much shopping you can do in this place."

They sat down for a light lunch.

"What are your plans for the future?" said Sol.

"I haven't really thought about it," said Dick. "Back to the private-eye job, I suppose."

"Perhaps I could help you with that. You know, look after the office while you're out on a case. A sort of Doctor Watson to your Sherlock Holmes."

"Yes, of course, if you don't think you'd get bored. It's not as exciting as this has been."

"Thank god for that," said Sol. "I don't think my old ticker could take another adventure like this one."

"You and me both," said Dick. "That cross has dragged us halfway across the world and nearly got us killed."

"Yes, and don't forget poor Marios. It actually did get him killed," said Sol.

"It's such a beautiful thing, crafted for the love of a beautiful woman, and yet sadness seems to follow in its wake," said Dick. "I can't think what could be keeping Ivana out this long."

Dick knew before he opened the wardrobe it would be empty. He noticed the cross was not on the shelf where he had left it.

He searched the room meticulously, knowing all the while he was not going to find it. He called Sol's room to give him the bad news. Sol sounded excited.

"Dick, I've got back to the room and there's half a million in sterling in one of Ivana's cases and a note for you. I haven't opened it."

"I'll be right up," said Dick.

He ran to Sol's room. "Ivana's gone. She's taken her things and disappeared."

Dick tore open the note and read it out loud.

Dear Dick,

I love you more than I thought it possible to love a man, but I made a promise that precedes our meeting each other. It's a promise I have to keep. I hope the money I've left with Sol will compensate you both for all your trouble.

My name as you know is Feodorovna…Ivana Feodorovna. You know that I was married and that my husband died of cancer several years ago. What you don't know is that my maiden name is, in fact, Dolgorukova, and I'm a direct descendant of the wife of the first Romanov tsar. The cross, as you know, was a gift to my ancestor and was only given away at the height of the tsar's grief on her passing. When I was a child, I was fascinated by a picture of her that hung in our drawing room in Ekaterinburg. In the picture, she wore this stunning jewel-encrusted crucifix on a chain from her waist. The cross belongs to the Dolgorukov family: my family. At nine years old, when my father told me the story, I had no idea I would one day be in a position to retrieve this family heirloom. When I was older, I learned that many treasures of old Russia had disappeared after the revolution. That one from even earlier times could be recovered and returned to the family would make my father very happy. He is in ill health and getting old, so I need to do this for him. I love him dearly, and his happiness is important to me.

My father believes the cross belongs to my family, and he made me promise to do all I could to find and return it. He doesn't want it to fall into the hands of the Russian government, who have already taken so much from us.

I don't imagine you'll be able to understand this, which is why I've considered it prudent to put distance between us.

I still love you and I always will. Please find it in your heart to forgive me my darling.

The Pilgrims' Bounty

Yours forever,
Ivana Dolgorukova

39

In the Office of Brady and Levy, London: One Year Later

"**D**ick, Dick have you seen the Times obituary today?" called out Sol.

"Not my favourite reading matter, Sol. Why? What's got you so excited?"

"It says here that the dying wish of Michailovich Dolgorukov was to exhibit the Romanov cross, which was a gift given to his family by the first Romanov tsar. It's going to be exhibited in London and New York. It's in London on Sunday, and his daughter, Ivana Dolgorukova, will be presiding over the exhibition."

Dick's stomach somersaulted, and his heart was racing. "But that's tomorrow," said Dick.

"I know," said Sol. "It opens at eleven a.m."

The exhibition was in the Russian section of the Victoria & Albert museum. As

Dick walked along the corridors to the showing room, his heart skipped and fluttered. As he opened the last door, he saw her standing next to the glass showcase looking even more beautiful than he remembered. He felt the sensation of dropping many floors in a fast-descending lift. She seemed to sense he was there, and she turned towards him. An involuntary smile creased her face, her eyes welled up, and a tear ran slowly down her cheek.

"How very touching. That's a forty-five you can feel in the small of your back, and my colleague, Mr. Wince here, has a similar weapon aimed at your lady friend."

Dick looked over his shoulder into the beady little eyes of Ben Scrud.

"What we're going to do now is move slowly into the next room, where we can discuss our little problem without disturbance. If you make any move that I consider dangerous to myself or my friend, Mr. Wince will shoot the lady. Do you understand?"

"Perfectly," said Dick. To Ivana he said, "Don't worry, we can sort his out."

She looked terrified. There were no visitors in the next room as no special show was to take place there, and normal visiting time was not for another hour. Scrud waved them over to some seating near a display of Japanese armour.

"Now, if you're sitting comfortably, we can discuss how you're going to bring me the cross to repay the outstanding debt."

"What debt?" said Dick. "I thought I made it clear at our last encounter that all debts were paid. The injury to my friend, remember?"

"How could I forget, Mr. Brady? My shoulder still aches from the repayment. An eye for an eye, as you said, but then if it's an eye for an eye, that still leaves my original debt outstanding. The only way I can see you repaying that debt, for which I hold you totally responsible, is to give me the cross. Once I have it in my possession, I shall consider the debt paid, and I promise there will be no further retribution."

"You're playing a dangerous game, Scrud. The cross doesn't belong to me, and I owe you nothing."

"Mr. Brady, as you like to say, let's not waste any more time. Miss Ivana…I hope you don't mind me calling you Ivana because your surname's quite a mouthful. If you do not get me the cross, I'll kill Mr. Brady. There, that's simple and to the point."

"Ignore him," said Dick. "He wouldn't dare fire a gun in a public place like this."

Ivana looked at Scrud and then at Dick, with fear in her eyes.

"I can't take that chance, Dick. You're more important than an old jewel."

"Let's get on with it, then," said Scrud. "I'll wait here with him while you go with Mr. Wince and bring back the cross."

There was little Dick could do. He watched as Ivana crossed the room and went with Wince through to the exhibition room.

Scrud sat next to Dick with his gun pressed firmly against his ribs, a look of satisfaction on his ugly face. He obviously felt that he had won and that victory was at last within his grasp.

That sneering grimace was to be his death mask. Following an almost silent cough, a red hole appeared in his forehead so suddenly that his expression did not change, even in death.

Dick looked over to the door and saw the reason for the change of circumstance. Standing in the doorway with Ivana in front of him, holding Wince unconscious or dead—he couldn't tell—by the scruff of his neck in one hand and a smoking, well-silenced gun in the other, was none other than Yakovlev, alive and well.

"Well, Dick, we meet again," said Yakovlev.

Ivana ran to Dick and hugged him, not wanting to let go.

"So we do, but I never imagined you'd come to my rescue."

"It's not exactly a rescue...more a removal of competition," said Yakovlev.

"With Noskcaj out of action, it's a case of 'the king is dead, long live the king'.

My orders from the new boss are still to obtain the cross...sorry."

"That's okay." said Dick. "At least we might survive now. With those two, I don't think that was the plan."

"Don't worry on that score. All I want is the cross, and nobody needs to get hurt. I haven't forgotten that you got that ambulance when you could have just let me die."

"You know I'll have to come after you if you take it," said Dick.

"That's not a problem because by the time you find me, I probably won't have it anymore. If we do meet again, though, remember I've repaid my debt and will have no reason not to kill you." He smiled.

Dick was still angry with the man. He had, in this instance, almost certainly saved his life and probably that of Ivana, but Dick had a nagging suspicion it was Yakovlev who had beaten Marios to death and dumped his body in Kyrenia Bay.

"I'll tell the police that three people stole the cross and that one of them shot his two partners and ran off with it alone," said Dick. "I'll give a misleading description of the third, so you'll be safe from them, but I'll be coming for the cross."

"That sounds fair to me," said Yakovlev. "I'll be on my way then."

"Is there no way you'd consider leaving without the cross?" said Ivana.

"Young lady, I'd like to please you, but what kind of a man would it make me if I reneged on a promise?"

"I understand," said Ivana. "Promises should be kept."

"I never learned your first name," said Dick.

"It's similar to your lady's. It's Ivan."

"Good luck, Ivan. If we meet again, let's hope we're on the same side."

Ivan turned and disappeared down the corridor, with only the smell of cordite as evidence he was ever there.

The police took some convincing of Dick's version of events, but with Ivana's testimony as the owner of the cross, they had no option but to accept it.

"Ivana, where are you staying?" said Dick.

"At the Grosvenor House on Park Lane. Will you come back with me?"

"Of course, but you could stay at my place. It's not far and more personal don't you think?"

"Dick Brady, is this some sort of covert way of asking me to move in with you?"

"You saw right through me!" They both laughed.

"First, I'll have to explain to the museum authorities that the exhibition will have to be cancelled, and then I'm all yours."

"Okay. While you're doing that, I'll give Sol an update and ask him to meet us for lunch."

"Sounds like a great idea, I'm looking forward to seeing him again."

"Have you been to the London Planet Hollywood?"

"Can't say I've had the pleasure."

"It's one of Sol's favourites, so I'll book us a table there."

While Ivana went off to deal with the museum, Dick got on his mobile phone, made the booking and then rang Sol.

"Sounds like I've missed all the excitement," said Sol.

Planet Hollywood was on the corner of a street just off Piccadilly. The taxi dropped Dick and Ivana off, and they climbed the winding staircase to the restaurant on the first floor. The whole place was decorated with film memorabilia, relics from Star Wars, James Bond, Elvis, etc., and Sol was sitting there in the middle of it all, beaming.

"Ivana, it's so good to see you again," he said while stage-kissing her and shaking her hand at the same time.

"You look very smart, Sol," said Ivana.

Sol had taken to wearing a blazer and trousers similar to Dick's since working in the office of Brady and Levy. Along with a white shirt, tie and black Oxford shoes, it made him almost unrecognisable from the old Sol. Strange thing was Dick had started to wear blue jeans and T-shirts under an old leather jacket—almost a reversal of styles.

"Thank you," said Sol. "And you look as beautiful as always."

The waitress arrived, and they ordered their meals. Ivana was fascinated by the surroundings, the unusual décor, lighting and memorabilia. The waiters and waitresses were mainly resting actors or drama students. They gave the place a jovial atmosphere, and as the food was also good, the three friends had an enjoyable afternoon.

At around three thirty, they said their goodbyes, and Sol went back to man the office. He would lock up and spend the night at the apartment he had taken in a little mews, just a short walk from the office. Dick and Ivana, meanwhile, collected her things from the Grosvenor House Hotel and took a taxi back to Dick's apartment on Baker Street. Ivana was impressed. He had a good eye for design, and though a little masculine for her taste, she couldn't deny it had been very well done. The lounge was mainly in black and white with a large, comfortable, sofa dominating the room. In one corner, there was a white baby-grand piano, which Dick didn't play but had been left by a previous tenant. It looked very elegant and stood on a zebra-skin rug. There was a Danish-style fire inset in one wall and over it, a large black-framed mirror on the white wall.

The drapes were in heavy white damask, edged in black, and the décor was further complemented by unframed paintings by Jack Vettriano. There were two comfortable white armchairs and a Bang and Olufsen TV and sound system in a viewing corner. An arch at one end led to a dining room, where the same colour scheme had been used but in reverse, with black contrasting with the white. Somehow, it all seemed to work very well.

The bedroom, however, was in shades of dark red and burgundy with satin silk sheets on a large sledge-type bed. One whole wall was covered by mirrored wardrobe doors, and the floor was covered in a thick-pile dark-red carpet. Concealed lighting behind the cornice gave the room a warm glow. The whole apartment lounge, bedroom, kitchen bathroom looked like it had been done by a designer, and yet the ideas were Dick's alone.

"It's beautiful, Dick. I'm going to love it here," said Ivana.

"I'm glad you like it because I'm going to love you being here," said Dick.

"So what's our next move? When do you want us to leave and where to?"

"One night's not going to make much difference, so I think we should worry about it in the morning. In the meantime, let's get you settled in and then maybe go out for tea before coming home for an early night."

"There you go again."

"What do you mean?" said Dick.

"Walking around with that silly big grin on your face. There's more to life than sex, Dick Brady," she said, smiling.

"I'm sure I don't know what you mean." He tried to look hurt, but they both collapsed laughing.

"I'm sorry you've lost the cross again," said Dick. "But I'm so happy to have you back."

"The cross is just an object, Dick. In the whole scheme of things, it's not that important. I realise that now. People are what really matter, the people you love. And I love you, Dick Brady." She kissed him hard on the lips, and they made love on the sofa. It was hot and intense as if they were trying to make up for their time apart. Lying there, safe in each other's arms, the battles over the cross seemed to be from another lifetime.

They showered together and then dressed and went to the Ritz for tea. The tea room was of timeless elegance, further enhanced by an accomplished pianist filling the room with beautiful gently echoing notes of a concerto. The service was attentive but discreet, and the sandwiches and cakes to die for.

"You're spoiling me, Dick. If I eat all this, I'll never get in my bikini again."

"If that's the case, I'll order you a plate of lettuce. There's no way I want to miss out on you in a bikini. I've seen it before, and it's a sight worth seeing."

"You're incorrigible. Now stop flattering and pour the tea."

They walked back from the Ritz to the apartment, and by the time they got home, they were both ready for that early night. After a brandy nightcap, they snuggled up together between the silk sheets and hardly moved until the phone rang at eight thirty the next morning.

Dick reached sleepily for the phone. "Hello?"

"It's me. What time are you coming in?" said Sol.

"Oh, give me an hour or two. I think we've overslept," said Dick. "We'll get showered and dressed and come straight in."

Stepping into the Brady and Levy office was like stepping back in time. It was accessed from a door in the Burlington Arcade on Regent Street and up a long winding staircase to a corridor, off which were doors to individual offices. One of these read: Brady and Levy, Private Investigators. This was etched on the glass door in gold leaf in old-style script, which was incongruously fresh and new. Inside, it was like revisiting Scrooge's office in A Christmas Carol. The walls were wood-panelled in old oak with shelves full of leather-bound books. There was a small reception with an antique writing desk and a boarded floor that was nearly black with age. Candle sconces on the walls from another age had not been removed, and even the current electric fittings looked ancient. The back room was larger, with two well-used desks and two old Victorian captain's chairs behind the desks. In front, were a few spoon-back client chairs that had seen better days. All the walls were heavily panelled in cream-painted wood, probably in an attempt to brighten the place up, as there were no windows. The only light came from a small skylight in the ceiling and some Marconi/Edison-era brass lighting. This was the head and only office of Brady and Levy, private investigators extraordinaire.

"It's very quaint," said Ivana.

"That's a kind way of saying small," said Dick.

"Well, it's big enough for our needs," said Sol. "And anything bigger in the middle of the West End of London costs a fortune and I hate wasting money."

"That's one thing," said Dick to Ivana. "I don't have to worry about wasting money while Sol's around."

"Good job I am, or he'd be skint in a month," said Sol

"I'm sure you'll keep him on the straight and narrow," said Ivana.

"Right. Let's make some plans for re-covering the cross," said Dick.

"If Yakovlev's got it, I'd better book some flights to Moscow," said Sol.

"Yes, but first let's see if we can get some help from our friends in the FSB. If someone's taken over from Noskcaj, they'll know about it. Who, when and where."

"I've got Dimitri, Andrei and Bogdan on file," said Sol. "Give me a minute and I'll get their contact numbers."

It was arranged that all three of them would fly to Moscow. Dimitri would pre-pare a file on Noskcaj's successor, and Bogdan and Andrei would meet them at the airport. They had been given permis-sion to assist Dick on the condition they kept their superiors informed of developments at all times.

At eleven fifty the next morning, they boarded an Aeroflot flight for Moscow arriving at six thirty p.m. Moscow time. They were to stay at Ivana's apartment, and Andrei and Bogdan collected them from the airport to take them there. There was much excitement and laughter at the meeting. They had all been through a lot together; their experiences promoted strong bonding and friendships that would last a lifetime.

They dumped their belongings at the apartment and agreed to decide their next move over dinner. Dinner was to be as guests of Bogdan and Andrei or, to be more accurate, the Russian government, as they were on authorised expenses.

"So where are you taking us tonight?" said Dick.

"We're going to take you to Shinok, a restaurant which has recreated a Ukrainian peasant farm in central Moscow. The staff wear traditional dress, and while you dine, you can observe the babushka as she tends to the farm animals next door."

"Oh! I love Shinok—their Varinki is delicious," said Ivana.

"I'll take your word for that, but I'm still a bit wary of trying foreign dishes, even though I enjoyed the food in India," said Dick.

"Don't worry. It's not sheep's eyeballs or anything like that. It's just filled dough parcels. I suppose the nearest English equivalent would be dumplings, but with fillings."

"Doesn't sound too frightening to me," said Sol. "Let's live dangerously. We have been, lately."

"You'll love it," said Andrei. "Ivana's right—it's absolutely the best."

And it was: wonderful, tasty and delicious. They ate heartily and consumed more than a few bottles of Stolichniy sparkling wine from the Ukraine.

Feeling slightly the worse for wear but happy with it, they said their goodbyes to Andrei and Bogdan and merrily made their way back to Ivana's. Sol went straight to bed with a very large brandy. Very soon his snoring was reverberating loudly from his room, so Dick closed the door discreetly.

Alone at last, their attraction for each other surfaced in a flurry of passionate hot kisses as they stepped hungrily towards the bed in Ivana's room. They were oblivious to the destruction of buttons and zips as they tore the clothes from each other in their haste to get naked. When they were free of these encumbrances, his body pushed against hers while she pulled him ever closer. He fondled her firm and full breasts as she reached down to squeeze his erect and straining penis. Guiding it towards her, she plunged it hungrily into her already wet and throbbing vagina, moaning with desire and delight. There was no slow build-up this time. Their bodies were hot and their passion on fire as they slammed against each other in violent convulsions. Their panting came thick and fast as the sweat of their exertions mingled and heightened the sensation. Their orgasm was in unison and surprised them both with its power, leaving them quivering from their sudden and fierce encounter.

"Oh my God," sighed Ivana. "I thought my head would explode."

"I think mine did," said Dick, smiling contentedly.

They feel asleep instantly until the ringing on Dick's mobile woke them the following morning at eight.

"It's Dimitri. I came in this morning, and the information you require has arrived in my inbox. Are you coming in?"

"Yes, of course," said Dick. "Just give me time to shower, dress and grab a bite, and I'll be there."

"You'll be where?" Ivana yawned.

"FSB headquarters. It's Dimitri. He's got information on Noskcaj's successor. I need to check it out."

After a hot shower and a quick breakfast with Ivana, Dick dressed and left to meet Dimitri.

Sol hadn't stirred, still sleeping off the effects of the previous night's drinking. Dick decided not to disturb him. He would leave him with Ivana and explain what he learned on his return.

The drive to FSB headquarters was wet and dismal but still only took a short time from Ivana's apartment. Dick ran up the stone steps, eager to find out what Dimitri had found out. They met in the main office, where Dick was given an ID tag to wear while in the building. In the lift on the way up to Dimitri's office, Dick could not contain himself.

"What have you got for me?" said Dick.

"I'll show you the file, but it's strange. The man who appears to have taken over has no criminal record. Nor has he been subject to any investigation. Rather odd, don't you think?"

"For someone who's heading a branch of the Russian Mafia, I agree. It's very odd," said Dick.

They left the lift and entered a large office painted in a green-grey gloss from floor to ceiling. It was filled with racks of files and had two grey steel desks that were clear except for a computer screen on each and one open file on the desk nearest the door.

"Make yourself comfortable, Dick," said Dimitri. "That's the file on the desk. It's thin because we know very little about this character."

Dick read through the file. Dimitri was right. A name, an address, the names of various companies, all thought to be clean and very little else. The informant was adamant this was the new leader of the local Bratva.

"Boris Rurik Godunov—a name that's hard to forget," said Dick.

"And yet there's nothing untoward about him in our database. Let me tell you we're very thorough," said Dimitri.

"Are you sure he's taken over from Noskcaj?"

"That's what my informant tells me, and he's always been reliable in the past, so I've no reason to doubt him."

"I think our first move should be surveillance," said Dick. "Do we know where to find him?"

"I'm ahead of you. I've already put a team on it...they're due to be relieved at two p.m., so if you wish, we could take over then."

"Sounds like a good idea. I'd like to get a look at this man at least."

There wasn't enough in the file to keep Dick's attention for much longer, so they spent the next few hours drinking coffee in the building's canteen and watching the clock.

40

The new antagonist

At one thirty p.m., they took the lift down to the car park and took Dimitri's Lada to the office block where Boris Godunov was under surveillance. Two agents had parked opposite, and Dimitri pulled up behind them. As he walked to the driver's door, the window slid down.

"Anything to report?"

"Yes, sir. The target arrived at eight thirty a.m. in a black people carrier accompanied by two men, whom we presume are bodyguards. He entered the building and hasn't left since. Other officers are at present trying to set up listening and video equipment in the building opposite."

"I see," said Dimitri. "We'll take over now. Tell the other officers to report to me by mobile as soon as they have secured a position."

"Yes, of course, sir."

Dick and Dimitri settled in for a long shift. They were not due to be relieved until at least ten p.m. Luckily, they did not have to wait that long. At around five o'clock, the black people carrier emerged. Boris Godunov was sitting in the passenger seat. As he passed, he looked straight at Dick and nodded, as if in recognition.

"So much for remaining undetected," said Dick.

"Don't beat yourself up," said Dimitri. "He'll be expecting extra attention having just taken such a high-profile position."

"I know, but it would have been nice to stay incognito for a little longer."

From what Dick could see, Boris was a middle-aged stockily built man with a shock of blond hair worn long and tied in a ponytail. He had a ruddy complexion and piercing blue eyes. Dick was sure Boris would have gained an equally detailed description of him.

"What is it with these gangsters and their ponytails?" said Dick. "If they're trying to give a macho image, the ponytail seems a contradiction."

"I know what you mean," said Dimitri. "I think it's just a fashion thing with them."

"Bit girly, if you ask me. Let's see if the sound and vision guys have set up."

The building across the street from the office Boris was using was a grey, dismal apartment block that looked like it had been there untouched for a hundred years. The windows hadn't been washed, probably ever, and most of them were splattered with dried bird droppings. The inside, however, although not pristine, was reasonably clean and acceptable. Luckily, the fourth-floor apartment overlooking the Godunov office had no tenant, and the caretaker had given the keys to the FSB agents to gain access. They set up a tripod, on which there was an HD video recorder. It had a huge zoom lens and a directional parabolic dish that would ensure even whispered conversations could be picked up from the office across the way. On the window through which the equipment was directed, they applied a film allowing them to see out while preventing anyone being able to see in.

"Looks like everything's in place here," said Dick. "Not much we can do until tomorrow, so we might as well call it a night."

"I agree," said Dimitri. "Let's meet here tomorrow at eight a.m."

"Will do. If you could just let me pick up my car from your office, I'll be on my way."

"No problem. Let's go."

When Dick got back to the apartment, Sol and Ivana were anxious to hear his news.

"Not much to report, I'm afraid," said Dick. "I've seen the man in question. Problem is, he got a good look at me, so no chance of any undercover work. We've got a good chance of picking up some information tomorrow, though, as the FSB guys have set up a video and listening station to bug his office."

"Mind if I tag along tomorrow?" said Sol. "This Russian TV gets boring after a while."

"Don't see a problem with that, but it's not much livelier on surveillance, believe me."

"I'll take my chances."

"We leave at seven a.m. We must be settled in position at eight without fail."

"That's fine," said Sol. "I'll have an early night." Dick winked at Ivana.

"Sorry." She grinned. "I'm on a night out with the girls."

"Guess I might as well have an early night, too," said Dick, faking a sulky expression.

When the alarm went off at six, Ivana was lying naked next to him. Dick hadn't heard her return, and delicious though she looked in the early morning light, he felt he should allow her the same courtesy and let her sleep on.

He met Sol in the kitchen, showered, dressed and ready to go.

"You're determined not to miss anything, aren't you?"

"It's all fuel for my memoirs," said Sol. "Writing's much more realistic if you were actually there." Without waking Ivana, they left the apartment and drove to meet Dimitri at the surveillance flat.

"You're only just in time," said Dimitri. "Their car's just turning into the underground garage now."

Sure enough, when Dick looked through the window, he saw the rear of the black people carrier disappearing into the building across the road.

"Is everything set up?" said Dick.

"Yes, we're ready," said Dimitri. "I just need to turn on the recorder."

Dimitri had rigged the equipment so that the sound being picked up was relayed to speakers set up in the surveillance flat. Sol made coffee, and they sat and listened to what was to become two days of boring, everyday, business conversations. All that was discussed were orders and deliveries for Godunov's legitimate companies, the everyday discussions of an innocent man.

"I'm not buying this," said Dick. "He's been forewarned. He must know we're taping him."

"Well, well, Mr. Brady," a voice boomed into the room. "It took you far longer to work it out than I expected. Perhaps I overestimated you."

The sound was coming from their own speakers, but there was obviously a listening device hidden somewhere in the room.

"Mr. Godunov, I presume," said Dick.

"Who else? I thought that, as you were so interested in listening to me, I'd return the favour. However, I found your conversation considerably lacking in excitement."

"And I found yours," said Dick, "more of a theatrical performance than real life."

"And yet it took you two days to come to that conclusion." Godunov sniggered.

"It looks like round one to you, Godunov, but the game's not over."

"Be very careful, Mr. Brady. As they say in America, you're on my turf now, and I don't allow any interference in my business."

"Then let's make this easy," said Dick. "You give back the cross and I won't interfere with your business."

"Why would I give back something that's rightfully mine?" said Godunov.

"Yours? And you believe that because…"

"Ask your girlfriend, Mr. Brady. Let her enlighten you while she still can." There was a loud crackling from the speakers and then nothing.

"I think he's pulled out the microphones," said Dimitri. "There's nothing more we can do here."

"So," said Dick. "Two days wasted. A clever man, our Mr. Godunov but not an innocent one. We just weren't listening in the right place or at the right time."

"I wonder what he meant by 'ask your girlfriend'," said Sol.

"I don't know. There's one way to find out. Let's go back to the apartment and ask her."

When they arrived, Ivana was in a very good mood. She had been shopping. She showed off her purchases to Sol and Dick, who tried their utmost to show interest, but the nagging question persisted in their minds. In the end, it was Sol who broke first.

"Ivana, your clothes, shoes and bags are beautiful and we're pleased to see you so happy, but we need to ask you about something."

She stopped modelling a new pair of stilettos. "What is it, Sol? What do you want to know?"

"The man we've been watching, Ivana, the man who has, according to the FSB, taken over from Noskcaj, is a Boris Godunov. He's laid claim to the cross and told us to ask you for an explanation."

"Boris Godunov," said Ivana. The blood drained from her face and her happy disposition evaporated in an instant.

"The very same," said Sol.

She flushed from her neck to her forehead and had to put out a hand to steady herself. Dick saw her distress and quickly helped her onto a chair.

"What is it?" said Dick. "You've gone very pale."

"Can you get me a brandy? Give me a minute and I'll explain."

Dick poured a large brandy and placed it into her trembling hands. After several minutes, during which nobody spoke, Ivana managed to get a grip and calmed down enough to tell them about Boris Godunov.

"As you already know, I'm closely related to the Romanov dynasty from the very beginning of their reign. Though not always the best of rulers over the centuries, they were loved by their subjects, for the most part. There was more good than bad amongst them. However, before they came to power, there was another house of tsars. If you look at the history, you'll realise even now, many centuries later, that you still recognise the names of some of them, such is the extent of their notoriety. Their family name was, I imagine you'll have guessed, Godunov. Boris Godunov is a direct descendant of that line. In his twisted mind, he still blames the Romanovs for stealing the crown from his family, and as the cross was made for a Romanov, he wants to believe it should really be his."

"How do you know so much about him?" said Dick.

"From my father. He warned me that the current Boris Godunov burns with resentment and hates the Romanovs and all their connections and has vowed revenge. He told me to always be on my guard, as our family was a target. If you ask in the right places, and you live to tell of it, you'll hear many stories of his brutality. In official circles, though, nothing. Anyone who tries to make an official complaint or investigation into this man disappears and is found brutally mutilated. He has informers and people installed at the highest level of government and allows no untoward records concerning him in any department. He's amassed exceptional wealth through his nefarious activities, and those he can't intimidate, he buys. There are few he can't intimidate, and he'll only pay as a last resort. Even then, that person won't be safe. He's personally competent in all kinds of combat, is highly educated and also a skilled pilot and flies himself when he can. The most important fact I have to tell you, as far as I'm concerned, is that he's completely ruthless in his quest for vengeance. His hatred of my family has been known to us for years and there have been several members who have disappeared and then been found with his signature mutilations. Proof that he was the culprit was never found, but he made sure we knew. For that reason, we've had to be on our guard continuously." She broke down sobbing.

"Why the tears?" said Dick. "You're safe here with me."

"He terrifies me. You don't understand just how evil he is."

"Maybe it's time somebody did something about it," said Dick.

"I'd rather you went back to England, both of you, safe and out of harm's way."

"What about the cross?" said Sol.

"Let him have it," said Ivana.

"Look, you're obviously upset. Let's drop it now and decide what to do tomorrow," said Dick.

"Okay, but I won't change my mind."

She slumped in the chair and looked exhausted. So different from the woman who had greeted them such a short while before.

Sol and Dick went into the kitchen to make some tea and sandwiches while Ivana dozed fitfully in her chair.

"What do you make of it?" said Sol.

"Sounds like he's some mean son of a bitch and well connected too."

"Do we give up, then?" said Sol.

"Let's sleep on it, but I'm leaning that way. I can't see it's worth putting Ivana at risk even if we were prepared to take him on."

"It just irks me that Marios will have died for nothing," said Sol.

"I agree, but think how much worse it would be if we lost Ivana too."

"You're right, of course. Maybe we should discuss it with Dimitri tomorrow?"

"That makes sense. Let's see what he makes of it before we decide."

Ivana tossed and turned all night. The events of the previous day were obviously playing on her mind. She eventually dropped off early the next morning while Dick was in the shower.

"I don't want to disturb her, Sol, now she's finally got to sleep. Let's leave her a note not to answer the door to anyone but us and lock her in."

After they were sure she was secure, they set off to meet Dimitri.

It was another dismal day on the Moscow streets, and the rain pounded down endlessly as they drove to FSB headquarters, causing the wipers on the car to squeak and squeal in protest. Dimitri was already in his office, waving away a cloud of tobacco smoke, revealing he had already broken the law that day. After exchanging greetings, Dick got down to business.

"Considering all that we've learned about this guy from Ivana last night, we're considering pulling out of this investigation," said Dick.

"What exactly did you learn?" said Dimitri.

Dick repeated what Ivana had told them and stressed how terrified she was.

"That explains a lot," said Dimitri. "I can't find any information on this man. It's like he never existed before taking over the Bratva. In that regard, my informant's disappeared and has failed to make contact or pick up his pay. I'm seriously concerned for his safety in the light of what you've told me."

"Will you continue your investigation?" said Dick.

"That's a problem. Without any incriminating evidence against him, it's just a matter of time before I'm taken off the case. He's already made a complaint about the surveillance, and my superiors have condemned my actions and offered him an apology."

"If it was just me," said Dick, "I'd stick with it, but I don't want to put Sol and

Ivana in danger, and this guy sounds very dangerous."

"So you're going to drop it?"

"Don't think I've got any option. It's not just my life I'd be playing with."

"I understand. I'll try and keep an eye on him, but I've got to be careful myself. If what you say is true, and I don't doubt Ivana, he's probably got people on his payroll here. The least that could happen is I could lose my job."

"It looks like evil triumphs over good this time," said Sol. "He seems to have all the cards."

"He does at present, but life has a strange way of turning the tables at times. Let's keep our options open. One day he might drop his guard and reveal his Achilles' heel," said Dimitri.

"Until that day then, we'll say goodbye," said Dick, offering his hand

Dimitri accompanied them both to the lift, and they descended in silence, both lost in their own thoughts. When they arrived back at the apartment, Ivana was just waking up.

"Where have you two been?"

"Just to say goodbye to Dimitri," said Sol.

"Yes, we're going back to the UK," said Dick. "And I'd very much like you to come too."

"You're going to leave the cross?"

"I'm not going to risk your life for a bit of metal and a few stones."

"Don't worry," said Ivana. "I think you're doing the right thing."

"So, you'll come with us?" said Dick.

"Of course, but not right away. I have to visit my family and warn them of Godunov's current whereabouts."

"Okay, if that's what you have to do, but don't be long. I'd feel safer having you with me." She touched his arm and kissed him gently on the lips.

"I love you so much, Dick Brady."

41

A new client asks for help

Dick and Sol booked the Aeroflot flight to Heathrow the next day and arrived, tired, at Dick's apartment on Baker Street. After a quick meal at the TGI Friday's close by, they decided to have an early night and face the world in the morning.

When they got to the office, a small mountain of mail was waiting for them, piled up by the door. Most of it was junk, but there were a couple of prospective jobs.

"This looks interesting," said Sol. "A guy in Exeter thinks his brother may be poisoning him. He's willing to pay good money and expenses for you to check it out."

"Or there's a woman," said Dick, reading another letter, "who's sure her husband's cheating on her, and she says money's no object if she can get to the truth. A Lady Matilda Savage."

"I think the poisoning sounds more exciting."

"I'm inclined to agree, and I've always fancied visiting Devon—I've never been there."

"Looks like next stop Devon, then," said Sol. "I'll call the number he's given us and tell him we're on our way."

"Let's go back to the flat and throw a few things in a bag first. I'm not at my best without a razor and a change of clothes," said Dick.

"Okay, I'll switch the phone to answerphone and we'll go."

Dick was glad to have something to take his mind off Ivana. He still felt uneasy about leaving her behind, but she had been adamant, and he understood her concern. Godunov was an evil and maybe mentally deranged individual, so it was probably the right thing to do, to take time to warn her family. Nevertheless, his stomach still turned as he thought of her two and a half thousand kilometres away in the same country as a man who hated her.

They returned to the flat and packed. Dick forced his worries from his mind as he heard Sol calling him from the lounge.

"What's up?"

"That was a very strange phone call. A woman answered the phone and said that Mr. Dorian Somersby wasn't well enough to come to the phone. When I told her we'd received a letter from him, posted only yesterday, she seemed surprised. When I went on to say we intended to visit him to discuss some business, she appeared quite taken aback."

"How do you mean 'taken aback'?"

"You know, stuttering and being sharp."

"You're getting good at this PI stuff, Sol, and with no training. I'm impressed."

"Never mind that. I think we should get down there as soon as possible."

"Don't get too excited. She's probably worried about him, and he's most likely a nutter."

"You always say don't jump to conclusions, so let's at least talk to him before you write him off as a nutter."

"You're right. I should know better. Where do we get the train for Devon?"

"From Paddington, and it's about two and a half hours on the Atlantic Coast Express."

Just then, the phone rang. It was Ivana. "Just to let you know I've arrived home safely, darling."

"Thanks for that. I can't say I wasn't worried," said Dick.

"No need. I'm here with my family and all's well. What are you up to?"

"Trying to get back to normal. We've got a case in Devon, and we're leaving on the next train."

"Good luck with that. I'll call you when I'm on my way."

"This shouldn't take too long, so hopefully, we'll be back in London when you arrive."

"Bye for now, darling. Love you lots."

"Me too. Bye!"

After a delightful train journey through the beautiful green and glorious scenery of the English countryside, they arrived at Exeter. A taxi took them from the station to the little village of Deddleham, where they approached the grade-one-listed Elizabethan manor house that was home to Dorian Somersby, the writer of the letter. A more picture-postcard destination could not have been imagined. The house had been built on a hill overlooking green meadows that were populated with young horses, roaming free, it seemed. The mile-long drive was lined with daffodils sprouting up between patches of rosemary, the scent wafting in through the open windows of the taxi. Chalfont was indeed a fine example of Elizabethan architecture. As they drew up outside the impressive entrance, they almost expected to be received by a character from a Brontë novel. Instead, a male teenager dressed in T-shirt and jeans opened the door and after a 'Can I help you?' ushered them into a drawing room.

The young lad was the son of Dorian's brother, Marcus, who appeared soon after.

"My wife's told me of my brother's request, gentlemen, but I'm afraid you've had a wasted journey. My brother's been ill of late and has this crazy idea that it's of my doing. However, I love my brother. I have independent means and would much prefer to have my brother around than be saddled with the running of this estate. I'm standing in for him at present, and to be honest, I don't enjoy it, nor am I any good at it."

"Why do you think he has developed this suspicion?" said Dick.

"I think it's because he knows I stand to inherit and because this illness hasn't been diagnosed by his doctor. The fact that he's unwell is affecting his judgement, I'm sure."

"You could well be right," said Dick. "I'd like to talk to him, if you don't mind."

"Of course, and I've asked his doctor to call and give you his opinion. He should be here within the hour. Just follow me."

He led them up a grand staircase lined with portraits, most of them darkened with age.

"Not a very handsome lot, I'm afraid," said Marcus. "But all ancestors I must confess. My family have lived here for four hundred years."

"You can almost feel the history," said Sol. "I love places like this."

As they reached the top, a young woman came out of the first door on the landing.

"This is Anna, our cook," said Marcus. "How is he today?"

"Much the same. A little grumpy and not feeling well. I did get him to eat a little, though." Marcus introduced Dick and Sol.

"Can you tell me, Anna," said Dick, "when you prepare his food, do you always take it to him?"

"Unless I'm on a day off, yes, always now. He's insisted that nobody else be allowed to touch his food."

"Does everybody else eat the same food?"

"Yes, everybody, and I even eat a little with him to set his mind at rest. There's nothing wrong with the food, Mr. Brady. I'd stake my life on it."

"What about before you prepare it? Where does it come from?"

"I do the shopping myself and harvest any vegetables or salads from the garden myself. Nobody gets to touch it before or after it's prepared, and everybody eats the same food."

"Thanks for your help, Anna. Now I'd like to talk to Mr. Somersby and then the doctor when he arrives."

"No problem," said Marcus. "I'll bring the doctor up as soon as he gets here."

He opened the bedroom door, and there, in a huge four-poster bed, lay Dorian Somersby. He had the look of a sick man with sunken eyes, pale skin and a sheen of sweat, even though the room was not warm. Despite this, his hair was trimmed and tidy, and he was clean-shaven.

"Have you brought someone else to prod and poke me?" he said, scowling.

"On the contrary, Dorian. This is Mr. Brady and Mr. Levy, whom you asked to see."

"Good," said Dorian, visibly brightening. "Leave us then, Marcus."

"Of course." He sighed and closed the door.

"Welcome to Chalfont, gentlemen," said Dorian. "I wish it could be in less distressing circumstances."

"You mean your allegation of poisoning?" said Dick.

"What else? Don't be taken in by his kindly manner. He wants me gone and no mistake."

He looked very pale when they first entered, but his agitation had brought a little colour to his cheeks. Nevertheless, he did not look a well man.

"We won't take anything at face value, Mr. Somersby. You can be assured of that," said Dick.

"Once we've made our enquiries, we'll advise you of our conclusions," said Sol.

"Don't take too long about it, or I may not be around to pay your fee," said an irritable Dorian Somersby. "I'm sorry if I appear sharp, but my condition isn't conducive to a cheerful disposition."

"We understand," said Dick. "We'll take our leave now and get to work."

As they left the room, Dick turned to Sol. "I'm going to make use of my contacts in London to check out the financial position of Marcus and his wife. While I'm busy with that, I think you should interview the staff."

"We've already spoken to the cook."

"I know, but interview her again and write down everything she says. I'll be waiting in the drawing room when you've finished and we can review the statements together."

On their way downstairs, Marcus went to meet them. "How was he?"

"Like you'd expect a man who thinks he's being poisoned to be—irritable."

"You believe him then?"

"I neither believe nor disbelieve him, Mr. Somersby. I'm just here to get to the bottom of what's ailing him. Whether that's something natural or poisonous has yet to be confirmed."

"I see, of course," said Marcus. "The doctor's arrived and is waiting for you in the library. That's the room to your left."

Doctor Chance was a tall, distinguished-looking man, probably in his early fifties, with greying hair and very white teeth. He shook hands firmly with Dick and Sol in turn.

"I'm Doctor Chance, and I've been Mr. Somersby's doctor for nearly thirty years."

"Dick Brady. This is my colleague, Professor Sol Levy, who has some pressing business elsewhere, I'm afraid."

"Of course," said Sol. "I'll catch up with you later."

Sol closed the door behind him, and Dick and Doctor Chance took a seat each beside the fire.

"I'm sure my patient will have told you of his concerns, Mr. Brady, so I'll get to the point. Mr. Somersby does seem to be gradually deteriorating.

"On his direction, I've done many tests for toxic substances or poisons. So far, all have come back negative. That doesn't mean it's still not possible—contrary to popular belief, some poisons are undetectable. My own view, however, is that it's far more likely he's suffering from a wasting disease. It could be one of many, so I'm currently trying to narrow it down with the use of the local university laboratory facilities. Unfortunately, these diseases are notoriously difficult to diagnose. The fact that he's deteriorating is evident, of course, so it's obvious there's a problem. Whether that problem's in your sphere or expertise or mine is at present open to conjecture. My money, though, would be on the medical condition."

Dick listened intently to the doctor's summary of the problem.

"I see, Doctor Chance. Thank you for being so forthright. May I ask…are you also Marcus's doctor?"

"Yes, and of the rest of the family. If you're about to ask if I think Marcus is capable of killing his brother, the answer is an emphatic no. I've known them both nearly all their lives, and until this present situation, they've always been close."

"What would Marcus have to gain by Dorian's death?"

"Their father appointed Marcus as heir if Dorian didn't marry. Dorian's a very wealthy man. He owns ten thousand acres of prime land and many properties in and around Exeter. Even his hobby of collecting rare cars has resulted in a collection worth millions. The problem with that as a motive is that Marcus is nearly as wealthy, if not more so. Though Dorian got the house when his father died, the rest of the assets were split more or less evenly, and Marcus is a shrewd businessman."

"You're right. There doesn't seem much of a motive for murder. What about Marcus's wife?"

"Another dead end, I'm afraid. She's independently wealthy, too, and is heiress to a Danish lager company worth billions. Though not rich myself, I believe there must come a time when an extra million here or there makes little or no difference to the lives of these people. Added to that, it's a real love match between her and Marcus. It's obvious to all who know them, and when little Oliver came along, it was the icing on the cake. They really are nice people."

"You've given me a lot to think about and, I must confess, not made my job any easier."

"I wish I could be of more help, Mr. Brady. Now I must take my leave and visit my patient."

"Of course and thanks for the information."

Dick followed Doctor Chance from the room and made his way to the drawing room to wait for Sol. When Sol arrived, he was still there, lost in thought.

"I've interviewed all the staff, and there's a record of each interview in this notebook," said Sol.

"Right, let's go through them one by one."

At that moment, Anna entered the room. "Can I get you some refreshments, gentlemen?"

"That would be most welcome," said Sol. "If it's not too much trouble, a cup of tea, perhaps?"

"No trouble at all, I'll just be a minute."

"Let's wait until she's brought the tea. I want to concentrate without interruptions."

Just a few minutes later, Anna returned with a silver tray carrying the tea and some fresh sandwiches.

"Mr. Marcus has asked if you'd like to stay for dinner this evening."

"We'd be delighted. Please thank him for us," said Dick.

"Of course." She left, closing the door behind her.

"Are we staying on then?" said Sol.

"At least until dinner. You said you've interviewed all the staff, but that still leaves Mrs. Somersby. Perhaps we can remedy that at dinner. Now let's start on your notes."

"Okay, first I re-interviewed Anna, basically asking the same questions as before. She confirmed that only she prepares the meals, that she eats from the same plate and that she has given residues from these meals to Doctor Chance for testing. I asked her to describe a normal day. She says she visits Dorian first and helps him to the bathroom, where he showers and shaves and puts on fresh pyjamas for the day. Then she sees him settled at the breakfast table in the adjoining room and goes to prepare and fetch his breakfast. Normally, this is cereal, and once again, she shares this to put his mind at rest. She does the same at lunch and again at dinner. She says she has observed him losing weight and has no explanation for it because he does eat in her presence. She says she's paid well. She has a cottage in the village that's been paid for from her wages and has a deposit account serviced from the same source. She admits she's not rich, but describes herself as happily comfortable. She's very fond of Dorian, for whom she's worked since leaving school. She's known him and Marcus since childhood and says they were close and happy brothers until these present problems. I asked if she thought it possible he was being poisoned. She said she assumed he was just very ill and started to sob, so I closed the interview."

"Very well done, Sol, and very thorough, I'm impressed. And next?"

"Next, I interviewed Johnson the butler-come-chauffeur, who was shopping in town when we arrived. Johnson is his first name. His surname is Abercorn. The family always refer to him as Johnson. I asked if he ever had access to the food. He answered he used to purchase certain items for the kitchen, but now all foodstuffs are purchased and prepared by Anna."

"He's worked for Dorian for more than ten years and has been very happy during that time. Like Anna, he considers he's well paid. Dorian has arranged and paid for healthy pensions for the staff, and Johnson has managed to save what he thinks is a considerable amount from living rent-free in a flat above the garage. He's obviously gay, but considers himself asexual, getting all the affection he needs from his dachshund, Sally. Asked whether he thought there was any substance to Dorian's suspicions, he says he believes not. His recollections over the last decade are of two brothers who loved each other, and this current situation can, in his opinion, only be down to Dorian's state of mind caused by his illness. Asked if he had ever had a sexual relationship with either of them, he replied no and informed me, with some disdain, that not all gay people were sexual predators."

Dick laughed. "You're not frightened to ask the tough questions then."

"I thought it pertinent." Sol frowned. "If there had been a relationship, it might have given us a motive and that's something that seems decidedly lacking at the moment."

"Is that it?" said Dick.

"There's just the maid who helps Anna with the cleaning in the kitchen and looks after Mrs. Somersby and the general housework. To be honest, her answers just mirrored those of the other two, so I learned nothing new."

Just then, Dick's phone rang. "It's the information from my contacts. Let me have your notebook for a minute."

Sol passed it over, and for the next few minutes, Dick made several pages of notes. When he eventually put the phone down, he looked thoughtful.

"What did you find out?" said Sol.

"Only that it's looking more and more as if this is a case of illness, not poisoning."

The door opened and Johnson walked in. "Mr. Marcus asks if you would like to stay the night. We have plenty of rooms available, so it wouldn't be a problem. Also, it would give you an opportunity to rest before dinner."

"That sounds like a good idea. I *am* feeling a little weary," said Sol.

"Yes, we'd like to take him up on his offer, Johnson. Lead the way," said Dick. He turned to Sol. "I'll fill you in on the phone call before we go down for dinner."

Dick dropped off to sleep quite easily and was awakened by the sound of a gong from downstairs signalling dinner. A few minutes later, Sol appeared at the door.

"So, you were going to tell me about the phone call."

"Ah, so I was," said Dick. "My contact has researched Marcus' and his wife's finances. It appears they are, if anything, in a better financial position than Dorian. Apart from Marcus Somersby's own wealth, Mrs. Somersby is incredibly wealthy in her own right. That means money's not a motive."

"I'm not surprised," said Sol. "Marcus obviously loves his brother. He'd have to be an amazing actor to be able to fake his concern so convincingly."

"Perhaps he really has got an undiagnosed illness," said Dick. "It wouldn't be the first time doctors have been unable to find an explanation."

"Let's go and eat," said Sol. "We can discuss our next move after dinner."

Sol agreed Mrs. Somersby was quite charming and Marcus came across as a warm and loving brother. Dorian's condition really was a mystery.

After dinner, the Somersbys retired and Dick and Sol were shown into the library, where they sat by the open fire and enjoyed a large brandy each.

"There's just one more thing I'd like to try before I tell Dorian I think he's wrong," said Dick.

"And that is?" said Sol.

"I want you to accompany me tomorrow morning to see Dorian. While we're there, I want you to keep him entertained while I have a look round his rooms."

"What for?"

"I want to install some secret recording devices just to be sure we haven't missed anything. I've got incredibly tiny devices, yet they can send full video and sound to my laptop up to half a mile away."

"Do you suspect something's amiss? I thought we'd discounted foul play."

"We have, but it's my army training going belt and braces just to be sure."

As agreed, they called on Dorian in his rooms the following morning. He seemed a little better and was pleased to have the company. Sol kept him occupied with their story of the Romanov cross while Dick looked around the rooms ostensibly, but was carefully placing his devices. An hour later, they said their goodbyes and went back to Dick's room, where he set his laptop to record from the devices. Once set they both went downstairs for breakfast.

At breakfast, they informed the Somersbys that they would probably be leaving the next day and that they believed the most likely explanation of Dorian's illness was natural causes. This was a great relief to them, but it was tempered by Marcus' sadness at his brother's condition.

42

A mystery solved

"Let's check it's recording okay," said Dick when they returned to his room.

"It's a bit soon," said Sol. "There hasn't been time to record much."

"I just want to be sure it's working. Just a quick look."

As the screen opened up, three pictures appeared: views of the bed, the breakfast room and the bathroom. They could see Dorian in the breakfast room being served by Anna and saw her eat a little of each dish in front of him before he ate. At the same time, they saw someone enter the bedroom and make for the bathroom. Once in the bathroom the person approached the soap dish Dorian used for mixing his shaving soap and from a small paper packet tipped what looked like dust inside. As the person turned to leave, the face was clear on the screen. Dick and Sol gasped. Up until then, they had been transfixed at the scene being played out before them. They suddenly burst into action and headed for Dorian's rooms. The visitor had long gone, by the time they arrived, but Dick went straight to the bathroom ignoring the surprised looks of Anna and Dorian. He scooped up the soap dish and wrapped it carefully in a dry towel.

In answer to Anna and Dorian's confusion, he said, "Maybe you haven't been as mistaken as we all thought, Dorian. I need to take this to be analysed, and I'll return later with my findings. In the meantime, do not, under any circumstances, shave today, and do not mention this to anyone until I return. I promise we'll explain everything later. I can tell you now that you can trust Anna one hundred percent, so eat and drink well. I'm sure it'll help your recovery."

They left and drove into Exeter and went to the laboratory Sol had located via the internet, which would be able to analyse the substance in the soap dish. After what seemed like an interminable wait, but which was probably little more than an hour, a technician presented them with the laboratory's findings. With the information in hand, Dick made some telephone calls, and they returned to Chalfont.

Dick asked all the family, including Dorian, to assemble in the drawing room.

"As you know," said Dick, "we've been asked by Mr. Dorian Somersby to investigate because he believed he was being poisoned."

"Something we all know to be untrue," said Marcus.

"On the contrary," said Sol. "We have absolute proof he was indeed being systematically poisoned."

"Then where are the staff concerned?" said Mrs. Somersby.

"They're not here because no member of staff was involved." said Sol.

"Can I ask you," said Dick, "what you majored in at university, Mrs. Somersby?"

"Of course. I majored in chemical engineering."

"So can you tell me if a salt dust can be made from mercury and if such a dust would be toxic?"

"Of course. Mercury salt can be made quite easily and it would definitely be toxic."

"It would appear, Mrs. Somersby, that your expertise has been put to use."

"How dare you accuse my wife," said Marcus.

"It is not your wife I'm accusing," said Dick. "I want you now to look at the surveillance tape I made of your brother's rooms earlier today."

They all crowded round the laptop screen to watch the action Dick and Sol had observed earlier. It showed a person entering the bathroom, tipping the salt dust into the soap dish and then turning to face the camera. There, staring at them quite clearly was Oliver Somersby. All eyes turned to Oliver, who had been sitting silently in a chair and who was now blushing furiously.

"It seems," said Dick, "that young Oliver inherited your prowess with chemicals, Mrs. Somersby, and managed to make mercury salt in small quantities. Although his uncle has left him his vehicle collection in his will, I believe he got impatient and couldn't wait to have access to these undoubtedly exciting vehicles. I'm sure their monetary value hadn't escaped him either. Anyway, he ingeniously came up with the idea of placing a small quantity of mercury salt in his uncle's shaving-soap dish every so often. Just a small amount each time so that the deterioration was gradual and could be attributed to natural causes. Such an unusual substance is easily missed in tests for poison by a doctor. Whether he intended to kill his uncle or just to make him incapable of visiting his collection is for a court to decide. You see, he'd already taken out a very valuable vintage corvette and written it off. Something that couldn't be hidden indefinitely."

There was silence in the room except for the ticking of the mantel clock. The

Somersbys looked devastated at the news. The first person to speak was Marcus.

"I don't know what to say. I'm just so very sorry, Dorian. I had no idea."

"I can't believe I could have given birth to someone so evil," said Mrs. Somersby.

Oliver just sat there staring at the floor.

"The first thing I need to do is to see if the effects can be reversed, then we'll decide what to do about Oliver," said Dick.

"Do you want to have him arrested?" said Sol.

"I'd rather you left this to us now, if you don't mind," said Dorian.

"That's entirely up to you," said Dick. "We're not the police. Our job's done here. We'll leave you a copy of the surveillance tape and take our leave."

"Take this with you then, and accept my grateful thanks. It's not something I can be happy about. Nor, as you can appreciate, can my brother and his wife, but I do understand it's a job well done." He wrote a cheque and handed it to Dick.

They decided to give the train a miss and hired a car for the return journey.

Once they were packed and on the road, Sol looked at the cheque Dick had passed to him.

"Wow, that's some payment. It seems this business can be very lucrative."

"We *did* save his life."

"I know, but what unhappiness will there be in that house now?"

"Better a little unhappiness than a funeral."

Almost on cue, Dick's phone rang.

43

The evil returns

Dick answered on hands-free.

"Mr. Brady. I was so disappointed you left our shores so abruptly. I was expecting you to become a worthy adversary instead of running away with your tail between your legs."

"And you are?" said Dick.

"You know exactly who I am, Mr. Brady, but I'll play your game for a little. I am Boris Godunov."

"And why are you taking the trouble to call me? I'm sure you have far more important things to do with your time."

"You underestimate yourself, Mr. Brady. You see, I get bored easily, and I find my current adversaries in Russia lacking in imagination. There's no challenge with these people. They're predictable and easily outmanoeuvred. I'm an accomplished chess player, and I require a player of equal ability as my opponent."

"I'm not interested in what you require, nor do I have any intention of joining in your games," said Dick. "I've heard most of them end with fatalities, and the fact that you consider it a game just emphasises how sick you are."

"In that case, I'm going to have to use some persuasion." There was a slap and a loud scream in the background

"Dick! Don't come to Russia!" It was Ivana.

The phone went dead, and Dick moved into the fast lane with his toe to the floor. "Where's the fire?" said Sol nervously.

"That was Godunov. He's got Ivana. We've got to get over there as soon as possible. That animal's capable of anything."

"Slow down then, or we'll be going in a box. It won't help her if we're the victims of a car crash."

Dick eased off. Sol was right. Few minutes one way or another would make no difference. He had to think it through and come up with a plan.

"Okay. Get on the phone and book us on the next flight to Moscow. Then call Bogdan and Andrei, and ask them to meet us on arrival."

Dick shook his head to clear it. A fine film of sweat appeared on his forehead. He had to get a grip, keep control. Hearing Ivana's scream was a shock, but he had to be strong if he was to remove her from the clutches of this monster.

By the time they were back in London, all had been arranged. They would catch the six p.m. flight from Heathrow and meet Bogdan and Andrei in Moscow at around ten. They didn't go back to Baker Street but went straight to the airport to catch, what seemed to Dick, the longest flight of his life.

They were first off the plane, and with no luggage, they were soon getting into the car Andrei had arranged. Bogdan stayed behind at HQ, trying to use their equipment there to locate Godunov and, hopefully, Ivana. The mood in the car was sombre.

"I didn't expect to see you back in Russia so soon. I would wish it was in better circumstances," said Andrei.

"I blame myself," said Dick. "I should have made her come back with me."

"She's an intelligent woman, Dick, with a mind of her own. It was her decision to stay."

"And look what that decision has brought her," said Dick, angrily.

"Look," said Sol, "if it's anyone's fault, it's the fault of the jerk who abducted her, so don't start laying blame elsewhere. What we need to do is get to him and find her."

"He's right, Dick," said Andrei. "You need to calm down if you're to make sound decisions."

Dick's head was spinning. He wiped hot tears from his eyes and shook his head to clear it. They were right. He needed to get a grip if he was going to be able to help Ivana.

"Okay, let's get back to your place and see if Bogdan has any idea about this arsehole's whereabouts."

Andrei put a magnetic blue light on top of the car and switched on a siren, moving fast through the traffic as the vehicles ahead made way for him. It seemed an age to Dick, but it was only a short while later when they pulled into the FSB car park. Dick got out and sprinted for the lift with Sol and Andrei following in his wake, trying to keep up.

As they entered the main office, they saw Bogdan sitting before a range of computers making notes.

"Have you got anything?" said Dick.

"Everything and nothing," said Bogdan. "I've noted all his known addresses and organised surveillance on each of them. Unfortunately, he doesn't appear to be at any of them."

"What about rented houses?" said Dick. "He'd need to be somewhere where a scream would go unnoticed, so it'd probably be in its own grounds."

"I'll get on to the agencies and see if anything like that's been rented recently," said Andrei, reaching for the phone.

"Let's think about this logically," said Dick. "I know he's twisted, and I know he wants to play out this sick game with me, but I doubt he's going to let it interfere with his business. If I'm right, we need to be talking to some informants to find out what deals he's planning next. That way, we might get a chance to grab him or at least follow him to his lair."

"I'm on it," said Bogdan. "If you grab a coffee in the canteen, I'll come and get you as soon as I have something."

"Sounds like a good idea," said Sol. "I'm parched."

Bogdan never arrived to collect them, but as they walked back to the office, he had the phone to his ear and was waving them over frantically, with his hand over the mouthpiece.

"It looks like we've struck lucky. This guy says there's a huge exchange—drugs for money—the day after tomorrow.

There's so much involved that it's unlikely Godunov will trust anyone with the money."

"Will the guy come in and give us all the details?" said Dick.

"No chance. His life's on the line, but he'll tell me everything on the phone. He's a clever guy and never meets in person, that's why he's still alive. I pay his fees over the internet, and I always get value for money. The information will be accurate."

"Write everything down, and then we'll see what the possibilities are. He's a very clever fucker, this Godunov, so you can bet it's not going to be easy."

They sat and waited while Bogdan spoke into the phone and scribbled away furiously on his notepad. When he hung up, they all shuffled into the nearby conference room and sat at the table while Bogdan relayed what he had been told.

There was going to be a meeting at the Ne Regrette club the following evening. If all went well, an exchange would take place at an underpass next to the old KGB headquarters opposite the Children's World Department Store at midnight the next day. The deal was for a large suitcase packed full of heroin, street value in the millions.

"Sounds to me like the underpass is the best bet because we can seal each end as soon as he goes in," said Dick.

"I agree," said Andrei. "But it would be interesting to visit the club. You never know what information you can pick up when you're undercover."

"Do you think you could manage to go unrecognised," said Sol.

"I think it could be possible with a little help from our disguise department," said Bogdan.

"You actually have a department dedicated to disguise?" said Sol, his eyes large with disbelief.

"But of course," said Bogdan. "Doesn't everyone?"

The next couple of hours were spent with Uri Malenkin, the FSB expert on disguise. He took photos of each of them and put them through a computer programme he had devised to ascertain the minimum changes needed to facilitate an effective disguise.

"I'll sit this one out," laughed Sol. "I'm too old for clubs, and I'd be laughing too much at you lot, anyway. Although, I must say, some of these disguises are a distinct improvement."

"So why are you laughing then?" said Dick.

"If it pleases him, let him have his fun." Andrei smiled.

"Sol, what are you going to do while we're in the club?"

"I'll sit outside in the car with the motor running in case you get spotted and have to make a quick exit."

"I never had you down as a getaway driver. Do you think you're up to it?"

"Let's say you might be pleasantly surprised," said Sol, grinning broadly.

"We might as well go back to the apartment and get some rest," said Dick. "Perhaps it would be wise to reconnoitre tomorrow just in case you're right and we do have to escape in a hurry."

"You'll need to do a little shopping too," said Bogdan. "They have gorillas on the door, and if you're not wearing designer clothes, you're sure to be turned away."

"Designer clothes? You mean Dolce and Gabbana, Tom Ford, that kind of thing?"

"I most certainly do."

"But they cost a fortune," said Dick, looking at Sol for support.

"Ah, but you see, that's not our problem…we're on expenses," said Andrei, smiling.

"Looks like we'll have to break the piggy bank," said Sol with a shrug.

They spent the next couple of hours on Petrovka Street in the Dolce & Gabbana store. Dick bought a whole new outfit, including a leather jacket and shoes, while Sol sat flinching as the price of every item flashed up on the till.

"You're sure there's nothing else you need?" said Sol, sarcastically.

"Now, now Sol, there's no need to be like that. It's all for a good cause."

"But so much money!" said Sol shrugging his shoulders and gesturing with his hands.

"Never mind," said Dick. "That's everything. Let's go back to the apartment and get some rest. Tomorrow we'll go and check out the club and decide where the best place is for you to wait. Until then there's not much we can do, so we might as well recharge our batteries." Sol was still muttering under his breath as they made their way out to the street to hail a taxi.

"Don't worry, Sol. It's all tax deductible."

"We'd have to make a profit for that to be any help," moaned Sol.

They grabbed a pizza and a bottle of wine on the way back to the apartment, and after one glass and a couple of bites, Dick went to bed leaving Sol to finish off the rest.

Dick had hardly been able to eat and now found it almost impossible to sleep. When he did manage to drift off, he had horrible nightmares involving Ivana and

Godunov. He woke twice from a short fitful nap, trembling and covered in sweat. The second time, he took a long hot shower and tried to make himself calm down.

His current state wasn't going to help anybody, least of all Ivana, he told himself. If he could remain calm and objective for just a while, he had a far better chance of snatching Ivana from the clutches of this deranged gangster. If he carried on letting his emotions get the better of him, he would be playing right into the monster's hands. Godunov said he was a chess player. So was Dick. The visit to the club was just his first move.

44

A job in disguise

The next day was wet with dark, overcast skies and pounding rain, ideal weather for checking out the club, which did not seem that impressive in the grey daylight. Probably at night, with all the neon and laser light, it would have been different. There was a small street opposite, which they thought would be an ideal place to park the car. On investigation, they found the street led onto a main dual carriageway that led across a river and out of town: perfect for a fast getaway.

Rather than take a chance that the optimum parking spot would be taken in the evening, they called Andrei and he took the car down. Bogdan followed in another. They parked the car, boot facing the club, so that no time would be wasted in manoeuvring.

Bogdan then dropped them off at the apartment. They arranged to meet at the club at midnight, so Dick and Sol chilled out in Ivana's apartment until late evening. Dick watched TV, and Sol listened to Ivana's classical music selection on headphones. Sol booked a taxi for eleven forty p.m. Sol was wearing his normal clothes and a pair of driving gloves. Dick could not help but grin. Dick himself was resplendent in his new Dolce & Gabbana outfit, even down to the shoes. He looked amazing, especially with the disguise Uri had prepared for him. It consisted of a small moustache that matched his black hair exactly, blue contact lenses and a pair of horn-rimmed spectacles.

He had combed his hair into a side parting rather than the swept-back style he normally had. It wasn't too heavy a disguise, yet the transformation was complete.

They met at the car; it was a good thing they did because the job Uri had done on Andrei and Bogdan was more thorough than that on Dick, and he doubted he would have recognised them. They got Sol settled in the car and then approached the club entrance. The two burly doormen looked them up and down, and deciding they looked the part and were likely to spend money, they let them in.

The inside of the club was richly furnished with thick carpet, expensive furniture and crystal chandeliers. Around the edges were velvet-covered booths, which looked onto the dance floor. There was a roped-off VIP area, and they settled into a booth opposite but to the side of it; they didn't want to be too obvious, but they still needed a good view. Andrei ordered drinks, and they sat back to enjoy the evening. Godunov's party had not yet arrived.

"Do you think your guy got it right, Bogdan?" said Dick. "It's well past midnight and I can't see him here."

"Don't be impatient, Dick. He'll be here. Midnight's early for a club in Russia."

"He's right," said Andrei. "We probably could have come later, but I didn't want to risk missing him. I'm interested to see whom he's meeting."

"We have a big problem here in Moscow," said Bogdan. "Heroin is being brought into Moscow in unheard of quantities from Tajikistan. Our government estimates we now have sixteen and half million hooked on it, that's one point six percent of our population. It's serious and won't get better unless we do something about it. If we can spot a new face in the business and take him down, it could help us in the battle."

"Is this guy a new face?" said Dick.

"So my informant tells me. He says he has a large suitcase packed with ninety-percent-pure beige heroin. Even I can't begin to guess what that's worth on the street."

"A word of caution, Dick," said Andrei. "A man who can afford to buy that suitcase is a very, very wealthy man, and money here in Russia can buy almost anything and almost anybody."

He had just finished speaking when Godunov's party arrived. Somebody, probably the manager, led them through the now-thickening crowd to their VIP seats. Boris was dressed like most of the current Russian millionaires, in a smart Savile Row suit.

Unfortunately, the image was spoiled by the stupid little ponytail and the way the jacket buttons strained to contain his girth.

Dick had to restrain the urge to launch himself across the floor and rip his throat out. He was just considering how that might feel, when the same manager as before led a tall, dark, balding man in a white suit to Godunov's table. The man was not alone. He was accompanied by two very fit bodyguards in similar attire. They couldn't hear the conversation, but they saw Godunov and the man shake hands; they were obviously making introductions.

Andrei was surreptitiously taking photos on his mobile, and so far nobody seemed to notice. He immediately emailed them to his people at FSB headquarters from his phone, who would see if they could come up with a name for this new supplier.

"We've got what we came for," said Bogdan. "We should make a move before we get seen or before Dick snaps and tries to kill the bastard."

"He's right, Dick," said Andrei. "You keep glaring at him like that and he's going to realise something's up."

"I know you're right," said Dick. "Come on, let's make a move."

They forced their way through the crush to the door and slipped out into the cold wet Moscow air. Sol was sitting comfortably across the road, listening to Beethoven on an iPod he had borrowed from Ivana's apartment.

They burst into the car. "Get us out of here fast," shouted Dick.

Sol had kept the engine idling. He put his foot to the floor, and the car flew forward. He careered down the little street at breakneck speed and sped onto the dual carriageway hardly slowing for the turn.

The engine screamed and the car seemed about to take off. When they had got their breath back, the three disguised men started laughing.

"What's funny?" said Sol, beads of sweat beginning to show on his forehead and a grim, determined look on his face.

"We're in no rush," said Dick. "But I'd love to know where you learned to drive like this."

"What do you mean...we're not being chased?"

"Afraid not, old chap. All went rather well actually."

"You rotten bastards," said Sol, slowing down. "I could have had a heart attack."

"But you didn't. C'mon, where did you learn to drive like that?"

"It's no mystery. It was our hobby, Marios' and mine. We went stock-car racing when we were young. I was quite good at it, I've even got trophies."

"You dark horse," said Dick. "You kept that one quiet."

"Not really. It never came up in conversation and I'd almost forgotten about it, anyway."

"Didn't look like you'd forgotten much to me."

"Or me!" chorused Bogdan and Andrei.

"Just take it easy on the way back," said Dick. "I thought I was going to be sick." They all laughed, even Sol.

When they arrived at FSB headquarters, there was news. The head of the drug taskforce updated them.

"Good morning, gentlemen. My name is Ilya Rakhmonov, and I'm in charge of the Moscow anti-drug taskforce. I was called from my bed because the photo you sent was of great interest to me. Drugs, especially heroin, are causing havoc here in Moscow. It's like Afghanistan is taking its revenge for the Russian invasion by destroying the Russian youth with this poison. The person in your picture is a Tajikistan warlord. His name is Faruh Vafovich, and the fact that he's here personally to make this deal means we're one step further towards the Armageddon that drugs will bring to Russia."

"Why is this particular guy so important?" said Dick.

"This man has access to unlimited tons of pure heroin. He's now meeting with the top drug retailer in Russia. If this deal is successful, it'll be the prelude to massive deals in the future. That can only bring horror to our streets. Already we have children as young as twelve becoming addicted. If they operate as they have in the past, heroin will become as cheap as a bag of sweets. Then when they feel they have the maximum number of addicts, the price will go up. At that stage, when they are hooked, they just can't do without it. Imagine what that'll do to our nation. The crime rate will soar and there'll be anarchy."

"There's some good news then," said Dick.

"And that is?" said Ilya, raising an eyebrow.

"This deal is most definitely not going to be successful."

"You think you can stop it?"

"With the help of my friends in the FSB, I think I can, but we have to plan carefully. I don't know about the Tajiks, but this Russian is as slippery as an eel."

"So what's the plan?" said Ilya.

"First, no disrespect, but I don't want you out of my sight from this moment on, and I want your mobile phone locked up here in headquarters. You can do the same with mine. We'll manage with two-way radios."

"You don't trust me?"

"I don't trust anybody. Information can be leaked either intentionally or accidentally. I don't want to take the chance on either. If we're careful, neither of these bastards will get away."

"I'm up for it," said Bogdan. "Here's my mobile. We're going to need Kapitan Igor's SWAT team though."

"Yes, but we don't need to tell him what for or who's involved yet. Just get him and his team on standby for now."

"Here's my mobile," said Andrei.

"And mine," said Ilya.

"Let's go into the conference room and form a plan of action."

Andrei opened out a large map of Moscow and set it on the table marking the underpass where Bogdan's informant had told them the exchange was to take place.

"Right," said Dick. "Where nearby is there parking for the SWAT team where they can be out of sight until the last moment? We need two different positions—one near either end of the underpass."

They scoured the map. "At this end they could park in the retail car park. It should be empty at that time of night," said Bogdan.

"And the other end is near the pumping station's car park. Another good position," said Ilya.

"I can't see a problem with either of them, so let's settle on that," said Dick.

"Okay," said Andrei. "We'll wait until both parties are in the underpass and then call on Igor to seal the ends."

"We'll have to give him a picture of Godunov for his men. We want him alive. If he gets killed, we may never find Ivana," said Dick.

"Of course. I'll organise copies now. We need to decide where we're going to be to direct the action."

"I suggest you find a vantage point in the Children's Department Store with a good pair of binoculars. I'm going to be with Igor."

"Okay, listen in while I give Igor his orders," said Andrei. "Then I suggest we all retire to the canteen until about eight p.m. I think if we leave, then we'll be early enough to escape detection."

45

The trap is set

At seven thirty p.m., Andrei ordered the armoury to issue weapons. Normally, he would have left Dick out, but he made an exception this time.

"Right, everyone. You've heard me order the transport," said Andrei. "We'll all travel together, Sol will drive. He'll drop Bogdan and me off at the store and then take Dick and Ilya to meet up with Igor. We've all got radios, so we can keep in touch. Good luck, everyone."

At eight, they were all in place. Andrei and Bogdan were on the store roof, and Igor's men were in unmarked vehicles at the designated car parks. Dick was with Igor in his command vehicle, a matt-black four by four similar to an American Humvee. The rain had not let up and pounded on the bodywork, making it difficult to be heard and steaming up the windows. They sat in silence as the time ticked by, each lost in his own thoughts, only breaking the monotony with occasional radio checks. They were brought sharply out of their daydreaming as the radio crackled into life at two minutes after midnight. It was Andrei.

"Both suspects identified entering the underpass from opposing ends. They're both carrying suitcases, and there appear to be four guards with each of them. Allow them time to exchange and then move in using extreme caution. These are dangerous men, who won't hesitate to kill to avoid capture. Igor, remember we need Godunov alive if possible. A woman's life might depend on it."

Igor affirmed the orders and gave instructions to his teams. Among them was a three-man squad consisting of a highly skilled sniper with a spotter and a cover man. The sniper's weapon was loaded with stun darts similar to those used to bring down animals in the wild. His orders were to try and pick off Godunov if possible.

Dick's ideas were slightly different. He also needed to keep Godunov alive, but that could also have been done with a couple of painful, but not life-threatening leg shots. This, he felt, would be a far more satisfying result.

As it happened neither of them was to be successful. Igor gave the order to close the trap and not let anybody out of the underpass. As they began to enter, a barrage of firing erupted, deadly for both lots of combatants in the confines of the underpass. Soon, there was a smoky haze and the acrid smell of cordite drifting through the tunnel around their heads. The SWAT team fared better than the enemy, as they were wearing lifesaving ballistic body-suits and helmets.

Their opponents had much less protection; only a few of them wore even a bulletproof vest. Igor's men eventually prevailed and Vafovich, seeing more resistance was futile, surrendered to Dick. But there was no sign of Godunov. He seemed to have evaporated into the ether, but Dick couldn't work out how.

On searching the underpass, it became all too obvious. A service door leading to the drains and services that should have been locked was wide open.

"Where does that lead?" said Dick.

"To the main drainage system, I'd imagine," said Igor.

"So he could surface almost anywhere," said Dick despondently. "This was his escape route. He had this all planned out in the event things didn't go his way."

"Looks like it," said Igor. "But I don't think he was expecting us. More likely he planned to rip off Vafovich."

"He's slipped up there then because, if I'm not mistaken, in that suitcase over there is the heroin he came to collect."

"Let's check it out," said Igor. They unzipped the case which was unlocked. Sure enough, it was packed with ninety-per-cent-pure pale-beige heroin.

"So it hasn't been a complete failure then," said Dick. "He won't be happy this was left behind."

When they got back to headquarters and retrieved their mobiles, Dick saw he had a missed call. He didn't have to guess who it was from. He pressed the return call button.

"Mr. Brady," snarled Godunov. "It appears you have me in check, but not checkmate, I think. We both know I have something you also are desperate to retrieve." Dick could hear the sneering satisfaction in the gangster's voice.

Dick thought quickly. "You're quite right, of course," he said, his voice as controlled as he could make it. "And it's your move, I believe."

"Might I suggest an exchange? It would seem the logical next move, don't you think?"

"You think the Russian government is going to allow me to give you heroin worth millions, knowing you'll be distributing it on the streets?"

"That, Mr. Brady, is your problem. I'm enjoying every minute with the young lady staying with me. I could, however, get bored at any minute, and your friends will tell you how I dispose of people I get tired of and in what condition. I'll be in touch." The line went dead.

Dick's hands were shaking and his mind was racing.

"No need to ask who that was," said Sol. "You've gone as white as a sheet."

"The bastard was threatening to hurt Ivana. It's knowing that the sick fuck could actually do it and that we're powerless to stop him that's killing me."

"Not quite powerless, Dick," said Andrei. "We have the heroin we know he wants."

"Of course he wants it. He's just suggested an exchange, but there's no way your government would condone that."

"Not if our government knew we had the heroin, but I've just spoken to Igor and Bogdan, and none of us has any recollection of a suitcase of heroin being recovered. A few kilos, yes…enough to send Vafovich to Siberia for life, but what suitcase?"

"You'd take a risk like that for me?" said Dick incredulously. "You'll join him in Siberia if they find out."

"As I'm the one who writes the reports, that's hardly likely, especially as the two other senior officers at the scene will confirm my version of events. Mr. Rakhmonov wasn't aware of the recovery, and though I'm sure he's trustworthy, I don't intend to inform him."

"Sounds like you've got it all worked out. What happens next?"

"The case is in the boot of a car I've seconded for your use. It's parked in the garage downstairs. I suppose you've just got to wait for Godunov to make his next move."

And wait they did. It was eight a.m. the next day when Dick received his call.

"Mr. Brady, are you ready to make an exchange? I'm beginning to tire of your young lady. I've done most things to her I can think of, and now I'm running out of ideas. Painless ones, anyway."

Dick made a superhuman effort to remain calm and detached. "I'm doing what

I can, but stealing from the Russian government isn't easy."

"However, Mr. Brady, I'm sure you'll be able to accomplish it. Now let's say tomorrow evening at twelve for the exchange. I'll call you at eleven forty-five p.m. and give you the address. Of course, you'll come alone. If not, you'll receive your parcel in pieces. Do I make myself clear?"

"Crystal."

"Good. If you stick to these terms I guarantee the safety of you and your lady. Goodbye, Mr. Brady."

Andrei, Bogdan and Sol had been listening on the mobile's speakerphone.

"I think he's made his first mistake," said Sol.

"How do you mean?" said Dick.

"If he's going to call at eleven forty-five for a meeting at twelve, he's no more than fifteen minutes away. Probably exactly fifteen minutes. If we draw a circle on a housing map with headquarters in the centre, we'll be able to see which properties within the radius are our likely destinations."

"But there'll be hundreds," said Dick.

"It's better than thousands," said Bogdan. "It's worth a try."

Andrei found a map of Moscow on the computer, which he connected to a projector that displayed it on a large screen in the conference room. He drew a circle depicting the radius, and they all started checking the map and making notes.

"I'll be buggered," said Dick. "Why didn't I think of that before?"

"Don't keep us in suspense," said Sol. "What have you found out?"

"Right on the line...don't you see it? And it's the perfect place for the snake to hide." Sol followed where his finger was pointing. "Noskcaj's place, of course."

"That makes sense," said Andrei. "With Noskcaj out of the way, of course Godunov would take it over."

"We should have considered that," said Bogdan.

"None of us did but better late than never," said Dick. "Now let's make plans."

"Should we plan to attack before he calls, to catch him off guard?" asked Igor.

"I think I should go alone with the heroin just as he asked. It's the only way we'll have any chance of getting Ivana out alive," said Dick.

"If you do that, he'll just take the heroin and kill you both," said Sol. "He wouldn't give his promise a second thought."

"Then we have to give him a reason to keep his word."

"How could we possibly do that?" said Andrei.

"I suggest Igor and his men surround the house," said Dick. "I want a satellite feed showing the troops in place which I'll show him on a laptop I'll be carrying. When he realises he's trapped, I'll offer him a solution—my personal guarantee that he'll be allowed to leave with his heroin on a helicopter provided by us. This, on condition Ivana and I are visibly alive outside the house on the satellite feed. If we're not left alive as agreed, the helicopter will be destroyed by a shoulder-held ground-to-air device, should it try to leave."

"Why would he believe we wouldn't destroy the helicopter once you were safe," said Sol.

"Because," said Dick, "he knows that the house is in a built-up area and that we wouldn't risk damage to people or property just for a bag of heroin."

"I don't like it," said Andrei. "But I don't have any other ideas."

"Nothing we come up with is going to be fool proof," said Dick, "but I think this is as good an idea as any."

"It does mean that if he complies, he gets away with a huge amount of heroin. I'm not concerned with the monetary value, but I'm horrified at the amount of carnage it'll cause on our streets," said Bogdan.

"That's how it would appear, but as Godunov likes to be one move ahead of us, let's take a leaf out of his book," said Dick.

"How do you mean?" said Sol.

"If Godunov leaves by helicopter, his fastest route to safety will take him across the river, do you agree?"

"It would seem so," said Sol.

"I'm sure the FSB's experts can fit a remote-controlled device that can be detonated once he's flying safely over the river."

"I'll contact our explosives experts straightaway and get things organised," said Andrei.

"In the meantime, I've got a couple of calls to make. Then I don't know about you lot, but I could do with a drink," said Sol.

"Agreed," said Bogdan. "We'll meet you in the Dissident, a bar just across the street."

In the bar, they began chatting amongst themselves about the forthcoming action. Dick, though, was a little preoccupied. Should he carry a weapon? It would probably have been pointless, since someone like Godunov would ensure he was well searched. And what condition would Ivana be in? Distraught for sure, but would

Godunov abuse her physically, or was he just trying to wind Dick up?

All these thoughts and more were racing through his mind until Sol turned up and asked, "What are you drinking?"

"I don't know," said Dick. "A beer, I suppose."

"A beer in one of Moscow's best wine bars? Don't be a philistine."

"You order then," said Dick. "I'll have what you're having."

"I can see you're all tensed up, Dick, but you need to relax for a while. There'll be enough time for tension when you get the call."

"I know. You're right, but it's not easy knowing Ivana's at the mercy of that animal."

"Starving yourself and becoming a nervous wreck won't help. Now calm down and let's eat."

The afternoon passed as pleasantly as possible in the circumstances and for Dick, the rest of the time until the phone call, dragged by interminably.

The next evening, while they were assembled in the office at FSB headquarters, the phone rang at precisely eleven forty-five p.m.

"Mr. Brady." It was Godunov's voice, falsely pleasant. "I trust you're ready to deliver my property?" He then gave the coordinates. Dick had been right about the address. "You have fifteen minutes, Mr. Brady. Don't be late, or I shall have to take it out on my charge."

Dick grabbed the suitcase and ran to the lift. A short time later, he was driving towards the Noskcaj house. He made it with just a minute to spare. He pulled up at the gate, jumped out of the car and pressed the button.

A voice Dick didn't recognise answered. "Leave the car, Mr. Brady, and bring the case to the front door."

The gates swung open, and as he walked towards the house, the owner of the voice and another guard emerged to greet him. They patted him down thoroughly and professionally, leaving no chance for a concealed weapon. He had been right about that: it would have been pointless. When they were satisfied, they led him into a downstairs lounge, having relieved him of the suitcase. They asked him to take a seat and informed him Godunov would be along shortly. He started searching the house in his mind for where Ivana might be held. Would it be the bedroom where they had found the women? Would Godunov be taking her to see him now? What condition would she be in? While he was still considering these things and more, the door swung open and Godunov entered carrying Dick's laptop.

"What do we have here, Mr Brady? I've checked the contents of the suitcase, and all seems to be in order, but I'm surprised to see you've brought me an additional gift. Is that what this is?" he said, pointing to the laptop he had placed on a nearby table.

"It is indeed," said Dick. "It's a way you might walk away from this with your ill-gotten gains on the condition you honour your agreement to leave us alive."

"I see. So you doubted my word. What an untrusting soul you are. Very well, go ahead. Show me how you wish me to accomplish your salvation."

Dick proceeded to show the satellite feed revealing the troops surrounding the house and explained the plan for Godunov's escape. As he was doing this, the helicopter landed in the grounds, and they saw the lone pilot jump down and leave by the gate, which closed behind him.

"You seem to have it all worked out, Mr. Brady." Godunov smiled. "But you didn't observe my conditions. You didn't come alone."

Godunov winked. Dick felt a sharp pain in his shoulder and then nothing but blackness as he spun faster and faster into oblivion.

He realised, as he came to, that he had been drugged. A hypodermic plunged into his shoulder. He was secured and gagged and could move only a few inches. As his vision cleared, nothing could have prepared him for the sight before him.

46

A horrific ordeal

Ivana was tied naked to a wooden cross. She was gagged by a rubber ball in her mouth secured by a chain around her head. Her breasts protruded through strategically cut-out holes, and her vulva was accessible below the V of the cross which was arranged on a pivot. When turned, her buttocks were equally accessible. Across her back and her buttocks were red wheals. She had obviously been severely beaten. Bulldog clips were hanging from her nipples, and she was moaning pitifully. Dick went to help her, but he was securely chained to the wall, just out of reach. The contraption had been set up in one of the cellars. As he struggled and pulled on his chains, trying to get free, Godunov walked in naked carrying a bag and a cane.

"Now then, Mr. Brady. I'm going to re-pay your little gift with a gift of entertain-ment for you." He proceeded to beat Ivana with the cane and became noticeably aroused as she flinched and groaned from the beating. He then took what looked like a glass penis with a flat end and, with a rubber mallet, proceeded to hammer it into her anus, oblivious to her shrieks from be-hind the gag. Once this was accomplished, he spun the cross and began to beat her with the cane across her breasts and her vagina. Her eyes were wild with fear and pain. Dick strained at the chains with all his strength, to no avail. His eyes were red with tears, and his body quivered and shook with the effort as his brain screamed in horror at the abuse.

Godunov seemed to take pleasure in Dick's futile attempts to escape and grinned maniacally as he began to rape Ivana while throttling her viciously till her face turned purple and her eyes bulged. The rape was rough and unrelenting, and soon blood began to run down her legs.

How long it might have gone on was unknown because a series of explosions dragged Godunov from his lust-filled haze, and he quickly left the room.

Minutes later, Igor and several troopers burst into the cellar. Taking it all in at a glance, Igor sent the men outside while he released Dick and Ivana. Dick gently cradled Ivana in his arms, sobbing quietly.

Godunov had not reached the helicopter, so Igor ordered the pilot back to take her to hospital.

Godunov's guards had been quickly dispatched, but there was no sign of Godunov. They put Dick and Ivana on the helicopter and began a search of the house and grounds, which turned out to be fruitless.

Sometime later, Sol turned up at the hospital.

"How is she, my friend?"

"She didn't make it, Sol," sobbed Dick. "She was dead on arrival."

"I'm so sorry," said Sol. "She was a wonderful woman."

"I can't believe what that bastard did to her. It was beyond evil. How can anybody develop such a sick and twisted mind?"

"From what Ivana told us, it's in his genes," said Sol. "He's the product of generations of evil bastards."

"I just can't believe he's got away with it. There's no justice in the world."

"Got away with it? I think I've got a surprise for you."

"What do you mean? What surprise?" said Dick.

"He didn't get away with it," said Sol. "I was thinking about what you said about him being a chess player, and I considered his MO. I wasn't about to let him fool us with the same move twice. I telephoned Spud and Danny before we went to lunch yesterday. They came over and we made plans."

"What plans? Get to the point. I'm not in the mood for long stories."

"We checked out the drainage system at Noskcaj's place, and sure enough, there was a main sewer running beneath the property. I got a copy of the plans with

Bogdan's help, and we traced the exits on the far side of the wall. There were two, but one had a roof collapse the municipality were scheduled to dig out next week. That left only one viable exit, and when we went to look, lo and behold, there was a locked Mercedes parked right beside it. A bit unusual as it was on a school playing field.

"So I played a hunch, and Spud, Danny and I waited there while Igor made the attack on the house."

"So where is he now?" said Dick.

"Spud and Danny have him chained up where you were in Noskcaj's place, and they're standing guard."

"Do any of our Russian friends know about this?"

"Not officially. You see, they've recovered the money and the heroin, so they're quite happy with what they've got to report."

"I see. Right, take me to him."

"Right away. The car's outside."

They arrived at Noskcaj's in double-quick time. Dick ran to the cellar, and there he was, a little battered and bruised. Spud and Danny were not renowned for their gentle nature. Still, though, he had that arrogant grin.

"Why so happy?" said Dick.

"You may have won this round, but not the match. My lawyers will get me out, and then the game begins again."

"Lawyers? Who said anything about lawyers?" said Dick. "The authorities aren't aware you're here, and to be honest, they're not interested."

"I know your sort, Brady." Godunov sneered. "You'll have to do the right thing and hand me in."

47

Retribution

"**O**bviously, you knew me before I watched you desecrate and murder the woman I love. I can assure you I'm a very different man now. Spud, Danny, tie him to that cross contraption while I look for my laptop. Strip him naked first."

"No problem, Captain."

A few minutes later, Dick went down to the cellar with the laptop he found in the lounge, along with a pen and paper.

Godunov had been stripped and tied to the cross so tightly that his hands and feet were going blue. He was as naked as the day he was born and had lost some of the arrogance he had displayed earlier.

"Now, Mr. Godunov, let's start with details of your bank accounts," said Dick. Godunov gave a half-hearted laugh.

"You know I won't tell you anything," he snorted.

"On the contrary. I know you will, and my friends here will check the truth of what you tell me on the laptop." To Spud, he said, "You and Danny go out for a smoke. I'll call you when I've got information for you to check."

"Okay, Captain. Here's a two-way radio. I've tuned it into mine. Just call when you need us."

"I hope that won't be for a while," said Dick. "I really want this scumbag to try and hold out."

"We've got food, so there's no hurry on our part," said Danny.

They heard the first screams before they had even got outside the house. They exchanged a glance. "Don't sound like he's gonna hold out long," said Spud.

Not much later, Dick called them back down. He was covered in splashes of blood, but his demeanour was as cool as ice, his jaw set firm and his hands steady.

Just a film of sweat on his forehead betrayed the fact that whatever he had been doing had required some physical exertion.

"Here are the details of his bank accounts, Spud. I know you and Danny have offshore accounts for your Special Ops payments, so I want you to transfer every penny out of his accounts and into yours. We'll decide how to reallocate it later."

"No problem, Cap. I'm onto it."

"And Danny, I want you to fetch me a blow torch from the garage and whatever tools you can find. Then I want you to go and get a bottle of vodka and some salt from upstairs."

"Be right back, Captain."

Dick went back into the cellar where Godunov was strapped to his machine and bleeding onto the cellar floor.

"I almost hope you've lied to me," said Dick. "I was so enjoying it before you caved in."

Godunov spat blood and saliva from his mouth. "You'll have to kill me because if

I ever get out of this, you can't imagine what I'll do to you."

"Oh, I'm not going to kill you," said Dick. "Once I'm finished with you, though, you'll very much wish I had."

Danny arrived with the vodka, salt, tools and the blow torch. "The torch's a bit old," he said. "I've tried it, though, and it still works fine."

"How's Spud doing with the money?"

"He says that so far, the information seems kosher. He's already transferred several million."

"Good. Tell him to keep going until all the accounts are cleared, and I want to know if any of the user names or passwords are false while Mr. Godunov is still in a position to correct his mistakes."

He needn't have worried. Like most bullies, Godunov was good at dishing out pain, but not so good at taking it. He was not likely to risk more punishment by holding out.

Dick went back inside the cellar, and as Danny made his way upstairs, even he flinched at the bloodcurdling scream he could hear through the door.

Dick had poured the bottle of vodka spirit over the open wound that had been Godunov's back and buttocks. He followed that up by emptying the salt on the damp blood- and vodka-soaked wound and was repaid with a long low moan as Godunov's body convulsed with the excruciating pain. When the cries were reduced to a whimper, Dick resumed his unrelenting questioning. "Where's the Romanov cross?"

"It's here in the R-Russian Commercial Bank in the World Trade Centre," stuttered Godunov.

"But you never told me you had an account in the Russian Commercial Bank. So you lied to me."

"No, no, it's not an account. It's a safety deposit box, number two zero two one."

"So, where's the key, and what name or password do I need to retrieve it?"

"The key's on my keychain. It's in my name, but you only need the key to open it." Dick found Godunov's clothes and the keychain was attached to his waistband.

"Is this it?" said Dick, holding up the most likely key. "Be sure you tell the truth because I'm going to send someone to retrieve it. If they fail I'll need to convince you of the consequences of lying. Do you understand?"

"It's true, I swear. You'll have no problem."

"I'll be honest with you, Godunov. I intend to do some brutal things to you, all well-deserved in my opinion, but I have a blow torch here to cauterise the wounds. If you've lied and my colleague has any problems collecting the cross, I will simply leave you to bleed to death."

Dick left Godunov contemplating his fate while he went to find Danny.

"Danny, call Sol, give him this key and tell him to go to the Russian Commercial Bank in the World Trade Centre. He has to ask for the Safety Deposit Box Department, box two zero two one. I want it emptied and the contents brought back here. If he has any problems, I want to be informed immediately."

"No problem, Captain. Oh, Spud asked if he could have a quick word."

Dick found his way to the lounge where Spud was furiously tapping away on the computer. "How's it going?"

"It's going great, but do you have any idea of the magnitude of these assets?"

"Not exactly, but I imagine it's sizeable."

"Sizeable isn't the word. It's bigger than some countries' national debt."

"We'll be able to put it to good use then. Keep stashing it away. I bet your bank managers will think all their Christmases have come at once."

They laughed, and Dick made his way back down to the cellar. Godunov had lapsed into unconsciousness. Dick got a bucket of ice cold water from the kitchen and doused him with it to bring him round.

"This won't do, dropping off just when the fun's about to start," said Dick. "Try and keep alert. I don't want you to miss a thing."

Dick's mobile rang. It was Sol. "Just leaving the bank. No problems…the box had around a million dollars in cash and the Romanov cross."

"That's good news. Bring it back here and we can get back to the business in hand." He hung up and turned back to his captive. "Right, Mr. Godunov, back to business."

"What do you mean?" he whimpered. "I've told you the truth. I've given you everything."

"Oh, not quite everything. Not retribution for the pain and suffering you put Ivana through. And all those other poor souls you've murdered over the years."

"Okay, so I'll go to prison for life," said Godunov. "You've had your revenge."

"Prison? You think prison's a just punishment for someone like you? Oh no, I have something much more suitable planned."

He took out a large hunting knife Spud had given him and lit up the blowtorch. He then heated up a nine-by-two-inch box spanner from the toolbox Danny had taken with him. Godunov watched his preparations, his eyes widening in fear and his body trembling in anticipation. When the spanner was glowing red hot, Dick positioned the cross frame so that Godunov's buttocks were easily accessible, and then holding the spanner with pincers, he positioned it at the entrance to Godunov's buttocks and drove it home with the same rubber mallet that had been used on Ivana. The screams were loud enough to rock the building. Dick pulled out the spanner and stood back to check the results. There was an angry red burn around the anus but no blood, and Godunov was still screaming.

"I'm going to have to take a break," said Dick. "Your screams are giving me a headache. Don't worry, though, I'll be back, and we'll have some more fun."

Upstairs, Spud was staring at the laptop in amazement.

"I've never seen so much money, Captain. You could pay the regiments' wages for five years and still have change. Sounds like you're having fun downstairs, too."

"Oh, I'm just getting warmed up. There's a lot more to come before I've finished with him. See if you can book us a private jet with his money. Get us a medical helicopter from here to the airport and then a private jet from here to New Delhi."

"New Delhi?"

"Yes, and make sure it's big enough to take you, me, Danny and Sol, as well as a stretcher."

"Consider it done. When do we leave?"

"When I've finished with that evil bastard downstairs."

Dick walked back down to the cellar. "Now then, have you missed me?" he said, closing the cellar door.

"Just kill me and get it over with. I can't take any more."

"Oh, I really hope you can because there's more. Now, let's see, what did you do to Ivana? You touched her vagina, and you'd need fingers for that, so let's start there."

After the first three fingers had come off, Godunov needed the bucket of water over him each time to bring him round.

Because of this, the removal of all fingers and thumbs took nearly twenty minutes. Each time one was removed, the wound was seared with the blowtorch to stem the bleeding and prevent infection. When Dick was finished, all that were left were two stumps with five blackened circles on each. The hunting knife was sharp so each amputation was quick, but the cracking of bone and sinew could still be heard as it sliced through.

"Right," said Dick, "so far so good. You won't be touching another woman ever again. Now, to continue."

"Enough," wailed Godunov. "Mercy!"

"Did you ever show any mercy to any of your victims? I don't think so. You killed and you mutilated whether they begged or not. Now it's your turn. Some people would call it karma. What's next? Oh yes, you raped her. Well, for that you need a penis."

"No!" screamed Godunov. "Not that."

"Can you think of any other way I can be sure you'll never rape again? I don't think we can rely on your promise. No, I think it's the only way to be sure."

Godunov sobbed while Dick heated the knife until it was white hot. He pulled on Godunov's penis and sliced through it nearest to the body. Fortunately, for Godunov, he passed out and was unconscious while Dick cauterised the wound.

When he came round it was with a low continuous moan that could have been for the pain or sorrow at the loss of his penis but was probably for both.

Dick left him alone and went to see if the travel arrangements had been made. It appeared they had, and Sol arrived on the medical helicopter.

"Ask the medics if they have anything for shock. I don't want to lose him at this stage."

"What do you plan to do with him?" said Sol. "Don't you think you should hand him over to the Russians?"

"What and risk some do-gooder giving him prison where he can live in some comfort? No way. He's going to pay for his crimes this time."

"But what's it doing to you, Dick? You look awful."

"I've just witnessed the woman I love tortured to death by this pervert. How do you expect me to look?"

"Why don't you just shoot the bastard," said Spud.

"That would be the easy way out, for him and for me. It's not what I want, and he doesn't deserve it. Give me an hour, and he'll be ready for the journey."

When Dick returned to the cellar, it stank like burnt pork. He wanted to throw up, but he was determined to see it through. He heated the knife once more.

"Right, now, where were we? Ah yes, you called her filthy names, and for that you need a tongue. Something we can remedy right now."

He forced Godunov's mouth open and pulled out his tongue with the pincers. It sliced more easily and quickly than the fingers had, and he dropped it on the floor alongside the penis. A rat ran out and grabbed the penis. Godunov looked on in horror as though it could still be of use to him. Dick smiled because he knew that, thankfully, it could not.

"Just one last thing and you're ready to travel," said Dick. "You stripped her and looked upon her naked body, taking away her dignity. For that you need eyes." Godunov howled as his eyes evaporated in clouds of steam.

The thump-thump of the helicopter arriving grabbed Dick's attention, and he decided that maybe he had gone far enough. It was time for Godunov to take his last journey.

The stretcher was strapped into the helicopter and Godunov was given the treatment required to keep him alive. It was a short trip to the airport, and Andrei arranged clearance for them so that very soon they were on their way to New Delhi.

With the million dollars Sol had taken from the bank, it was no problem getting assistance and confidentiality from the medics on the helicopter and the crew of the private jet. Dick radioed ahead, and they were met at the airport by a friend, who was, he said, a fixer. From the airport, they were taken to a run-down district of New Delhi, and Godunov was left in a clinic there to recover from his wounds. They were in a district that was run by 'The King of Beggars', and through the fixer, Dick arranged for Godunov to become one of his beggars on his release from the clinic.

"He has no money, he can't see, he can't speak or write, and he doesn't understand the language," said Dick. "It will be like a living death and is no more than he deserves."

"I think we all agree with that," said Spud.

48

A funeral and a dream fulfilled

"Tell the pilot next stop Ekaterinburg," said Dick. "We're going to put Godunov's money to good use.

"Sounds like an adventure. Give us a clue," said Spud.

Dick explained. "Did you know there are nearly a million orphans in Russia?"

"You're kidding. I thought Russia was a wealthy country," said Danny.

"Wealthy or not, there are nearly a million abandoned children and orphans, and it was one of Ivana's dreams to open an orphanage in Ekaterinburg, where she was born. We're going to use Godunov's money to open an orphanage in her name for the children of the Sverdlovsk region."

"Beats getting shot at." Spud grinned.

"I'll second that," said Danny.

"It's a great idea," said Sol. "I can't wait."

The plane landed in Ekaterinburg in a flurry of snow. Dick had contacted Andrei, who arranged for them to be met by an FSB agent, who had been instructed to liaise with the local authorities for them. While he was ascertaining what licences were required by the municipality, they contacted several estate agents to find a suitable property. On the day of Ivana's funeral, they left the agents to do their job while they went to pay their respects.

The funeral service was conducted in the cathedral on the Blood, in Ekaterinburg. The cathedral was built, aptly, on the site of the murder of the last tsar, Nikolai Romanov II. It was obvious from the turnout that Ivana had not only been well known, but was also well loved in her home city. Crowds lined the streets on the way to the church, which was packed with people in mourning.

The funeral carriage was white and drawn by four black horses that gleamed

in the morning sun as if they had been pol-
ished. White-feathered plumes adorned
the head harness of these magnificent animals, and the driver and footmen wore
black capes trimmed with white-and-black
silk top hats. The carriage carried both the
Dolgorukov and the Romanov coats of
arms. On arrival at the cathedral, the casket was carried in by six Russian cavalry
officers of Ivana's brother's regiment. A
full troop stood either side of the entrance
with raised sabres as an honour guard. Her
family had her casket left open as it lay in
the cathedral before being removed to the
family mausoleum, and Dick and the others went to say goodbye. She was dressed
in white fur and looked incredibly beautiful.

Dick was the last to approach the casket. He leaned down and kissed her gently,
tears unwontedly welling in his eyes, his
shoulders heaving from involuntary sobs.

"Goodbye, my darling," he whispered
softly. He turned and walked back up the
aisle to where the others were waiting.

"Aren't you staying for the funeral?" asked Sol, quietly.

"I don't think I can face seeing her sealed up in some musty old crypt. I think I'd rather go now that I've said goodbye."

"Okay, my friend, then let's go back and build her an orphanage to be proud of."

Back in the city, a property had been found just behind Lenina Street. It was situated in the large premises of an old wholesale fur merchant that had been derelict for some time. They rushed the purchase through, and in a few short weeks, they were in the throes of renovating and refurbishing the old building with the assistance of a first-class architect, who had been recommended by the municipality.

With much hard work and lots of help from local people, tradesmen and builders, they completed the project and were ready to open the doors just twelve weeks after the purchase. Again with the help of the municipality, they had a full staff of qualified, kind people, who would run the orphanage under their directorship.

The first children arrived almost immediately, and Dick, Sol, Spud and Danny were there to welcome them. Although the building was huge, they had asked the architect to split it inside into separate family-sized apartments so that the children would have as normal a life as possible. Each apartment would have designated 'parents', who would have special responsibility for the children under their care. They couldn't pretend it would be the same as having a blood family, but it was the nearest they could get to it. With all four of them taking an active interest, however, they were confident no child under their care would be allowed to be unhappy.

On the opening day, the city dignitaries turned out in numbers, and Ivana's brother attended to cut the ribbon to officially open the Ivana Dolgorukova Romanov Orphanage.

"It's a great day to remember," said Sol. "She would have been proud of what you've achieved."

"What *we've* achieved," said Dick. "You, me, Spud and Danny."

The orphanage filled up rapidly, and it soon became clear that, though they had made an excellent start, it was never going to solve the problem of unwanted children in Russia.

Nevertheless, to do nothing was not an option. The four of them did their absolute best to ensure that, at the very least, Ivana's orphanage was a haven for the children they could care for.

Just before Christmas, however, the general situation in the country worsened.

"Have you seen the news, Sol?" said Dick.

"I haven't had time," said Sol. "I'm busy with the accounts today."

"You're not going to believe it. The government has passed a law banning the adoption of children by anyone from the US."

"You've got to be kidding," said Spud, who had just walked into the office.

"Do I look like I'm kidding? Over a million kids living on the streets and some

idiot comes up with an idea like this."
Dick was fuming.

Danny had followed Spud in and heard
Dick's rant. "I watched it on CNN at
breakfast," said Danny. "I couldn't believe it. They've even given it a name—
the Dima Yakovlev Law, as if they're
proud of it."

"Proud of it?" said Dick still angry.
"With government orphanages struggling
to cope with over six hundred thousand
children, according to UNICEF, and over
a million still living on the streets, what
have they got to be proud of?"

"It seems," said Danny, "it's retaliation
for some US legislation they consider anti-
Russian."

"And they think the best retaliation is to
harm their own children?" said Dick in
disgust.

49

An old adversary

They often talked about returning to the UK and their own business. The London office had been unused for some while, but an early return seemed unlikely. Looking out for the children kept them all very busy. The actual timing of their return, however, was taken out of their hands by a single phone call.

"Hi, Dick, it's Bogdan. How are you all?"

"We're fine. How about you and Andrei?"

"Both well, but we've got a problem."

"Okay, shoot. Don't keep me in suspense."

"Noskcaj's escaped from prison."

"Escaped? How?"

"Do you remember Andrei telling you that people with the kind of money these guys have can buy almost anything in Russia? Well, it looks like that includes prison breaks."

"I suppose there's no point in going over the details of his escape," said Dick. "That's history. Where is he now?"

"According to our information, he's in London. I thought he might be looking for you. Revenge wouldn't be out of the question for someone like him."

"I'd hate to disappoint him, so it looks like I'd better head over there and see if I can draw him out."

"I thought you'd say that, so Andrei and I have booked seats on tomorrow's flight. I'll send you the details so you can join us."

"You do that. I'll tell Sol and the boys."

"Our people here are quite capable of managing without us. They have been for some while," said Sol.

"It's probably about time we got back to some real work," said Spud. "I've loved helping the kids, but it's all set up now. We're not really needed."

"That's settled then," said Dick. We're all on tomorrow's flight with Andrei and Bogdan."

They arrived in London on a typical January day. It was dark, cloudy and drizzling with rain.

Andrei and Bogdan were met at the airport by a chauffeured limousine from the embassy and arranged to meet up later.

The others took a taxi and were the first to arrive at the office. It was damp and smelled musty.

"Blimey, you two know how to live, don't yer?" said Spud. "This must be what the nobs call bijou, Danny."

"Bijou, is it?" said Danny. "I'd have thought bloody small was a better description."

"It's not overly large, I agree," said Sol. "But it has a certain character, don't you think?"

"About as much character as the old gents' toilets at Paddington Station," said Spud. He collapsed laughing with Danny.

"Okay, you two, you've had your fun," said Dick. "Don't laugh too hard because, for the time being, you'll be sleeping here."

The laughter stopped abruptly. "Do what? Tell me you're joking," said Spud.

"If Noskcaj's looking for me, he'll either come here or to the apartment. I can't be in two places at once, so that means you two are staying here."

"Looks like the last laugh is on you," chuckled Sol.

"All joking aside, I want you all to be on your guard," said Dick. "Let's not kid ourselves. Just because we bested him once doesn't mean Noskcaj's not a dangerous man."

"I think we'd better go eat," said Spud, "and then pick up a couple of sleeping bags."

"That's the spirit," said Sol still chuckling. "Here's the key to the gun cabinet. There's a selection of weapons inside."

The next day, Andrei and Bogdan arrived at Dick's apartment at eight a.m. Sol slept on the couch, so they all got in a taxi together and went to pick up Spud and Danny for breakfast.

Their night in the office was uneventful, cold and damp. They were not quite their usual chirpy selves.

"There's no way I'm spending another night in there," said Spud.

"Nor me," echoed Danny.

"Yeah, well, I thought maybe it wasn't such a good idea last night," said Dick, grinning. "But I thought you'd be settled, and I didn't want to disturb you."

"Oh, he's decided to be a comedian now, Danny. Ain't he bloody funny?"

"Yes, ever so," said Danny. "A laugh a minute."

"Come on you two…I'll make it up to you by buying breakfast."

"It'll take more than breakfast to make up for a night in that mouldy shoebox you call an office."

"Bijou." Sol grinned. "Remember fellas, it's bijou."

They met up with Bogdan and Andrei for breakfast. The six of them discussed their predicament.

"Do you have any idea where he might be holed up?" said Dick.

"My informant tells me he should have the actual location in a few days," said Bogdan. "All he can say at present is that it's somewhere in the West End of London, probably a hotel."

"Right," said Dick. "In that case I'm going to call in some favours from my old firm and see if they know of any Bratva bolt holes in London."

"That's a good idea," said Spud. "From my recollection, those pals of yours know just about everything that's going on."

Dick made the call, and Bogdan emailed over his photo and file. Three uneventful days later, he received an answer to his enquiry.

"They own some property in Maddox Street that they've turned into apartments," said Fergus Walsh, one of Dick's old colleagues. "Problem is we've put surveillance on it since your call, and there's been no sign of him."

"Okay, Fergus," said Dick. "Can you email me over the exact address, and is it possible for you to continue the surveillance for a little longer?"

"It would help if you could get me a request from your Russian friends. I'm sure the boss would authorise the overtime without a fuss then."

"I'll get that organised immediately. Thanks again for the help."

"No problem. That's what friends are for, but you owe me one. Bye for now."

Dick was puzzled. "If he has his own place, Sol, why isn't he there?"

"Maybe because he knows it's the place where you'll be looking for him. I think he wants to take you by surprise."

"You're probably right, but how can we find him before he finds us. It's like finding a needle in a haystack."

"Maybe," said Sol, "we should stop wasting our energy in trying to find him and instead make sure he can find us."

"And how do you propose we do that?"

"I think we should give him the opportunity to retrieve what he's lost."

Dick looked curious. "Go on, I'm listening."

"I think we should advertise a showing of the Romanov cross at the Victoria and

Albert museum, just like Ivana planned. Only this time, we'll be prepared."

"The problem with that is that we no longer have the cross to exhibit."

"True, but only Andrei, Bogdan and the four of us are aware of that, and none of us is likely to apprise Mr. Noskcaj of the fact."

"How will we organise an exhibition without the cross?" said Dick. "He won't be fooled by an empty cabinet."

"That's not easy, I grant you, but I have very good photos of the cross and some very talented friends in Hatton Garden. I'm sure, for a consideration, they'd be able to produce an excellent facsimile that would pass all but the closest inspection."

"Do you know, Sol, you never cease to amaze me. If your friends can pull it off, I think he'll find the challenge of the cross on exhibition irresistible."

Sol went home to the mews and retrieved the photographs he needed. He headed off to Hatton Garden to find his friends.

In the meantime, Dick contacted the Victoria & Albert and made arrangements for the exhibition. He told Spud and Danny of the plan but suggested keeping it between them for the time being.

Sol met them all back in the office and informed them that all was in hand. It was going to cost a not-inconsiderable amount of money. Sol was sure the result would be well worth the expense.

"I doubt we'll be able to tell it from the real thing," said Sol.

"If it can fool us," said Dick, "I've no doubt it'll fool him, so well done, Sol. When will it be ready?"

"With today's modern technology, it'll take only a few days to duplicate, they tell me. It all depends, however, on how long it takes to get the imitation stones delivered to the workshop and then matched to the photos. I'd allow a week to be on the safe side."

"Right, I'll contact the V and A, and advertise the show to take place in a week's time. Then we just have to hope he takes the bait."

Noskcaj had still not appeared at the Maddox Street apartments, and where he had gone to ground remained a mystery. Bogdan's informer came up with no new information, nor had any of Dick's contacts, and the trail seemed to have gone dead.

Dick decided to use some of the waiting time to return the hospitality Andrei and Bogdan had shown to them while they were in Moscow. London was his home town, and there were a million and one places he could take them for dinner. He chose to take them to Le Gavroche. Although he considered it one of the best restaurants in London, he felt it was small recompense for all the kindness they had shown him and the others in Moscow.

The restaurant was housed in a Georgian building in Upper Brook Street in Mayfair. When they entered, they were greeted by Enrico, the immaculately dressed manager, who showed them to their table in the main dining room. In the sumptuous surroundings of greens, pinks and blues, they were given menus by identical twin girls, Ursula and Silvia. After ordering their food, David, the sommelier, guided them through the best wines to complement their meal. And what a meal it was. Served on large plates on pristine white tablecloths, each course was presented like a work of art.

"Bit posh in here, ain't it?" said Spud.

"Speak for yourself," said Danny.

"What's important," said Dick, "is the food. Now just sit back and enjoy yourself. If you've any complaints later, I'll be glad to hear them."

The Writers' Club in Moscow was good but was nevertheless no comparison to the epitome of culinary skill at Le Gavroche. Every course was perfect and delicious. There were, of course, no complaints, and Spud had to be told to shut up going on about how much he had enjoyed it. During the rest of the week, they visited various establishments, but it was always an anticlimax. None of them compared to the evening they had spent at Le Gavroche.

When Sol got a call to go and collect the cross, they had still heard nothing from Noskcaj or his cronies. He arrived back at the office with it, and they could tell by the smile on his face the venture had been successful.

"Come on, Sol," said Danny. "Let's see what you're smiling about."

Sol opened the package, and there was a hushed silence in the office as they all gazed down upon it.

"My god," said Dick. "It's identical. If I didn't know better, I'd swear it was the real thing."

Spud and Danny just whistled. "Looks worth a million dollars," said Spud.

"More than that I hope," said Sol.

"You've really pulled it off, Sol," said Dick. "It's an absolute ringer."

The newspaper advertisements had gone in: a full page in The Times, Telegraph and the Daily Mail. They had also taken a billboard on Piccadilly Circus.

"He'd have to be blind to miss it," said Sol. "If he's looking for revenge, it'll be hard to pass up this opportunity."

They were all sitting around a breakfast table on Saturday morning, and the show at the V&A was booked for the following Monday.

"I've arranged with the museum to get access on Sunday," said Dick. "That gives us a day to prepare a little surprise for Mr. Noskcaj."

"Okay," said Bogdan. "We'll rest up today, and I'll do a weapons check in the morning while you lot prepare the trap."

"I'll set up some surveillance cameras," said Sol. "And monitor all that goes down."

"Sounds good," said Dick. "Make sure that we've all got two-way radios and that they're all working too."

"Will do."

Sunday morning arrived, and the exhibition room was bustling with activity. The cross was placed in the glass exhibition case immediately under a strong downward-pointing spotlight. The resulting effect was an astounding myriad of sparkling coloured light that danced across the ceiling and around the room.

Spud and Danny set up several concealed positions, from which they could survey the room. From these positions they could give cover fire without being seen until they actually opened fire. The room was huge and the layout such that concealment was not difficult. The hope was that Noskcaj would think he was not expected and so would not be looking for retaliation.

When they were satisfied they had done everything they could for the perfect ambush, it was early evening. Dick took them all to one of his favourite restaurants nearby, the Petrus on Kinnerton Street. The Russians were as impressed with Petrus as they had been with Le Gavroche. The cuisine was mainly French, and Spud was about to turn his nose up until he spied the fillet of Casterbridge beef, which he and Danny demolished with obvious glee. The rest of the party were more adventurous, but all agreed the food was excellent and a great evening was enjoyed by all. They left the restaurant in good spirits and arranged to meet the next morning at eight a.m., two hours before the museum opened, to allow them time to get into their positions.

They quickly hid themselves in the pre-arranged hiding places and settled down to wait. They were still sure Noskcaj would find the opportunity impossible to resist. Thirty minutes before opening time, Noskcaj made his move. Unfortunately, all did not go as planned.

The first thing they heard was a number of small explosions, and then, in what seemed like seconds, the room filled with smoke. They had not gone prepared for this. Their plan allowed for a daytime attempt during the museum opening hours.

Noskcaj, however, had other ideas and was well prepared. While Dick's team was blundering around in the smoke, Noskcaj's gang, using special night sight and infrared goggles, made straight for the display case. It was just a matter of seconds before they retrieved the cross and made their escape.

As the smoke eventually cleared, it became obvious where their point of entry had been. A cover lay carelessly open on the entry to stairs leading down to the cellars below. It was a very old building, and the cellars were extensive.

"They must have had inside help and information to have access to the cellar exactly under this room," said Dick.

"I don't think that would be difficult to get with the kind of money this guy has to throw around," said Spud.

"Let's look on the bright side," said Danny. "At least he didn't get away with the real thing."

"But he did get away," said Dick. "And that wasn't supposed to happen."

50

To catch a thief

At the Regent Street office, they discussed the day's disaster.

"He's going to try and leave the country," said Dick. "He thinks he has his prize, and he'll want to get it somewhere safe before making his next move."

"Your friends have an all-points bulletin out for him at every airport," said Sol. "I doubt he'll be able to get through while they're on high alert."

"There are two things wrong with that," said Dick. "Firstly, as Spud recently reminded me, with the sort of money he can throw around, I'm sure he'd have someone in place somewhere. Secondly, why assume he'll leave by air? There are far fewer checks if he leaves by sea. That's my bet, anyway, so let's get a list of all ships leaving in the next few days."

"Leave that to me and Danny," said Spud. "If you've got a phone and a fax here, we can have it ready in a couple of hours."

"Get to it then. Sol and I'll get a takeaway and put the coffee on, so we can eat while we work."

When Dick and Sol returned, Spud and Danny had written a list of ships leaving over the following few days on the office whiteboard. It was surprisingly long.

"I never realised there were so many ships coming and going every day," said Sol.

"It will be like finding a needle in a haystack again," said Danny.

"I'm not so sure," said Dick. "I think Mr. Noskcaj's vanity might have been his undoing."

"How do you mean?" said Sol.

"Let's see…what's Noskcaj's first name?"

"Alexander," said Sol. "But there's no ship called Alexander shown here."

"But there is something strange," said Dick. "Why would a Russian-registered vessel have an American name?"

They all looked intently at the list. "You mean the Jackson?" said Sol.

"Exactly. The Jackson A. The A, I believe, stands for Alexander," said Dick. "And what does Jackson spell in reverse?"

Spud got there first. "It's Noskcaj."

"Exactly. Alexander Noskcaj, alias the Jackson A."

Fifth down on the first list it now seemed all too obvious:

Katharina B
Tamerlane
Grande Ellade
Jaynee W
Jackson A
Goliath Leader
Nagato Reefer

"If you're right," said Spud, "it's due to leave the day after tomorrow."

"I don't believe in coincidences," said Dick. "You should contact Badger, and we'd better make plans."

The Jackson A was a fine-looking ship and was originally one of the last tramp-design ships built by Charles Connell & Co. of Glasgow. She had sailed under many names over the years before finally being designated the 'Jackson A' in a self-imposed tribute to its current owner, Alexander Noskcaj.

Badger's team was fitted out in wet suits, the weapons waterproofed, ready for the assault. Spud, Danny and Dick were to approach from land once Badger was aboard.

For once, things went as planned. The guards on board were not expecting an attack and were completely taken by surprise. Just a few shots were taken, but more in disbelief than with any real intention to repel the boarders. Those shots alerted Spud, Danny and Dick.

They went aboard quickly, but the job was all but done.

"Blimey, you don't waste much time, Badger," said Spud. "You might have left some for us."

"But then you'd have moaned about how much you're paying us," quipped Badger.

"Let's get down to business. Where's Noskcaj?" said Dick.

"He don't seem to be aboard, boss," said Badger. "This one said he got a call about an hour ago and left in a hurry."

"Shit," said Dick. "How the fuck does he do it? He's as slippery as an eel."

"We might not have lost him, boss," said Badger. "This guy said he heard him shout 'Get me to London…Maddox Street'. Can't be many of them in London."

"You're quite right, and I think I know just the one," said Dick with a smile.

The race to London was unnerving, with Dick at the wheel, toe to the floor most of the way.

"Bloody hell, Danny," said Spud. "It's like being back in India."

When they arrived, Dick decided to start with surveillance on the Maddox Street building. "It'll be easier to take him on the way out rather than storm the building."

"You're right—less chance of casualties," said Spud.

They settled into their positions to keep watch, and less than an hour after arriving, the door opened and out walked...Andrei.

"So that's how he got so lucky at the museum. I bet that's who made the call to the ship," said Dick. "I don't believe it."

"Can't deny the evidence before your own eyes," said Danny.

"I guess you're right," said Dick. "Anyway, if he's just leaving, it must mean Noskcaj is still inside."

"Do we sit and wait, or are we going in?" asked Danny.

"We're going in," said Dick. "Badger, have you got any C Four with you?"

"Now c'mon, boss. You know I was a boy scout. I always come prepared."

"Okay then. I want someone at every window to throw in a stun grenade on my order, which will be at the precise moment you blow the door. And make sure there's a team at the rear. I want every exit covered."

"What about me and Danny?" said Spud.

"You two can follow me through the front door as soon as it's blown."

A few minutes later, the radio clicked, and Badger's voice crackled out. "In place and ready, boss."

"Right. On my mark…three, two, one, fire!"

The explosions were almost instantaneous and absolutely deafening, leaving their ears ringing. Dick burst through the demolished door, with Spud and Danny in hot pursuit. They cleared the building room by room, hand- and ankle-cuffing all those they encountered. There was little or no resistance. The stun grenades did their job, and most of those inside were completely disorientated. One guy managed to get out of a rear window, but he was quickly overpowered by the team outside.

When the people had recovered enough to be interviewed, they had a strange story to tell. It appeared that sometime earlier, they had been visited by a team who used far less violent ways to gain access. After opening the door to a gas-meter reader, a large force had followed in behind him. They discovered Mr. Noskcaj and took him and the package he had with him away with them. They warned those inside to say nothing of the incident. The last of them left not long before the attack.

"What the fuck's going on?" said Spud.

"I don't know, but I intend to find out," said Dick.

Dick drove furiously to the Russian embassy and stormed into Reception trying with great difficulty to keep his temper under control.

"Can you tell Mr. Andrei Gromyko that Mr. Dick Brady would like to speak with him?"

"Of course, sir. Please take a seat."

A few minutes later Andrei appeared and walked towards Dick with a smile and an outstretched hand.

"Never mind about the hand," said Dick angrily. "What's happened to Noskcaj and the cross?"

"Ah, so you know," said Andrei sheepishly.

"No, I don't bloody know. That's why I'm asking you, as you were the last one to see him."

"Yes, I'm afraid that's true."

"So enlighten me," said Dick, his voice full of suspicion. "Why would you be helping him get away?"

"Let me put your mind at rest," said Andrei. "Helping him get away is the last thing on my mind. My superiors spotted an opportunity to get inside information on the extent of the Bratva and their influence in my country. We informed Noskcaj that all his assets had been confiscated. We told him we were, however, prepared to allow him to leave with the cross he's recently acquired. In return, he's agreed to submit to a full debriefing, revealing all he knows of the Bratva network and activities."

"But the cross is worth very little," said Dick. "And even so, he doesn't deserve his freedom."

"Firstly, he doesn't know the actual value of the cross. He thinks it's worth at least two million pounds. Secondly, once we have all the information we require and it's been verified, we'll release him. Before we act on that information, though, it might easily become known how happy we are with the assistance he's given."

"But that will be like guaranteeing a death sentence." Dick understood now.

"That's unfortunate, but then again, you did just say he didn't deserve his freedom."

They smiled together, grimly, and shook hands.

"It seems there is some justice in the world, after all, Andrei."

"In this particular instance, it would appear you're right."

Dick used his mobile to call Sol and the boys, and they arranged to meet back at Dick's apartment to freshen up before going out on the town to celebrate.

"Ask Badger along, too," said Dick. "Let's make a party of it."

51

Conclusion: Three Weeks Later

Dick, Sol, Danny and Spud were in the Regent Street office discussing plans to make a short visit to the orphanage. Spud was at the old-fashioned gas burner making coffee while Sol read the newspaper.

"That didn't take long," said Sol.

"What are you on about?" said Danny.

"It says here a body of a man's been pulled out of the Thames. Police are not yet revealing how he died but are asking for anyone who has any information to come forward. He's been identified as Alexander Noskcaj, who, they are informed, was an adviser on crime at the Russian embassy in London. The embassy says that, as far as they know, he was supposed to have left for Russia a week ago."

"So the story ends," said Dick.

"Not quite."

Andrei and Bogdan entered while they were all engrossed in the news report.

"We managed to retrieve this and thought you might like to keep it as a memento."

It was an unprepossessing package. Just brown paper tied with string. However, inside was, of course, the exquisite replica cross.

"That was very thoughtful of you," said Dick.

"It's almost as stunning as the real thing," said Sol. "It's a shame we can't compare them."

"That can never happen because the original is now where it should always have been," said Dick. "In the hands of a great and beautiful Dolgorukov Lady."

The End

Dear Reader,

I do hope you have enjoyed my book. I would very much appreciate it if you would take the time to leave a short review at the books page of the retailer you purchased it from.

If you wish you can leave your email on my website to be notified of future releases.

www.kenbloomfield-author.com

Thank you so much for your time,
Ken Bloomfield

The Pilgrims' Bounty

The Pilgrims' Bounty

The Pilgrims' Bounty

The Pilgrims' Bounty

The Pilgrims' Bounty

Lightning Source UK Ltd.
Milton Keynes UK
UKHW010742050822
406887UK00001B/170